LOVE AND LATTES AT PUMPKIN HOLLOW

VICTORIA WALTERS

Boldwood

First published in Great Britain in 2025 by Boldwood Books Ltd.

Copyright © Victoria Walters, 2025

Cover Design by Alexandra Allden

Cover Images: Shutterstock

Chapter Image: Shutterstock

The moral right of Victoria Walters to be identified as the author of this work has been asserted in accordance with the Copyright, Designs and Patents Act 1988.

All rights reserved. No part of this book may be reproduced in any form or by any electronic or mechanical means, including information storage and retrieval systems, without written permission from the author, except for the use of brief quotations in a book review. This book is a work of fiction and, except in the case of historical fact, any resemblance to actual persons, living or dead, is purely coincidental.

Every effort has been made to obtain the necessary permissions with reference to copyright material, both illustrative and quoted. We apologise for any omissions in this respect and will be pleased to make the appropriate acknowledgements in any future edition.

A CIP catalogue record for this book is available from the British Library.

Paperback ISBN 978-1-80557-084-4

Large Print ISBN 978-1-80557-083-7

Hardback ISBN 978-1-80557-082-0

Ebook ISBN 978-1-80557-085-1

Kindle ISBN 978-1-80557-086-8

Audio CD ISBN 978-1-80557-077-6

MP3 CD ISBN 978-1-80557-078-3

Digital audio download ISBN 978-1-80557-081-3

This book is printed on certified sustainable paper. Boldwood Books is dedicated to putting sustainability at the heart of our business. For more information please visit https://www.boldwoodbooks.com/about-us/sustainability/

Boldwood Books Ltd, 23 Bowerdean Street, London, SW6 3TN

www.boldwoodbooks.com

To my agent Hannah Ferguson for the phone call that birthed this story!

1

Autumn had always been my favourite season for three very important reasons:

1. My mother loved this time of year and named me Willow after her favourite tree from her childhood.
2. I grew up on Birch Tree Farm and watched the trees that lined the drive up to the farmhouse change to stunning colours each year autumn came around.
3. I was born in October.

So, when I looked out of the window as we were about to start the penultimate week of September over breakfast and saw that the birch trees were starting to change colour, I couldn't help but smile despite the fact the current mood on Birch Tree Farm was far from the happiest it had ever been. The birch trees, which had given our farm its name, lined the long, sweeping drive up to our farmhouse, and they stood tall and proud, come rain or shine. But they always came into their own once October arrived and they transformed into a beautiful, golden hue.

A heavy sigh from my father, who sat at one end of our long, pine table in the kitchen, drew me from gazing out at the trees to look at him. We were having a late breakfast as it was Sunday and although there was always something to do on the farm, it meant a day of taking things slightly slower than we did the rest of the week. Fresh eggs from our chickens, tomatoes grown with our own hands along with homemade bread with tea and orange juice made for a hearty start to the day. And a cosy one as the Aga in the corner made the kitchen the only room in our farmhouse that was always warm.

'What's wrong?' I asked my dad nervously, as he went through our post, wondering if yet another bill had come. They seemed to be coming more often and for more money than we could keep up with. He had read the same letter three times now, and I braced myself to hear what was causing him to frown quite so deeply.

'I think you should read this,' he said, sliding the letter down the table towards me. His face seemed to look permanently concerned now. He had aged a lot since my mum got ill and passed away five years ago but over the past twelve months, I had seen more wrinkles appear and his hair, once the same dark-brown shade as mine, was now salt and pepper grey. Even his eyes, also matching my mahogany colour, had lost the twinkle they had had when I was younger. I hated to see how worried he was about the farm, and I always tried to keep things optimistic but it was becoming harder to put a smile on his face. 'Willow,' my father said with a tut, noticing that I had drifted into my head, which I was prone to doing. 'The letter,' he repeated, nodding towards it.

I eyed the letter on the table like it was a bomb that might go off. 'Why do I need to read it?' I asked him, wondering if I could escape and avoid having a look. It couldn't be good news.

'Willow, I know that you prefer to bury your head in the sand, you're a dreamer and a romantic, just like your dear mother was, but you can't hide from this,' my dad said, gesturing around us. 'We've barely scraped by this past year, and I can't see things getting any better. Plus, we can't keep pretending that I'm not getting older and finding it harder to work with my arthritis. That letter...' He trailed off for a moment, seeming to find the words difficult to get out, '...it could be the answer. Please read it for me.'

Reluctantly, I picked up the letter, not wanting to disappoint my dad more than I felt like I already was, and saw the letterhead at the top said *Henderson Homes*. I already felt on edge as I started to read and when I reached the words, *we would love to discuss adding Birch Tree Farm to our property portfolio*, I dropped the letter back down onto the table.

I shook my head. 'They want to buy the farm. No way, Dad. They will build their identical, small, new-build houses over all our land,' I said, pointing out of the window. 'And what about the birch trees?' I cried, my heart quickening at the thought of anyone taking down my beloved trees. 'You can't seriously be considering this?'

'They say they are willing to make us a very generous offer,' Dad said. 'We can't afford to just dismiss this out of hand. We are struggling, and I might have to give up working soon; how will you manage the farm on your own if I do? We need to be sensible here. As hard as it is.' He reached over and picked the letter back up. 'They want to send one of the Henderson brothers to the farm to look around and talk about what they might offer us. I think we need to say yes to the meeting.'

I stared at my father in horror. 'But where would we go?' I

asked, trying not to panic. I had lived on Birch Tree Farm my whole twenty-five years on this earth, my parents having inherited it soon after they got married. It had been my only home, and I had worked on the farm since I was old enough to; I literally had no idea what my life would look like anywhere else. 'What would I do?' I could hear the selfishness in my words but I couldn't help it. I had lived and worked here all my life so the thought of it being taken away from me was terrifying.

Dad leaned back in his chair, looking as lost as I felt. 'I don't know, love, but we can't carry on the way we are, can we?'

2

Dad's question hung in the air for a few moments. I could see in his eyes he was finding this idea as hard as I was but it looked like the fight had been sucked out of him. I hated to see that.

'What if I come up with an idea to help?' I blurted out in desperation.

'What do you mean?'

'An idea that will turn things around, something that will make us more money at this time of year, a way to clear our debts and fix things up around here,' I said, thinking about the long list of things that needed repairing. The problem was our farm did okay in spring and summer when the pick-your-own season was in full swing and people came from the town and surrounding areas for our fruit and veg, but there wasn't enough to offer as we moved into autumn and winter to encourage people to make the trip out to the farm. So, for the rest of the year, we had pretty much no income.

Yet the bills never stopped.

'Is that even possible, love?' Dad said, gently. 'We need to face facts and I think we should at least meet with Henderson Homes to find out what our options are.'

'You won't give me a chance to think of something?'

Dad sighed. 'You can try but I'm going to ring them tomorrow morning and arrange for someone to come to the farm. I don't see any other option at this point.'

I stood up, scraping my chair back noisily on the stone tiles that lined the kitchen floor. 'This is crazy. What would Mum have said about this?' I questioned, knowing it was a low blow but I couldn't stop the words from coming out of my mouth. I instantly regretted them when my dad looked crestfallen. I felt deflated and claustrophobic. I needed to get out of here.

'Willow...'

'I need to go for a walk and think,' I said, cutting him off. 'I'll see you later.' I whistled for my dog and left the kitchen, torn between anger at Dad, sadness at the thought of what my mum would think about how things were going, and determination to do something that could save our beloved farm. Maple, my Border Collie, trotted after me loyally as I walked out of the farmhouse and exhaled shakily once I hit the fresh air.

Birch Tree Farm was over three hundred acres in size. When you drove through the gate, you went up the sweeping drive lined by birch trees to our farmhouse – a low, long building, red-bricked. And then behind the farmhouse were acres of land that stretched out as far as the eye could see, separated into fields of different fruit and vegetables and then on the other side were our polytunnels, bigger and more cost-efficient than greenhouses, that kept our crops sheltered and warm, and to the side of the house was where we kept our chickens. We had thought we could make some extra money selling eggs but the profit margin was so low, it hadn't worked. Still, it meant we had free eggs to reduce some of our food bill.

I walked that way, with Maple close to my heels keeping an eye on everything like she always did.

It was a cool morning, watery sunshine peeping through the clouds, and I was glad I had on my beaten but still hardy Barbour coat, inherited from my mum, along with wellies and a thick jumper and leggings. My long hair was in its usual messy bun.

My eyes drank in the farm. At this time of year, there were no visitors and no seasonal workers so I had the space to myself. This I was used to but occasionally, I did feel a pang of loneliness. Maybe I was feeling slightly sentimental about my upcoming birthday, knowing I didn't have anyone special to celebrate it with. But today, it ran deeper than that. I missed my mum. She would have known what to do. I had no idea how to change my dad's mind about meeting Henderson Homes, and what if they made us a really good offer? Could we realistically turn it down? But then I would have to leave the place I loved most in the world.

'Oh, Maple, I wish there was a way to make money around here before spring comes around,' I said, as we walked towards the field behind the chickens, which was empty of any crops. It didn't have the best soil or light so we usually kept it empty and sometimes in peak summer sold ice creams from it. Today, Maple ran across it joyfully as I tried to walk off my melancholy. I stared out at the land and willed a good idea to come to me but I was feeling too sorry for myself to think clearly. I pulled out my phone to message my best friend Sabrina.

> I'm in need of girl talk ASAP please.

Sabrina replied within a minute, as I was following Maple across the field.

> I have it on good authority that Birchbrook Café will have their seasonal food and drinks in from tomorrow.

Sabrina's reply made me smile. We loved the café in our hometown and met there frequently in autumn and winter for a hot drink and sweet treat.

> Just what the doctor ordered! When can you meet me?

As I waited to see when she'd be free for a chat, I turned to look back at the farmhouse. I saw Dad walking outside and round to one of the crop polytunnels. He walked slowly now, ever so slightly stooped, and I could often see him wince, early in the morning or late at night when his joints ached. It pained me to see it. I also hated to see him so worried. I knew he was right that we couldn't carry on how we were for much longer. I was just at a loss to know what we could do. I didn't want to entertain the idea of selling, especially not to Henderson Homes.

Maple came up to me and sat down, leaning against my legs, following my gaze.

'Well, Maple, get your thinking cap on; we have to find a solution so we can stay here. Because we love this farm, don't we?' I reached down to run my fingers through her fur, something which always made me feel better.

Maple gave a small bark, which I took to mean she agreed.

'God, I've been single for too long,' I muttered, shaking my head for thinking I was having an actual conversation with my dog. She was very clever so you never knew. 'Come on, Maple, let's get our chores done so we can watch a Sunday movie on the sofa in front of the fire,' I said, setting off for the chickens.

My phone beeped with a response from Sabrina who told me to meet her in the café on Tuesday morning as her mother was looking after Dottie, her baby. I really hoped Sabrina might help me come up with an idea because the clock was definitely ticking.

3

'Will you be here later then, love?' Dad called out to me on Tuesday, coming up to lean on the fence as I scattered feed for the chickens.

I glanced behind me at his nervous face. I tried not to grimace but it was impossible. 'I don't know,' I said. I whistled for Maple as I saw our naughtiest chicken, Hetty, heading towards the hole in the fence. That was next on my list of jobs to fix. Maple darted over to sit in front of it, forcing Hetty to let out a frustrated cluck and wander back towards the other chickens for more food. 'I have to fix that fence then I'm meeting Sabrina in town for a coffee. I haven't seen her in two weeks,' I added. I had spent every hour since my conversation with Dad on Sunday trying to think of ideas for the farm but I knew I hadn't hit on anything that would work yet and I was getting increasingly annoyed with myself.

Dad frowned. 'I think you should be here to meet with Henderson Homes, Willow. You need to hear them out along with me. See what their plans are, what the offer is, and I thought you were worried about the trees?' he asked, gesturing to the birch trees in his eyeline.

I sighed. Meeting one of the Henderson brothers to hear how they would destroy our farm was probably the thing I wanted to do the least in the world but I hated to keep disappointing my father. And I *was* worried about the trees. 'I suppose I could come back for the meeting,' I said, begrudgingly. I was shocked at how fast it had all been set up. Dad had phoned them yesterday and learned that one of the brothers would be in the area and could meet us early this afternoon. Dad said there was no point putting it off, we needed to have all the facts before we could make a decision, so he had agreed to it, and that ticking clock suddenly had gone into overdrive.

'You said you'd let me come up with an idea to help the farm, though,' I reminded him again as I went over to the damaged fence to inspect it. We needed a whole new one but couldn't afford it so I'd have to patch it up like I had done countless times by now.

'Have you? Come up with an idea?' he asked, coming over to look at the fence with me.

I shook my head sadly.

He turned his attention to the fence and not my lack of bright ideas, which I appreciated. 'It was that storm last week that did it; I don't think it'll last much longer.'

'It'll be fine,' I said stubbornly. 'I'll go get some wood and my tools, then I'll head into town. You need anything?'

Dad looked at me like he wanted to say something but shook his head. 'No, thanks. I'm going to go inside and get changed, and tidy up the kitchen ready for the meeting. Mr Henderson will be here at one thirty so make sure you're back from seeing Sabrina for then, okay? And give her my love.'

As I started to walk off, Dad called my name.

I looked back at him. 'Yes, I'll be here,' I said, through gritted teeth.

I just knew this Henderson man would be what I hated most in the world: suited and booted, arrogant and rich, no idea what being a farmer or running a farm was about, and wouldn't see how special this place was. He would have no heart, I was sure, so I really didn't want to meet him but I also didn't want my dad to agree to anything without me being there. I was also hoping that I could put Dad off the idea of dealing with Henderson Homes in the meeting, throw as many spanners in the works as possible to give me more time to come up with an idea that would solve our problems and let us avoid having to sell.

Okay, so it wasn't a great plan, but right now, it was the only plan I had.

* * *

Once I had completed all my chores, I walked into town to meet Sabrina late morning. I changed out of my work clothes into my better ones, which, to be honest, weren't much different but they were clean and without holes. Birchbrook was a half-hour walk from the farm and I had done the walk so many times throughout my life, I could probably do it in my sleep. It was slightly downhill as our farm stood at the top so the journey into town was always more enjoyable than the way back.

Summer had definitely faded away now with autumn drifting in. The leaves were all starting to change, a few conkers were falling in my path, and the air was crisp as I strolled towards our quaint hometown.

Birchbrook was small, with most of the locals knowing each other, but it was popular with tourists as it was so pretty and had a lot of independent businesses, which was becoming rarer with each passing year. I always felt a warm flood of pride whenever I walked through it. Today, the pride was mixed with sadness that this might not be where I lived for much longer. I couldn't imagine living anywhere else, though.

When the town came into sight, I turned off the main road and into the High Street, my boots making noise on the cobbles. Birch trees ran in a line on each side of the road and, like our ones at the farm, were starting to turn. At Christmas, fairy lights were hung in them, and in summer, they were lush and green, but soon they would be a burst of autumn colour, something people loved to come and take photos of. Each shop had something outside to mark the seasons – once September moved into October, the businesses put pumpkins or autumn flowers outside their doors, and I smiled to see them already starting to appear.

Halfway down the High Street was the Birchbrook Café, which had been here for my whole life, run by a husband and wife, both called Pat (yes, it was confusing), along with their son now. It was a cosy haven and declared by all to make the best coffee and cakes for miles around. They had already decorated for autumn, I was happy to see. I slowed down to walk inside and passed a hay bale by the door that had a pile of orange and white pumpkins on top with two pots of dark-orange chrysanthemums in front of it. On the door the open/closed sign had changed to one that was pumpkin-shaped, and when I walked through, a delicious cinnamon smell hit me.

Inside the café, there was more autumnal-themed décor. The small, round tables now had beige and cream gingham tablecloths on them with three Munchkin pumpkins in the centre of each. I went up to the long counter, which displayed the cakes, and my eyes widened to see the delicious offerings. Behind the counter worked the three family members, and hanging across the back wall was a burlap banner with a square for each letter spelling out *Hello Autumn*.

'It's very, um, festive in here,' a deep voice rang out.

I looked at the man ahead of me in the queue and instantly pegged him to be an outsider. He wore a suit and ordered an espresso, ignoring all the autumnal-themed drinks and treats on the menu.

'We like to celebrate the seasons around here,' Pat, short for Patricia, said in her usual kindly way.

'Overkill.' Her son, Paul, glowered as he made the man's espresso using the fancy coffee machine behind the counter. 'It's the same every year – like we don't know what month it is unless we decorate the café within an inch of its life.'

Pat, short for Patrick, his father, met my eyes and rolled his. I bit back a smile. The two Pats were always friendly, smiley and happy, but their son was the complete opposite. He acted like he hated every minute of working with his parents but if anyone dared to suggest he did something else, he'd bite your head off so we assumed secretly, he enjoyed it but liked to wind us all up with his 'I hate this town' attitude. It meant that you not only got a tasty drink and cake in the café but entertaining conversation too.

'Haven't seen you here before,' female Pat continued as she took the man's money.

I eyed the new drinks and treats in for the autumn season and wished I could afford to try them all but I knew I had to be as careful as possible right now.

'I'm in town for a meeting,' he replied in a posh accent. 'Actually, do you know where this place is? I need to be there in a couple of hours – it's called…' He pulled out his phone to study it. 'Birch Tree Farm.'

4

I looked up as female Pat met my gaze. Paul stopped making the drink to stare, and male Pat looked over his shoulder at us. I also felt the gaze of several customers linger on me as this man asked about my farm. I knew instantly who this was then, and I was pleased I had got him completely right. Mr Suit Man, who ordered boring coffee, and couldn't remember the name of the farm he wanted to buy, was the Henderson brother I was being forced to meet soon.

'I know it,' I found myself blurting out before anyone else could speak. Again, I felt all eyes on me.

Mr Suit Man turned around, and I watched him take me in. He gave me a quick head-to-toe sweep and lingered on my scruffy boots, my baggy jeans and my cardigan that used to belong to my mum, which was so soft and cosy but definitely not high-fashion, and then up to my make-up-free face and messy bun. 'You do?' he asked, as if surprised that I would know anything. He looked about my age and was tall. I had to slightly look up to meet his rather startling blue eyes. He had broad shoulders and was conventionally handsome with a clean-shaven face and almost-black hair that slightly swept over his forehead. But the haughty expression on his face made sure that even if he was attractive, he most definitely would never be my type.

Instantly on edge at his disbelieving tone, I nodded. 'Sure. We all know the farm.'

The man glanced at the family behind the counter, who all quickly nodded then looked back at me, wondering where I was going with this. As I was too.

'Google Maps directed me to the town, not the farm, which is crazy,' he said, shaking his head in disbelief that a place could exist which Google couldn't find.

'Yeah, it does that, but we are all used to directing people who are lost,' I said, knowing the town was super helpful in summer when people were trying to find our farm, but I knew this guy didn't deserve any help. The way he said 'farm' just dripped with disdain. My back was definitely up.

I heard the bell on the café door jingle then and someone came in, stopping behind me. I could tell by the waft of a familiar floral perfume that it was Sabrina, probably wondering why everyone in here was looking at me and listening to my conversation with the stranger in a suit. I ploughed on quickly before she could say anything.

'You need to go through the High Street then take a right and go down the hill and the farm will be there; it's about a twenty-minute drive,' I said pointing to the opposite way the farm was. I knew it was childish but I just couldn't help it. This was all happening so fast and I felt like I had to do whatever I could to slow things down while I thought of a way to stop it altogether. I could tell everyone was confused why I had given the wrong directions but they had known me for all of my twenty-five years and they trusted me so no one said anything to disagree.

Mr Suit Man sighed. 'Great, another twenty-minute drive. Glad I went for the double shot then.' He gave a business-like nod. 'Thanks,' he said curtly to me, picked up his coffee in a takeaway cup and then strode out of the café, making the bell ring out shrilly by how hard he yanked the door open.

'Willow!' Sabrina chastised me. 'What did you do?'

Everyone in the café was quiet, waiting for me to explain myself. I turned to face the room. 'I know it looks bad but he's here because he wants to buy our farm...' I had to swallow down the lump in my throat. 'And build houses on our land. Dad is considering it as the farm isn't doing that well. I just need more time to come up with an idea to stop us from having to take his offer,' I added in a nervous rush.

'Oh, Willow,' female Pat said. 'I know what you need,' she said, immediately bustling around to get me something to eat and drink.

'Are things on the farm that bad?' Sabrina asked, reaching out to touch my arm. I looked at my best friend's anxious face. We had been close since primary school, growing up here together. She was even shorter than me, but curvy to my slim frame with blonde hair to my brown, and her eyes were a gorgeous blue. We always joked we were opposite in every way. She had married her school sweetheart and they had a baby last year. They lived in a cottage on the edge of town. She was a teacher at the school we had met at, and her husband worked for a big company in the next town to ours, and honestly, they were my favourite people. Her concern made the tears welling up in my eyes threaten to overspill, and I knew she could tell. 'Sit down at our table; I'll get this – no arguments,' she added when I opened my mouth to protest.

I nodded, knowing that firm tone of hers well, so I went over to the corner where our favourite table sat empty as if it had been waiting for us. As I passed people I had known for years, I received sympathetic smiles and nods, murmurs of, 'Anything we can do, let us know', and I sank into a chair feeling grateful for them all, slightly bad for sending the Henderson man in the wrong direction but mostly terrified for what the next few hours were going to bring. Because he would end up at our farm at some point, and it felt like a bulldozer was already heading towards us, threatening all I held dear.

'Okay, tell me everything while you enjoy these,' Sabrina interrupted my doom-like thoughts as she sat down opposite me, sliding a tray onto the table. 'We have a pumpkin spiced latte each, of course, and then I got us two sweet treats to share – an apple and toffee muffin and a slice of pumpkin spiced loaf cake.'

'I already feel better,' I said, smiling at what was on offer. It all smelled so delicious, my mouth started watering instantly. 'Thanks, Sabrina.' I looked over at the counter and gave female Pat a grateful wave too. She smiled back and then turned to tell Paul off about something.

I took a sip of my latte and let the sweet spiciness warm my body up. 'It gets better every year.'

'I look forward to autumn mostly for this,' Sabrina agreed, cutting the cakes in half and handing me a plate with my share on. 'And carving a pumpkin. And collecting conkers, and watching the *Gilmore Girls* and *Hocus Pocus*. There's too much to enjoy actually. I love it all.'

'The best time of year,' I said, taking a bite of the muffin. 'Oh wow,' I cooed. 'Just so good. I love it all too, although it's a shame it signals the end of our busy season on the farm.' Everything washed back over me and I sighed. 'I hate to think about having to let the farm go. I just don't know what to do.'

'Willow, you can't seriously be considering selling the farm and your home,' Sabrina said, looking shocked.

'We're really struggling. We only bring in money in spring and summer and bills are only going up and up; we can't rely on the summer season any more to see us through the rest of the year. Dad said if I could come up with an idea to help, he'd reconsider, but I'm worried this offer from Henderson Homes will be too good for us to turn down. I don't want to lose the farm; it's my home, you know how much it means to me...'

Sabrina nodded while I took another sip of my drink.

'But an idea that might turns things around just isn't coming to me.'

'We have to come up with something. That Henderson man looked like he'd never set foot on a farm. And he seemed to be turning his nose up at the town too.'

I nodded. 'He seemed to be exactly what I thought he'd be like. He'll find the farm at some point today so I probably haven't achieved anything sending him the wrong way but I couldn't help myself,' I admitted. 'I'm not usually petty but I'm not in my right frame of mind right now.'

'Of course not, you must be worried sick,' Sabrina said. 'I wish you'd told me how bad things had got on the farm, though.'

'I'm sorry. I suppose I have been doing what Dad has told me off for – sticking my head in the sand a little bit,' I confessed. 'I'm just scared. I never thought of doing anything, or living anywhere, else. Birch Tree Farm means so much to me.'

'I know it does, Willow. We can't let this happen,' she said firmly. 'Do you have any ideas at all?'

'Well, we do pretty well in the summer, as you know; we just need to think of something that could generate income in the colder months. Like this place.' I gestured around. 'They have really tapped into autumn, haven't they? Decorations, seasonal-themed drinks and food: it means that people come in to see what's new.'

'Especially us as we love autumn,' Sabrina agreed, nodding.

I stared at my best friend, my brain starting to tick over furiously. I looked around the café again, taking in the autumn theme they had going. 'That's it,' I said slowly. My eyes caught on the pumpkins outside the door. 'We do love autumn,' I added, moving my gaze back to Sabrina, who was looking at me worriedly.

'You've spaced out again; are you okay?' she asked.

'I think I just had an idea!'

5

'Don't keep me in suspense!' Sabrina complained after a couple of seconds' silence. I had spaced out again, debating internally whether this could actually work.

'Sorry,' I said, shaking my head so I could focus on her again. 'I was just thinking about what you said – we love this season and our town already celebrates it a lot. Look around at the décor and the seasonal treats, and the whole High Street gets into the spirit, doesn't it? Pumpkins are pretty much everywhere in Birchbrook in October.'

Sabrina smiled. 'And don't forget how crazy we go for Halloween with the parade,' she reminded me.

'How could I forget?' Every 31st of October, the town held a Halloween parade where everyone carried LED lanterns along the High Street. Local businesses set up stalls to sell food and drinks and people followed a trail that looped around. Everyone loved it. The reminder of the annual event made me think that my idea could actually work. 'What if the farm could join in with the autumn spirit? Bring people out to the farm at this time of year, not just in spring and summer?'

'That would be great. But what would they come for in autumn?'

'Pumpkins,' I blurted out.

'Pumpkins?' Sabrina repeated, looking a little worried at me again.

'Pumpkins,' I said firmly. 'Everyone needs pumpkins at this time of year. And right now, we all have to go out of town to get them, either from the supermarket or the fruit and veg market, which is only on twice a month.'

'Plus the ones in the supermarket aren't great; they can look a bit mouldy and they are expensive,' Sabrina added. 'I heard that a lot of the shops this year ordered them from a farm up north and all chipped in for the shipping costs,' she said, taking a sip of her latte.

My eyes lit up. 'So, having pumpkins much closer to home would be something everyone would want. Plus not just businesses, everyone I know likes to carve a pumpkin or pop one outside their house with a candle in for Halloween. There is a need for pumpkins in our town.'

'I guess there is. But how does that fit in with your farm?'

'We could sell pumpkins!' I said excitedly. 'We could create a pumpkin patch. Do you remember we went to one once, what was it now – three years ago?'

'Oh, yeah, we had fun,' she replied. 'It was miles away, though. They had pumpkins to pick outside but also that area where they had piles of all pretty, different kinds of pumpkins ready to grab, and they sold food and drink too, right?'

I nodded. 'I remember thinking, though, that it could have been even better. They could have had much more there. Like an autumn trail. And somewhere for people to take photos. Plus, it was a long way for us to go. What if I could do something like that at the farm? Not just a place to sell pumpkins but we could make it a destination for people to come to in autumn.'

Sabrina caught on quickly. 'That sounds like it would be lots of fun, and you love this time of year so I bet you'd be great at making everyone feel all autumnal. There's just one snag in your plan, though...'

'We don't grow pumpkins?'

'Yeah,' she said. 'You don't have any pumpkins.'

'We don't have any *yet*,' I corrected. 'That pumpkin patch we went to didn't grow all those pumpkins, some they had bought in like the supermarket does. So, I could do that too.' I stood up abruptly. 'I need to go and talk to Dad about this. Before Mr Suit Man gets there and starts to convince Dad we need to sell up. If I can persuade him to let me try to create a pumpkin patch, I can buy us some time.'

'Hang on, you mean you want to do one *this* year? As in for *this* autumn? We're already almost at the end of September, and wouldn't a pumpkin patch need to be open for October?' Sabrina looked up at me with wide, blue eyes.

I gulped. She was right. It was extremely late to even consider doing something like this. But what choice did I have?

'I'll work it out somehow, right? If I can get Dad to let me try. I better head straight back to the farm and talk to him about it before Mr Suit Man finds us,' I said, already moving away from the table. Now I'd had this thought, I couldn't let it go. Something like excitement was coursing through my veins. I had felt stuck for so long, so worried without knowing what the hell I could do about it. But now I had a slight glimmer of hope on the horizon. I just wished Sabrina wasn't still looking so anxious.

'It would be a lot of work, Willow,' she cautioned.

'I can work hard,' I found myself snapping at her, a little bit irritated that she wasn't as excited as me. 'You said it yourself – I love autumn. I am going to show my dad that if we do this, we could keep our farm. Wish me luck!'

I hurried out of the café before she could talk me out of it, which I could see by her face she was itching to do. I knew that my plan was outlandish even for me but something deep down in my gut told me that I had a chance to make it work.

I walked back through the High Street, this time really drinking in everything around me. The pumpkins outside the shops, the pretty autumnal flowers and the trees hinting at the golden hue they would soon become.

Everyone loved the seasons here. Christmas was insane in Birchbrook and every year, people seemed to get more into autumn and Halloween. Shops stocked more and more autumnal décor. Last year, I had bought an autumn wreath and a pumpkin-scented candle! There was no stopping the seasonal-décor trend so why not embrace it and do something at the farm that would bring in revenue at this time of year?

I strode quickly towards my farm, trying to imagine what a pumpkin patch might look like, and the work that would be involved. Sabrina was right that it could be a huge undertaking considering how close October was now. But we couldn't afford to wait until next year. Dad wouldn't let us, I knew that for sure. He was close to accepting this Henderson offer and we hadn't even heard what they had to say about it. I had to get to Dad and put the pumpkin-patch idea into his head before Mr Suit Man turned up. Convince him that I could do it and how popular it would be. My town loved seasonal things. Surely people would come? I just had to make a plan for how I could make it happen in a really short time.

My confidence faltered a little bit when my home came into view. I could see the farmhouse ahead and I thought about how the farm had changed since I was young. Dad had seemed to have always been cheerful back then, the farm had been thriving and the house warm and light. Everything was in good nick back then compared to how it was now. And, of course, my mum had still been alive.

Thinking about her made me sad but it did remind me that autumn had always been a huge part of my life. She had loved this time of year and had made me love it too. I remembered how she had always carved a pumpkin with me and how we carried lanterns in the Halloween parade together every year. And my mum loved the birch trees as much as me; she would sit under them on crisp, sunny autumn days to read her favourite books and watch me playing in the falling leaves. When we walked home from school, we'd both pick up conkers and put them in bowls to keep the spiders away. And for my birthday, Mum would always bake me a cake that was covered in leaves made of icing. 'Willow leaves for my Willow,' she would say.

Mum would have loved creating a pumpkin patch, I was sure of it.

'I hope you're looking down and cheering me on for this,' I whispered into the wind as I walked through our gate and up the tree-lined drive.

A joyful bark sounded then and Maple ran out of the farmhouse to greet me with a cheerful wag of her tail. Maple wasn't worried. She was always happy. Dogs were the best.

I ruffled her fur when she met me. 'Where's Dad then, girl? Because I have had an idea that could mean we can stay here.'

Maple barked and set off towards the house so I followed her and gathered my courage to talk to Dad.

As I walked inside, I glanced back and looked over at the field to the side of the farm that was currently empty of anything other than some mud and grass. We didn't use that area currently for anything because the soil wasn't good enough for our crops, so could that be where the pumpkin patch might work? We couldn't grow pumpkins there, of course, but there was no time to grow them for this year anyway. So, I could use the area to display pumpkins for people to pick up, and create an autumnal experience for visitors.

If it went well and we wanted to grow our own pumpkins, that could happen in one of our crop areas in the future.

I knew I was maybe getting ahead of myself but that was my fatal flaw – I was a dreamer and once I imagined doing something, I couldn't let it go. The patch was firmly planted in my mind now; I just needed a way to make it happen. If I could get Dad to let me at least try.

Following Maple, I found my dad in the kitchen. He'd changed into a jacket and tie ready for his meeting and he was putting the kettle on the Aga to boil. Guilt washed over me that I'd sent Mr Suit Man in the wrong direction. He was bound to be late now, and that would be my fault.

Was I being selfish trying to do all I could to save the farm?

6

'Can we talk?' I asked my dad nervously as I stood in the doorway to our kitchen.

'You came back.' Dad looked relieved to see me, and I felt guilty all over again. 'What's up, love?'

'I did something that was maybe just a tad childish...' I admitted, walking in and sitting down at our table. Maple followed, plonking herself on my feet. I reached down to pat her, glad of her comfort and support. 'Mr Suit... Henderson,' I corrected myself, quickly, '...is likely to be late for your meeting.'

Dad came over. 'What happened, Willow?' he asked wearily, sinking into the chair opposite me.

I told him what happened at the café. 'I just couldn't stop myself, I'm sorry.'

'Oh, love. I knew you were having a hard time with this but that was definitely a childish response.'

I winced. I hated disappointing him. 'I'm sorry. He just seemed to have his nose in the air about our town and the café, and our farm. He got my back up, and I just blurted out the wrong directions.'

'Did he? Or was that just what you wanted to see? I'll phone him and help him find his way,' he said, reaching for his phone on the table.

'Hang on just a minute.'

Dad paused and raised an eyebrow at me.

'I know I handled that badly but it's because I really don't want to have to leave the farm.'

'I know. I'm sorry, I've let you down.'

'What do you mean?' I asked him in surprise, certain that it was me who had let him down, not the other way around.

'I should have done more to keep things working well around here but maybe after your mother, I did lose my way a bit then it was too late; things just seem to get worse each year. And I'm stumped on what we can do to stop it. That's why I wanted to meet with Henderson Homes.'

'It's not your fault,' I told him firmly. 'It's been a hard few years. I have had an idea that might work but, Dad...' I trailed off to gather the courage to say the next part. I was terrified to hear his answer but I knew I couldn't be selfish. I loved my dad, and he had to come first as much as I was desperate to stay here. 'Do you want to save the farm? If you wanted to leave, it would be hard but I would understand, and I have to... I'd accept it,' I finished, swallowing the lump in my throat again.

'Willow,' Dad choked out, sounding like he had a similar lump to me. 'I don't want to leave but I don't know if we have another choice.'

'What if we did, though?' I cleared my throat, relieved that in his heart he didn't actually want to leave the farm. 'I was in town and looking at how the High Street is decorated for autumn, and the café has seasonally themed food and drinks on the menu now. Plus, we always go big for Halloween around here, don't we?'

Dad nodded with a smile. 'That we do.'

'Well, what about getting into the autumn mood around here too? Bring people to the farm for some seasonal fun. I was thinking we could set up a pumpkin patch.'

'A pumpkin patch?'

I nodded. 'We would sell pumpkins. We could have an autumn trail with lots of cool seasonal and Halloween-themed props, places for people to take pictures. We could have pumpkin and autumn-themed food and drinks, maybe the two Pats would want to get involved; it would be a fun place for families to come like when they visit for our pick-your-own. But it would be to pick a pumpkin and before you say it, I know we don't grow pumpkins but for this year, we could just buy them in and then in the future—'

'Love,' Dad interrupted me gently. 'I can see you're excited about this but not only does it sound like a lot of work for us, what about the costs involved? You're talking about buying in pumpkins, and creating a trail... How would we afford it? We're trying to make money, not spend more.'

I leaned back in my chair, the wind sucked out of my sails suddenly. Once again, I'd got carried away with something without thinking about the basic part, like how we'd afford to do it. The pumpkin patch was already forming in my mind; I could see it out there on the field. But how could I make it happen without money? 'I think it would be really popular, it would make money; I just know it, Dad.'

'I think it could too. People love autumn and Halloween, and there isn't anything like that nearby. It was a good idea, Willow. But I don't see how you could make it happen. Not only is it only a couple of weeks until October, but we don't have extra funds for it.'

'What about getting a loan?'

'No,' he said quickly. 'We can't take out a loan and risk the farm. I'm not leaving you with nothing for your future. If we can't save the farm, we need to sell it so we both have something to live on. We'd need to start over somewhere. You have to be more practical about these things.'

I bristled. I hated the implication that I was too much of a dreamer. 'Mum would have loved the idea,' I said. 'She would have encouraged me, not told me to just give up. You say you want to save the farm but you won't help me do it.'

'That's not fair. We have to be sensible. Think with our heads, not our hearts.'

'Why?' I asked stubbornly. I could tell he was losing patience with me but I just wasn't willing to give up. Then the lightning bolt came. 'What about the jewellery?' I asked, although my heart did ache at the thought of parting with any of it. I shook it off. 'You said I should be practical. I've kept hold of it for years even though we've needed the money.'

'No, Willow, you love those pieces,' Dad told me, alarmed.

I thought about the jewellery box in my bedroom upstairs handed down to me by my mother. Some of the pieces had been in her family for generations, and I knew selling a few would raise some much-needed funds. Neither of us had ever wanted to touch it before. My mum had adored her jewellery and I would hate to part with any of it but I also knew she would understand. 'I do love them, but the farm is more important, isn't it? We've both resisted even mentioning it. It's been a bit of an elephant in the room at times. But we are close to selling up, Dad. If this isn't an emergency situation, I don't know what is. Mum would want us to use the jewellery to save the farm, wouldn't she?'

My question hung in the air and before Dad could respond, Maple let out a warning bark. She looked towards the window and I followed her gaze. Then I could hear the sound of tyres on the driveway.

I stood up, looked out of the window and sighed. 'Looks like you don't need to phone him after all,' I said as I watched a fancy car make its way towards us. It had to be Mr Suit Man. No one I knew had a car like it; this was mostly a four-by-four area. This car was sleek and shiny and just screamed, *I'm not from around here.*

'Not much harm done in the end then,' Dad said, getting up from his chair stiffly. 'I'll put the kettle back on for tea. Let's just listen to what he has to say, okay? Then we can talk more later.'

'I already know what he will say, and the answer is no,' I replied, sitting back down and folding my arms across my chest. 'My idea can work, Dad, I just know it.'

Before Dad could answer, the doorbell rang and Maple let out a low growl.

'I know how you feel,' I told her.

Dad sighed. 'Be friendly, you two, please,' he said as he walked to the door.

'I wish we didn't have to be,' I confessed in a whisper to Maple. 'Stay though, girl,' I told her, knowing that after sending him in the wrong direction, I better not let my dog chase him out, although the idea of doing just that was appealing, I had to admit.

'Come on in,' I heard my dad say.

I braced myself as Mr Suit Man walked into my kitchen and saw me, his face dropping instantly once our eyes met.

7

'As I said, I would have been on time, but I was sent in the wrong direction,' Mr Suit Man said, arching an eyebrow. His large, bright-blue eyes were staring right at me.

I shifted on my feet, uncomfortable with his scrutiny. 'Yeah, that was my fault,' I admitted. Maple leaned against my legs for support. I reached down to pat her. Mr Suit Man glanced down at my hand then back up to my face. 'I suppose I wanted to put this meeting off for as long as possible.'

'Well, you sent me on an hour's detour. I managed to get correct directions from a dog walker,' he said with a shake of his head, clearly irritated. 'I don't understand why you wanted to waste my time.' He turned to my dad. 'You said on this phone you wanted this meeting.'

'I'll be frank, Mr Henderson,' my dad said. 'Neither of us want to sell our farm, but we might have to. Willow is sorry she sent you the wrong way. We're a bit out of sorts as you can imagine.'

I could tell Mr Suit Man was confused and I knew I had been slightly childish so I tried to explain. 'This farm has been in our family for generations; I've lived and worked here my whole life...' I began.

'But you said in your phone call, things have become too hard to manage,' the man said to my dad, ignoring me. 'That's why I'm here. This should be an exciting meeting for you.'

'Um...' Dad said, glancing at me, knowing I felt the same way – this was the farthest thing from exciting. 'You're here now anyway. So, have a seat, Mr Henderson, I'll make us tea, yes?'

'You should call me Dylan,' he said, sitting down at the kitchen table at the opposite end to me, thankfully. 'Mr Henderson sounds like my father,' he added, looking uncomfortable at the prospect.

'How old are you?' I blurted out.

'Twenty-seven,' he replied, but then carried on addressing Dad. I had been right that he was close to my age but the way he spoke and acted seemed older to me. 'I spotted your farm a couple of weeks ago while I was scouting for locations for a new development in this area. My brother has been looking for somewhere around here for a while as this area is so sought after, what with the good schools and the fact it's so popular with tourists. Birchbrook seems very... quaint,' Dylan continued briskly, saying the word 'quaint' with a definite snobby inflection.

'We love our town,' I told him pointedly as Dad made three cups of tea. 'It's sought after because it's a great place to live.'

'I think a development would do really well here,' Dylan said with a nod, seeming to miss my point. He glanced out of the window at the farm. 'Those trees would be really appealing to buyers too.'

Dad looked over his shoulder at me then turned to Dylan. 'You would keep the trees then? Willow has been very worried about them; she's loved them since she was a little girl.'

'Buyers love nature as long as it doesn't infringe on light coming into the houses so I think we'd keep them. We could name the development after the birch trees to match the town,' Dylan said. 'We think we could fit around ten properties on the farm and—'

'Ten houses?' I looked out at my farm and tried to picture it transformed into a development of ten new-build homes. My heart dropped down to my stomach. All that land gone.

Dylan pulled his phone out of his pocket. 'Now, I spoke to some estate agents in the area. We would of course need several surveys done on the land but at the moment, my brother, who runs our company, has instructed me that we could offer—'

'Here we are.' Dad brought over the teas and sat down in between me and Dylan. He glanced at him. 'It's a family business then? We like that, don't we, love?' he added, looking at me.

'Well, maybe it means you can understand why we don't want to sell our farm,' I said in a frosty tone as I could tell Mr Suit Man was just focused on his phone, and not us. 'So, Dylan, do you run the business with your brother then?' I asked him, forcing him to look up from the device.

'My brother, who is a few years older than me, owns the company; I just joined at the start of this year,' he replied.

I sighed. He didn't really know about running a family business then. I looked away from him. 'Dad, this is pointless; we don't want to sell and what about the pumpkin-patch idea? We're wasting time having this meeting.'

'But I thought you were interested in selling?' Dylan frowned. 'Mr Connor—'

'Adam, please,' my dad said as he took a sip of his tea. I hadn't bothered to have any of mine; I was too keyed up to drink. 'We are struggling with the farm, and that's why—'

'But I have an idea to turn things around,' I interrupted. 'And neither of us want to sell, do we, Dad?'

'This would be a great opportunity for you both,' Dylan said quickly.

I eyed him. 'And for you. As you said, this would be really popular for people; Birchbrook is sought after and hardly any new houses come onto the market. Our farm is really the only big patch of land around here that you could develop into your... homes,' I said, wrinkling my nose at the word 'homes' because the ones they had built, which Dad had shown me online, looked so uninspiring, I knew I wouldn't personally be able to enjoy living in one. I loved our old, chaotic, run-down house. 'This would make you a lot of profit, wouldn't it?'

'We would be able to ease all your money worries,' Dylan replied smoothly, like he'd practised this speech a hundred times. 'It would be a good opportunity for all of us. Why don't I put together a proposal so you can see exactly how much we could offer you for this land, and I think you'll be keen then—'

'Dad?' I broke in. 'Let me create this pumpkin patch. We could give it a go; give me a few weeks and I'll make it work. There isn't a deadline on your offer, right?' I demanded of Dylan. 'You want this place; you'd wait for us to decide whether to accept or not, wouldn't you?'

'Well, uh, if we weren't going to get this land, I'd have to find somewhere else for my brother...' Dylan shifted in his seat. Was it my imagination or did he seem a bit nervous suddenly?

'How long would you need for your pumpkin patch?' Dad asked me, leaning back in his chair to study me.

'It would need to open in October, and would be open for the whole month so we'd know by the end if it's going to be something that could generate enough income for us to be okay until the spring/summer season,' I said eagerly.

'Wait, you haven't even heard our offer...' Dylan hastily punched at his phone. 'I think my brother would offer something in this region, once we had all the surveys done, etc...' He showed his phone screen to my dad. 'Surely, that would be something that would interest you, Mr Connor?'

'Adam,' Dad reminded him as he looked at the number Dylan had written down.

I craned my neck but Dylan turned the phone so I couldn't see it, as if I wasn't allowed to know the details. I shook my head.

'It would clear all our debts and allow us to start somewhere new,' Dad told me as Dylan took the phone away. 'But, Dylan, my daughter is right – we really don't want to leave. Willow, would six weeks from now be long enough to know if the pumpkin patch could get us through the winter months? To make the money we need to get out of the hole we're currently in?'

'Maybe I should leave the room,' Dylan said. 'This is most unorthodox,' he added under his breath. He seemed alarmed by how this meeting was going. I wondered if he'd ever dealt with homeowners like us before. Judging by his wide eyes, the way he was pulling at his shirt collar and shifting in his seat, he hadn't. He probably thought we would bite his hand off to accept, and was now befuddled.

'Six weeks?' I checked with Dad, who nodded. 'If I can create and make enough of a success of the patch in six weeks, and prove that we could turn the farm's fortunes around, you won't sell?'

'But if not, then I'll accept this young man's offer,' Dad agreed with a nod.

'Hang on...' Dylan began.

I smiled. 'Six weeks. It's a deal.'

8

'Maybe you should show Dylan around the farm, tell him your idea; he might then understand why we want to hold off on responding to his offer.'

'Why me?' I asked, flashing a pleading look at my father. I really didn't want to spend any alone time with Mr Suit Man.

'My legs and feet are tired. I'm tired. Willow, show Dylan the farm then I'm sure he will be willing to wait six weeks for a final decision on this offer. You can send it over in writing, can't you?' Dad said in a tone that I knew meant I couldn't object. I wasn't sure Dylan would be able to either.

'Um...' Dylan looked thoroughly confused at what had just happened. 'Well, I can send the offer over but six weeks is quite a long time...'

'You'll understand,' Dad said simply.

I wasn't sure my father was right about that. This farm was clearly a million miles outside of Dylan Henderson's comfort zone but resigned, I stood up with a sigh. I supposed after my behaviour earlier, I couldn't refuse my dad this. 'Let's go then.' I nodded at Dylan and whistled for Maple, heading out before anyone could stop me. I felt relieved. Dad was letting me try at least. He didn't want to sell and he seemed to think maybe there was a chance I could do this. I really didn't want to let him down again. I wanted to make this work. And I needed to start by getting rid of Dylan Henderson as fast as I possibly could.

Outside, I looked behind me to see Dylan had followed and was hurrying to catch up. I took him around the side of the farmhouse to see the crop fields.

'You might get muddy,' I warned as Maple ran ahead of us. 'You aren't really dressed to tour the farm.' His suit and shiny shoes couldn't have been more inappropriate for our farm as we approached the autumn season. I pointed to the empty field. 'That's where I want to create the pumpkin patch. That field isn't doing anything for us right now so it's a great spot.' I folded my arms as he looked over at it, pausing beside me.

'What even is a pumpkin patch?' Dylan asked as he groaned, looking down at his feet, his shoes sliding into a muddy hole.

'Told you, you're not dressed for a farm. What do you do when you visit one of your building sites?' I asked, trying not to laugh at how horrified he looked at being outside on a field.

'I don't,' he said, surprised. 'My brother does all that. I scout for areas we can develop, do the pitches and write the proposals and make our offers. We haven't bought a farm before. But as I said, this place caught my eye.' He glanced at me. 'What's a pumpkin patch then?' he asked again, still looking like my dad and I had bamboozled him. Which we probably had, to be fair.

I explained the idea I had, getting excited all over again. 'I just love autumn, and so does our town. You probably noticed the High Street and the café?'

'I did notice a lot of pumpkins when I was there. I had no idea people celebrated autumn. It's just a time of year,' Dylan said, frowning. He looked at our empty field. 'Halloween and

Christmas, yes, but I don't get why autumn would be celebrated.'

'Why shouldn't it be celebrated?' I countered hotly. 'Autumn has always been my favourite time of year. A time of change. New beginnings. And the start of cosy season. Warm drinks, comfort food, the beauty of nature...' I gestured behind me. 'The way the leaves on the trees change into beautiful colours, don't you think that's magical in its own way?' I tilted my head as Dylan's eyes turned to me.

'You really are passionate, aren't you?' Dylan said, looking down at me, his voice softer for the first time since we met.

I looked back at him, startled again by the colour of his eyes, which were even brighter outside in the natural light. I took a second to compose myself to answer. 'I am passionate about this farm, yes.'

'Even though it's failing?'

I snapped. 'Hey! You can't just stand there and say our farm is failing; you have no idea what it's like working here day in and day out, living here too, trying to turn a profit when every day, something breaks or there's a storm or a crop fails, or...' I trailed off because I had been about to tell him about losing my mother and that was way too personal to share with Mr Suit Man. I took a breath and tried to calm down a little bit. 'I love this farm and I *have* to save it. Do you have any idea what it's like to feel that passionate about anything?' I put my hands on my hips, not believing that he was even capable of being passionate full stop.

He opened his mouth to speak but then he shook his head and looked away from me. 'Passion is overrated, Willow. It won't pay the bills. You need to think with your head, not with your heart. And our offer will allow to you start over somewhere, make a new life; why would you turn that down for a...' he trailed off, then glanced back at me. '...pipe dream?'

I was seething. This man was heartless. I looked out at Maple, who had noticed a squirrel running down one of the trees. She took off after it with a bark. She was what mattered. My dad mattered. My mother's memory mattered. This farm mattered. Not this man's opinion.

'You're wrong,' I told him shortly. 'I will make this work because I believe in this farm, and I will save it. You won't get to tear this down and build your identikit houses here. And you know what? You think it's a pipe dream because look at you...' I gave his suit a disdainful look up and down. 'You have no idea what hard work looks like. I bet you have never worked outside in your life before. You don't know what it feels like to get up at the crack of dawn in winter or see the tiny changes in the seasons every day, to grow things with your bare hands, to see what nature is capable of...' I trailed off to take a breath as I had got really carried away. 'You wouldn't last a day working here.'

Dylan spun to face me then and I could see I had finally managed to push his buttons like he had pushed mine. His blue eyes finally had a spark of fire in them. I had to take another breath because they took him from being conventionally handsome to being... attractive. And that was a thought I definitely didn't want to have. 'You have no idea how hard I work. I am working hard to prove to my brother that I can run the business with him, and this farm would be my biggest find so far.'

I tilted my head to look at him. It was interesting to see he clearly wanted to do a good job with his company and show his brother that he could.

Maple barked again so I turned from those blue eyes of his. 'This way,' I said, shoving my hands into my coat pocket to follow Maple around the farm. I pointed out the crop fields and the chickens and then we wandered around to the other side where there was a row of four cottages.

'These cottages are listed on Airbnb but they really needed renovating. It's been on our wish list for years but would cost a lot and neither of us really have the time to focus on them as a business to make it worth the outlay. We occasionally have people staying but mostly, we use them for our seasonal workers in summer to help us with the pick-your-own business,' I explained. 'If I could get more people to the farm outside of the summer season then maybe it would be worth fixing them up and people might want to stay here.'

'That could be an opportunity,' Dylan said. Then he shook his head. 'But a lot of money and work. There is just you and your father working here?' He gazed around. 'So much land for two of you to manage.'

'Yeah.' I sighed as we wandered back towards the farmhouse, the birch trees ahead of us swaying in the breeze. 'There were more of us back in the day. When my mum was alive,' I said with a hard swallow. 'But we had to let our full-time help go as profits went down and we lost my mum. We now employ seasonal staff in summer only so yes, there is a lot for us to do and my dad isn't managing as well as he used to.' When I said all this out loud, I wondered if Dylan had a tiny point about the pumpkin patch being a 'pipe dream'. 'As I said, it's hard work but I love it, and Dad doesn't want to lose this place either.'

We walked in silence for a bit, moving slowly back towards the house.

'I feel like you think I'm the enemy here,' Dylan said after a moment. 'But this offer could change your life.'

I stopped and turned to face him. Reluctantly, he did the same. 'I don't want it to change. I love my life.'

'Do you?'

I hesitated. Things certainly hadn't been the same since we lost my mum. And I did sometimes get a sharp pang of loneliness that took my breath away. Dad wasn't happy. But the farm still brought me joy. In summer, when the sun was shining and there were people here picking fruit and veg, eating ice cream, kids smiling... Maple came to me then as if she sensed I was feeling lost and I smiled down at her. She brought me joy too. There were parts of my life I loved and parts that were bloody tough, but wasn't that true for everyone? Although as I eyed Dylan, I did wonder if his life was at all tough. Or was it perfect?

'You don't understand. You can't know what it's like here. Or how I feel about it. I know you think I should bite your hand off for the money you're going to offer us but honestly, the thought of doing that just breaks my heart.'

There was a beat when Dylan absorbed what I'd said. I thought maybe for a moment he did understand but then he ruined it with his next words. 'It's going to be too much work for you to save it so why not just accept my offer now and not put yourself through these six weeks as your dad is suggesting?' Dylan said.

'I know you couldn't do it, but I can.'

'How do you know I couldn't do it?' he suddenly said, the fire back in those eyes of his. I had pushed his buttons again, I realised gleefully.

'Look at you, Mr Suit Man. You'll leave here and go back to your warm office while I'll be out here working to save my family's business. If there is a tiny bit of hope, I'm going to cling to it. And when my dad calls you in six weeks, it will be to say I've made the pumpkin patch a success and he won't accept any offer you give him.'

'You really are stubborn, aren't you? I kind of want to hang around and see what a disaster this will turn out to be,' he flung back. The he raked a hand through his hair. 'This meeting has not gone the way I thought it would,' he muttered. 'That was unprofessional of me. Why don't we go back inside and talk to your father and—'

'Why don't you hang around then?' I interrupted. 'And watch as I make sure my dad will never accept your offer?' I said, putting my hands on my hips in challenge.

9

Dylan stared back at me defiantly. 'What are you talking about, Willow?' he asked with an exasperated look. I wondered if he had anyone react to him and his brother wanting to buy their land like this before. Actually, I wondered if he'd ever met anyone like me at all. He seemed to be thoroughly confused. But I didn't care. I knew in my gut that making a last-ditch effort to save the farm was something I *had* to do, even if it would be bloody hard, and even if it didn't end up working out.

'Well, as you said, this will be hard work for me; why don't you help me with the pumpkin patch and I'll listen to your plans for this place and take your offer seriously? Then if you can persuade me, or if the patch doesn't work out, I'll sign on the dotted line. But if it does work out, then you agree the best thing is for me to keep the farm and walk away,' I blurted out without really thinking about what I was suggesting. I just found the idea of Mr Suit Man staying to help out on the farm hilarious and also a chance for me to make sure my dad wasn't persuaded to sell the farm to him. I also thought maybe I could subtly pick his business brain while he was here. I waited to see what Dylan would do with my outrageous idea.

'Why would I do that?' he asked slowly. 'This is your opportunity, not mine. I'm making you an offer.'

I raised an eyebrow. 'But you said this would be your biggest deal so far, right?' I asked. He gave a slight nod. 'And you want to show your brother you can do it. I can see that in your eyes – you want to prove yourself. Well, so do I.'

'But we're against each other?' he said, with an inflection that suggested he was checking.

I shrugged. 'Keep your friends close, your enemies closer. Right?'

'This has not gone the way I thought it would,' Dylan muttered. 'Are you serious? You want me to stay here for six weeks?'

'You can work remotely, can't you? Tell your brother you're working on the pitch for the farm, which technically wouldn't be a lie.' The more I thought about it, the more I thought this could be good for me. I'd get free labour, free business advice plus the chance to show Dylan just how much the farm meant to us. Maybe then he would withdraw his offer in six weeks' time anyway. 'You could stay in one of the cottages,' I added. That would keep him out of my way when I didn't need his help. I was sure neither of us would want to spend any time together socially based on how today was going. 'Or do you think I was right and you can't cut it living and working on a farm for six weeks?' I added then, with a smug smile. Was Mr Suit Man going to back down from my challenge?

'Oh, couldn't I?' Dylan countered. 'You're wrong. I'm not afraid of hard work. And you're right, I'm determined to prove myself just like you. So, why not? In six weeks' time, you'll bite my hand off to accept Henderson Homes' offer. Until then, I'll stay here and help out. And I will also persuade you that selling is not only the best idea but your only option at this point.'

I flung out my hand. 'Deal.'

We shook once, firmly, eyes locked. At the touch of his hand in mine, the smug smile faded from my lips. My hands were battered from outdoor life, his were smooth and soft but it wasn't that difference that shook me and made me quickly let go of him. It was how warm his touch had suddenly made my skin.

Flustered, I looked away, my cheeks turning pink. 'I have no idea what my dad will say about this,' I admitted.

'Or my brother,' Dylan said with a sigh.

'We better find out then,' I said, turning towards the farmhouse, ready to share our bonkers plan with my father. He would likely think I was even more of a hopeless dreamer than ever, but then again, if I could get Dylan on board with my pumpkin patch then surely Dad would have to get on board too?

I whistled for Maple and set off, Dylan hurrying after me, his shiny shoes completely caked in mud now, his hair tousled from being out in the elements, his tie slightly askew, but I had to admit just to myself that those blue eyes of his had looked the brightest they had since I first glanced at them in Birchbrook Café earlier.

* * *

'I'm sorry, what?' my dad said after I told him what Dylan and I had discussed. Dylan had gone to his car to talk to his brother. I glanced out of the kitchen window to watch him walking to his posh car looking like a real fish out of water. It was going to be interesting to see if he could even last a week here, let alone six.

'Willow, I am used to your slightly outlandish ideas and plans but I'm seriously worried about this. Not only do you want to create a pumpkin patch for October, just a couple of weeks away, but now you've invited this stranger to live and work on the farm and help you do it? Even though he actually wants it to fail and for us to sell the farm to him. Have I got that right?'

'I know it's a little bit out there,' I admitted, 'but I get free labour plus we could get some business advice from Dylan; we might be able to turn things around and then we won't have to sell.'

'And what if we do have to sell?' Dad countered.

I sighed. 'Well then, I'll have to accept it after these six weeks.'

'Will you?' Dad sighed. 'Why would Dylan even agree to this? Doesn't he need to do his job? How can he work here and for Henderson Homes?'

'I think he works mostly remotely anyway, plus this farm is his biggest idea; he wants to make it happen and is going to tell his brother he needs to be here to plan it all and pitch the idea to us. He's going to stay in one of the cottages. Look, Dad, I know you're not fully behind my idea but this is a great way for me to make it happen. And if it doesn't work out like I think it will, we just say yes to Henderson Homes. So, where's the problem?'

'Can you work and live with Dylan for six weeks? You sent him in the wrong direction earlier today. How will you deal with him being around all the time?'

'I'm going to think about the big picture,' I said, although I was a bit worried now that Dad had asked me that. Dylan was a stranger who had got my back up. I was unconvinced he could work outside so he could end up being more of hindrance than a help. Especially because he wanted my plan to fail.

Dylan walked in then. 'My brother thinks this is weird and I think he might be right,' he said, looking as stunned as me that we had got ourselves into this. But we'd shaken on it and I could tell that accepting a challenge meant something to us both.

'I'll show you the cottage you can have,' I said, hurrying past my dad before he could plant any more doubts in my head. 'Dad thinks the same as your brother,' I added when we were out of earshot. We left the farmhouse again and I led him to the cottages. 'You won't try to sabotage me while you're here, will you? You said you would genuinely help me with the pumpkin patch.'

'You seem to think I'll be useless at farm work,' Dylan replied. 'But I think I'll surprise you. And I want to win this fair and square, as I'm sure you do. I won't need to sabotage you; you are going to sell the farm to me in six weeks' time.'

I snorted. 'No way. This is going to work, and you will have to admit that I was right – this farm is worth saving.' I unlocked the best cottage we had and held out the key for him. 'Take a look around, go and get whatever you need and we can start work first thing tomorrow.'

'Stay here tonight?' Dylan asked, stepping through the door and raising an eyebrow. It was old-fashioned and lacked amenities but it was comfortable and cosy. 'Maybe we have a been a bit hasty...'

'Are you scared, Dylan Henderson?' I asked from the tiny hallway as I watched him look around the cottage.

'Honestly? My brother hating this idea only made me want to do it more. And I'm not scared of anything.' Dylan returned to me by the door. 'Why, you want to back out?'

'Nope,' I said, shaking my head firmly. 'It's the same for me and my dad. Him doubting me makes me just want to work even harder. So, first thing tomorrow then, Dylan Henderson?'

Dylan put the keys to the cottage in his pocket. 'First thing tomorrow, Willow Connor.'

I nodded and left the cottage, looking up at the sky darkening above me. The grey clouds started drizzling and I hurried back to the farmhouse, hoping the weather wasn't giving me an ominous sign.

10

That evening, I walked into the Birchbrook Arms, the local pub, in desperate need of a drink. After Dylan left the farm to pick up whatever he'd need for his stay, I completed my chores and then Dad and I had leftovers for dinner. Dad settled down with a puzzle, Maple lying down nearby to enjoy the log fire we had lit as the night drew in chilly, but I couldn't relax – I kept looking out of the window and listening for the sounds of the car on the driveway. I was torn between wanting to know exactly when Dylan came back to the farm to make sure he hadn't changed his mind about our pact, and not wanting to be sitting around waiting for him. So, in the end, I said I'd nip out for a drink and then hopefully, I'd be back just to see Dylan's car and him safely in the cottage.

Birchbrook Arms was on the edge of town and was incredibly old with low ceilings and wooden beams, and roaring fires in autumn and winter. I opened the door and recognised all the people inside. I liked that. It was comforting, and right now, when things were in such turmoil, I clung to the familiarity of my hometown more than ever. I waved at the landlord, Johnny, who had run the pub for as long as I was old enough to drink, and he walked over to my end of the bar.

'You got all the town talking today, Willow,' he said as he grabbed a wine glass, not needing to ask me what I wanted – my drink of choice had been long fixed. 'Sending some city boy away from your farm or something.'

I sighed. Of course, everyone had talked about what happened in the café earlier. Had that really been the same day? It felt like a week ago. I leaned against the bar, glad it could take my weight. I felt weary to my bones. I noticed a few other people listening in on us as well. 'Yeah, he wants to make an offer to buy our farm and bulldoze it all into new-build homes,' I said as Johnny slid a glass of wine across the shiny wood to me. I tapped my card on the machine and took a sip. 'I really don't want to have to sell. I was putting off the meeting but, of course, he turned up in the end anyway.'

'What are you going to do?'

'It wouldn't be the same without your fruit and veg in summer,' a woman sitting said behind me. I glanced over at her and smiled. She ran the florist's in the High Street.

'That's what the problem is – we're okay in summer, but less so the rest of the year. So, when I was in the High Street today, I thought maybe I could do what the town does and create something autumnally themed on the farm.'

'Like what?'

I looked over and saw the question had come from Paul from the café who was sitting with a couple of his friends, beers lined up in front of them. My conversation with Johnny had drawn the attention of everyone within earshot but I wasn't surprised – Birchbrook was a nosy town, although I knew they all meant well.

'Well, we all love pumpkins and as our pick-your-own does

so well in summer, I thought I'd make a pumpkin patch,' I said, beaming at everyone listening. There was silence and a few people looked at one another then back at me.

'You want to sell pumpkins? How will that save the farm?' Paul asked, confused.

'We wouldn't just sell pumpkins; it would be like a whole autumnal experience: a day out for families like when you come to the farm in summer. It will be... fun,' I said, finishing a little bit lamely as no one seemed to be into this idea. I gulped down more of my wine. 'The High Street is always decorated for autumn. You have an autumnal menu,' I pointed out to Paul. 'Maybe you could sell some food and drink at the patch; I'll come in and speak to your parents.'

'We'd need to be sure there would be enough customers to make it worthwhile leaving the café, though,' Paul said, looking less than thrilled but then he was often moody.

'Hang on,' Johnny said. 'You don't grow pumpkins, do you?'

'Not yet. I'd have to buy them in for this year,' I admitted.

'How will you make a profit by doing that?' Paul called over.

My heart sank. I supposed I hadn't actually run any figures. I could just picture the patch in my mind and I knew I could make it a place people would want to come and visit. That had made me think I could make money out of it. But now everyone seemed to be pouring cold water on the idea, just like my dad and Sabrina earlier in the café. Why couldn't anyone see my vision?

Before I could respond, the pub door swung open and everyone turned from me to the door. I looked as well and my evening got a little bit worse. Dylan strode in, seemingly oblivious to everyone staring at his entrance, and walked up to the bar. He had at least ditched the suit and was now wearing dark jeans and a dark shirt, although he still had shiny shoes on.

'Isn't that the guy from the café?' Paul asked, his voice carrying over to the bar.

Dylan turned then he saw me. 'Your dad suggested I come for a drink and some food,' he said, looking surprised to see me. I assumed Dad had failed to mention I'd be here.

'Right,' I said. 'Anyway...' I raised my glass to everyone then slid off to a free table in the corner near to the crackling log fire. I was going to drink my wine away from annoying questions. My head was starting to pound with things to think about and I was fed up with everyone making me feel like I was crazy to even try to make this pumpkin patch happen. I sat down and stared at my wine glass on the table dully. I was now regretting coming out. I should have stayed home and not told anyone about my idea.

'Do you mind?'

I looked up to see Dylan hovering by my table with a beer and a glass of wine.

'I hate drinking alone,' he added. 'I got you another glass...'

Staring at it, I was torn. This didn't feel like a good idea at all. Our conversation earlier hadn't exactly been polite and calm. We might have to work together for the next few weeks but I was at as loss about what we would find to talk about in the pub.

'Come on, Willow, we have to coexist for six weeks...'

I sighed, again regretting my impulsive proposal. 'Go ahead,' I said. 'This evening can't get much worse.'

Dylan sat down and slid my wine over to me then took a sip of his beer. 'What's happened?'

'I was telling everyone about the pumpkin-patch idea when you came in, and everyone seems to think it's a bit mad. Asking me about how profitable it will be. I haven't exactly worked out the details yet but that doesn't mean it can't work. No one has any imagination around here,' I grumbled.

'Imagination is great,' Dylan said. 'But you do need a plan so you can make a profit. Otherwise you might as well accept my offer right here, right now.'

I started to glare but he smiled and his eyes twinkled in the light from the fire. Was he teasing me a little bit? I was so stunned, I couldn't respond for a moment. I decided to turn the tables. 'So, what did your brother say when you told him you were going to stay on our farm?'

'It was along the lines of people here,' Dylan said. 'Wondering what on earth I was thinking. But I told Nate I'd do my usual work so there wasn't a lot he could say. I often work from home or remotely anyway, and this would be a great addition to our portfolio so it's worth the effort.'

'How come you haven't worked with him for long?' I asked, curious as to why it hadn't always been a family business.

Dylan gulped down his beer. 'I studied law at university, I thought I wanted to be a barrister, well, I guess my family pushed me in that direction... my brother is eight years older than me and after we lost our mother, he kind of took on responsibility for me along with our dad.'

I stared at him. 'I lost my mother too.'

'I gathered from what you told me at the farm,' he replied gently. 'I hated university. I hated my course, I couldn't focus, it was so soon after my mum died, and I was grieving but I also had so much pressure from my brother and my dad. God, is this being too honest?' he asked, suddenly stopping as if realising he was blurting out deep shit to a stranger.

'Oh no, I am used to spilling my secrets; I want to hear it all,' I encouraged him. My dad often said I talked too much for my own good so I was pleased to meet someone else with the same tendency. I smiled. 'Sometimes, it's good to just let it all out, right? So, university went badly?' I prompted.

'That's an understatement. I ended up leaving. And since then, I guess, I've been a bit unsure what to do. I've had quite a few jobs and moved around and my brother has kept on at me to work for him. This year, I gave in and said yes. So that's why I want to do well at this job.'

I nodded, understanding his determination to do well and why he wanted to make our deal happen. He wanted his brother's approval. I knew the feeling. I hated letting my father down. And Dylan felt like he had been doing that for years. 'I guess our crazy pact makes more sense now. I lost my mother and since then, the farm just seems to have declined and we've struggled. I hate the thought that I'm disappointing her.' I tilted my head to the side. 'She loved autumn. It was her favourite time of year, and she passed that love onto me. I want to make her proud, just like you want to make your family proud.'

He smiled across the table at me, holding eye contact. It was a weirdly nice feeling to connect with someone new like that. I was used to being around people I'd known forever. They all knew about my mother and rarely spoke about her, and I was sure that was because they didn't want to upset me but sometimes, I wanted to talk about her. Dylan was listening. And maybe that was making me be more honest than I probably should be. Particularly when we were on opposing sides.

'I get why you're determined to save the farm and why you want to make this pumpkin patch now,' Dylan said. 'And now you know why I want to get you to accept my offer to buy the farm.'

I finished my first glass of wine and started on the one Dylan had bought me. 'We know why we are doing this then. But there's a long way to go to get the other one to agree to the same point of view.'

Dylan shrugged. 'We have six weeks, right?'

'Despite the fact our families think this is completely mad, plus the whole town will be talking about it, I have no doubt. And neither of us have an actual plan of how we're going to win our pact.' I couldn't help but smile though because suddenly, I didn't feel quite so alone.

Dylan smiled back and then his food order arrived so our conversation paused and I was a little bit relieved it had. Opening up to Dylan might turn out to be dangerous.

11

After Dylan had finished his dinner, and our drinks were gone, we walked back to the farm together. We had been keeping the conversation away from deep subjects again, Dylan asking questions about Birchbrook and me waxing lyrical about my hometown.

'You really do love it here, don't you?' Dylan said after a minute of silence following me describing the lantern parade we had on Halloween. We were strolling up the hill towards the farm. The sky above us was clear, dotted with twinkling stars, the night air chilly, promising cold days and nights ahead, the light from the moon guiding our way. There were no streetlamps here, and no one on the road. I was used to the quiet, and to the dark, but Dylan kept looking around and I wondered if he was slightly spooked by it as a city boy.

'I know you think I probably haven't seen much of the world like you have,' I said, shaking my head. He opened his mouth to protest but I was sure that was going through his mind. I shrugged. 'I actually went to university myself,' I said, glancing across at him. He, as I expected, did look surprised, although he tried to hide it.

'Yeah, a few towns over so in the week I lived there and just came back to the farm on weekends and in the holidays. My best friend Sabrina came too. She's a teacher now. Anyway, I studied agriculture. I wanted to be able to run the farm one day. But after I left, my mum became ill and lots of things I had planned fell by the wayside. I did miss Birchbrook a lot too. This place is just in my blood.'

I could see the edge of the farm ahead of us now, lights left on in the farmhouse to guide my way. My dad had done that since I was a teenager and started going out at night. It was reassuring. Whatever happened, I could always come back home. But all that was under threat now. I wondered if Dylan could ever really appreciate the fear inside me that one day I wouldn't be able to return to this place.

Dylan stumbled beside me then, his shoes not as hardy as my boots walking in the mud in the dark.

Instinctively, I reached out to grab hold of his arm.

'Thanks,' he mumbled, righting himself.

'You need to get some decent footwear if you're going to live and work on a farm for six weeks,' I said, as he righted himself and avoided falling over.

'Hmm, you might be right. I'll order some tonight. Oh, can you get Amazon to deliver out here?'

We started walking again and I let go of his arm, trying not to think about the curve of his muscles that I had felt through his coat.

'Of course you can,' I said with a laugh. 'We are part of the modern world, you know. We have Wi-Fi too.'

We walked through the gate and I closed it behind us. I paused at the end of the path as I would go on to the farmhouse but Dylan needed to head the other way to the cottages. 'Can I ask you something?' I checked softly.

'Go ahead,' he replied, turning to face me. I could only make out his silhouette in the light coming from the house behind us. It made asking him this question easier.

'If you weren't involved in it, would you think I was crazy to be creating a pumpkin patch like everyone else seems to?'

'I've never been encouraged to use my imagination. My family are logical, my work is logical, but I wish I could sometimes. I admire people who can dream.'

'Everyone can dream,' I told him. 'You just need to let yourself.'

'Maybe you can teach me.' I saw his eyes catch the light. There was that twinkle again. It made me wonder if there was more to this man than the city, than his suit, than business, than the logical world he came from. Then I scolded myself. I shouldn't be wondering that.

'What will you teach *me*?' I blurted out the thought before I could stop myself.

'I'll have to think about that. Goodnight, Willow. I'll see you tomorrow.'

'Meet me right here at 9 a.m.,' I called as he started to slip away in the darkness.

His chuckle drifted back to me. 'Yes, ma'am.'

I smiled then let myself into the farmhouse. Maple was asleep in her bed but opened her eyes and lifted her head, her tail wagging as I went over to give her a pat. 'What a night, girl,' I said, softly. I gave her a kiss then headed upstairs to my room, my mind whirring with ideas of what Dylan could teach me while he was here. I needed him to get me back into the mindset I had at university. I needed my business brain alongside my imagination. I needed to be logical and make this a success. Turn a profit. I needed to use Dylan to help me do this. But as I got ready for bed, my mind wondered if he could teach me anything that wasn't business related.

'You've been single for too long,' I grumbled to myself as I went over to the window to pull my curtains closed. Just before I did, I peered out and looked over to the cottages which were just visible from my room. There was a light on in one of them. I wondered what Dylan was doing, and then the light turned off. He'd gone to bed.

Why did I feel lonelier all of a sudden?

I shook my head, pulled the curtains abruptly closed and then put on my pyjamas, trying desperately not to think about Dylan in bed.

* * *

My eyes opened before my alarm went off the following morning.

It was still pitch-black outside. I was used to waking up when it was dark and with everything on my mind, I wasn't surprised that I didn't need a wake-up call. The farmhouse was chilly as the heating always needed an hour to feel like it was actually doing its job so I didn't want to get out of bed just yet. I turned on my lamp, reaching over to my bedside table and opening up the drawer where I kept things my mother had left me. I pulled out the wooden jewellery box she had had since she was a teenager and put it on the bed so I could open it up and look inside.

When I was growing up, I loved looking at these pieces. My mum only wore them on special occasions. She told me once though when she was ill that she regretted that. 'Life is short, Willow. Don't save things for special occasions. If it brings you joy, use it or wear it now. The same goes for people. If they bring you joy, tell them.' I lifted out the gold and diamond necklace that her grandmother had passed down to her – it had been in the family for generations and I knew it was worth a lot – along with the diamond ring my mum had worn when she and my father had got engaged, and a string of pearls that had been a wedding present. I touched them, hating the thought of parting with them but Mum had told me she regretted keeping them in a box so much. Surely, she would agree that saving the farm was a reason to take them out?

I pulled out my phone and opened up an old email. A couple of years ago, when I couldn't ignore the fact we were struggling on the farm, I had taken the pieces to a jeweller's a couple of towns over to have them valued, and they had been willing to buy them at the time. But I'd walked away and like my dad said, I'd stuck my head back in the sand and ignored the valuation.

For now, I thought the diamond necklace would be enough to get the pumpkin patch started, along with the small amount left in the farm bank account. I typed an email to the jeweller's asking if I could come in with the necklace ASAP and then I put the necklace around my neck for what was probably the final time, getting out of bed to look at it in the full-length mirror.

My reflection reminded me instantly of my mum. We had looked so similar. I remembered seeing her wear the necklace for Christmas once. I couldn't wait to be old enough to wear it too. 'I'll get it back one day,' I promised us both now.

Downstairs, Maple clearly heard that I was up and barked and I knew that the moment to be sentimental was over.

We had work to do.

12

I met Dylan at 9 a.m. after finishing my morning chores.

'I hope you had plenty of coffee this morning,' I said to him as he walked up to me outside the farmhouse. Maple was at my heels and my dad was behind us, heading out to feed the chickens but pausing to watch Dylan meet me. He had ditched the suit completely this morning and again wore jeans but these weren't the stylish, designer ones he'd had on in the pub last night – they were faded blue with a couple of rips in them. He also had on a large, cosy-looking, brown jumper, a Barbour jacket, although his was clearly brand new, and a pair of trainers. His hair was tousled from the September breeze, his cheeks had more colour in them than yesterday and there was slight stubble on his chin, making me wonder if he hadn't shaved and why looking less than perfect as he had in the café worked so well for him.

'I've had two cups,' Dylan replied. 'Is that enough?'

'We'll see. Come on,' I said, walking towards the field with purpose.

'Good luck!' my dad called out with a chuckle.

'I think I might need that too,' I heard Dylan mutter from behind me.

I chose not to reply but instead pointed to the field. 'So, we need all this grass gone so we can create the patch. Our sit-on mower has died a death and I can't afford to replace it so...' I gestured to the lawnmower and the wheelbarrow I'd left next to it. 'What do you think?'

Dylan raised an eyebrow. 'I thought we could come up with a business plan today.'

I nodded. 'Yes, yes, but we can't get anywhere until this field is cleared. I'm on that,' I said, pointing to the bramble bush that edged one side. 'And I need you to take care of the grass. If can you handle it?' I questioned, putting my hands on my hips and raising an eyebrow at Dylan. Something told me his need to prove himself meant, like me, he didn't back away from any challenge if he could help it.

Dylan stared back at me then he set off towards the mower. 'Course I can bloody handle it, Willow.'

I watched him go with a smile. 'Maple, this is going to be fun. Come on, girl, let's get rid of this bush.' She followed me eagerly as I pushed another wheelbarrow over and pulled on a pair of thick gardening gloves. Thankfully, today was a dry day so rain didn't disrupt us and soon most of the morning had gone by in a busy blur.

I thrived on manual labour. It meant that I didn't need to think outside of the task I was working on. My body was working so my mind was silent. I ripped out the bramble bush bit by bit, pulling it by the roots and adding what I removed to the wheelbarrow while sometimes glancing at Dylan, who was mowing the grass. He had removed his jacket and rolled up the sleeves of his jumper, revealing arms that were as muscly as I thought they had been when I touched him last night. Maple ran back and forth between us, happy to be outside as she always was, and I caught Dylan patting her a couple of times when he paused to empty the mower into his wheelbarrow.

Checking the time, I stopped and stretched out my arms. They would slightly ache tomorrow, that was for sure, but I observed my work. I had almost cleared all the bush and that made the effort worth it.

There was a whistle from the farmhouse.

Maple set off with a bark as Dylan looked over at me quizzically.

'It's lunch time. Come on, we've earned it.'

As we walked back to the farmhouse, I looked happily at the field to see it half removed of grass.

'You've done great, thank you,' I said. 'After lunch, I need to go to another town. Do you want to come and we can talk about my business plan on the way?' I honestly didn't want to be on my own for this trip and knew my dad would find it too difficult to come with me.

'Can we also talk about my offer for this place and why I think you should accept it?' Dylan asked, looking over at me.

'That was the pact,' I said, although I already knew I would only half-listen to him. I had to focus on saving the farm, not get distracted by him pushing his agenda to take the place from us. I walked into the farmhouse and glanced back to see him rolling his sleeves back down. He then smoothed his windswept hair back, his cheeks pink from the manual labour, and I knew I needed to add all of it to the list of things I couldn't let myself get distracted by for the rest of the day.

'You two looked like you were working hard out there,' Dad greeted us in the kitchen as we went to the sink and washed our hands. He had laid out homemade soup and fresh bread on the table. It smelled delicious and the room was warm from the

Aga, welcome now we'd stopped working and could feel the chill of the sunny, crisp day. Maple ran to her bowl for her lunch as we sat down and tucked in.

'I haven't done work outside like that for a long time,' Dylan admitted as he poured himself a glass of water and almost finished it in one long gulp. 'My grandmother used to give me pocket money to mow her lawn when I was younger; I think that's probably the last time I did any gardening,' he admitted.

'You don't have a garden at home?' I asked as I buttered a slice of bread. I realised I had told him all about Birchbrook but I didn't know where he came from. I tried the soup Dad had had in the slow cooker all morning – it was thick and tasty vegetable soup, and the bread was perfectly crusty. It was just what I needed after working all morning and I glanced at Dylan to see him also tucking in with gusto.

'I live in a building with twenty floors,' he said. 'Right in the city – very different to here. But my grandmother's house was at the seaside and I used to love going there. I haven't been for a couple of years, though.' He frowned as if he hadn't realised it had been that long. 'My family home, where my father and brother still live, has a large garden but we have a gardener. I suppose I've been stuck in office jobs for a long time now. It did feel good out there though, I have to admit.'

Dad nodded. 'I have always loved working outside. It's good for your health. I only wish I could do as much as I used to. I hate that Willow has to take on so much more nowadays. It's good you're here, Dylan.'

'You do more than you should,' I said with a smile. I knew he felt bad that his arthritis prevented him for helping like he once had. I had to admit, two pairs of hands today had been really great. I could get this patch up and running so much quicker with Dylan pitching in.

'I just worry about you, love,' Dad continued. 'We want to save the farm, we both do, Dylan, but I worry about what happens when I can't work any more. If you take over, Willow, you'll need help like we used to have. But we can't afford any now.'

'But if I can make us more money outside of the summer season, I'll be able to afford help,' I reassured him although it was another worry on my list. I knew it wouldn't be long until Dad would be forced to retire due to his health, and the thought of being solely responsible for all of this, even though I desperately wanted to keep it, was terrifying. I occasionally felt lonely and that was with Dad still running things – how would I feel once he stepped aside?

'My daughter doesn't like to think about the future too much so I have to,' Dad said, turning to Dylan. 'That's why your offer is so appealing to me.'

'Life is so short; if we constantly worry about the future, it becomes even shorter,' I told him, remembering what my mum told me. She got cancer so young and it took her away so fast, I still had trouble accepting what had happened.

'But it also arrives sooner than you think,' Dad responded. Sometimes, we really were like chalk and cheese.

'I lost my mother too,' Dylan said then. 'It does make you think that it's important to find things you really love in life. I do understand why you both want to keep hold of the farm, more than I did when I first turned up. I have a confession: after I discovered Birchbrook and saw your farm and the land you had, I did some research. I got a sense the farm wasn't as successful as it once was, and I thought that would mean you'd jump at our offer.'

I narrowed my eyes. 'Does that mean you've made a low offer?' I asked, reading between the lines.

'I told you I spoke to estate agents locally; I think it's a fair offer but you could get it valued or look around for others, Willow,' Dylan said seriously. 'Ours comes with the bonus that we won't take down the birch trees; we'll write it into the contract.'

Dad beamed at him but I put my spoon down, not sure I could finish my lunch now. It felt like Dylan had preyed on us struggling by trying to swoop in and take the farm away from us. From me. And my dad was seriously considering letting it happen.

'I already have something I love,' I said shortly. I stood up, scraping back my chair. 'I need to leave for this appointment.'

'I'm still coming.' Dylan jumped up too as if sensing I was about to say I wanted to be alone, and I had been about to. 'You wanted to talk about the plan for the patch,' he reminded me.

I sighed. I did want to see if he thought it was doable. I wanted someone else to believe this was an idea that could work, not just me. 'Fine. I'll get changed and see you outside in twenty minutes. You can drive,' I said, walking up to my room. The jewellers had told me to come and see them this afternoon. I hoped they would want to buy the necklace today and I wanted to get the best price I possibly could, so I'd thought them seeing Dylan's fancy car might give me more bargaining power. The more money I could make, the better for the farm.

'I'm off, Dad,' I said after I'd I freshened up and changed, now hovering in the doorway to the kitchen.

He was clearing away our lunch things and turned to look at me. 'Are you really sure about this, love?'

I nodded. 'There's no point in keeping things when we could lose our home. And I know you think we can start over somewhere; maybe we can, maybe we might have to, but I don't want to.' I tried to push down the lump in my throat. I had always been a dreamer but I knew right now, I also needed to be practical.

Dad heaved a heavy sigh. 'I hate that you're in this position, I really do. But I'm also proud of you.'

'Mum would understand, wouldn't she?'

Dad came over and reached out to give my shoulder a squeeze. 'She would be proud of you too.'

God. The lump came back with a vengeance. I nodded, trying to hold it together. 'Okay then, I'm off. Wish me luck.'

'Good luck, Willow.'

I hurried out before either of us could start welling up and walked down the driveway. Dylan was in his car already, on his phone, not paying attention as I walked over to him. The window was open so I could hear his conversation coming out of the car speakers.

'You better not let me down with this, Dylan,' a gruff voice said.

13

I froze and listened in, as Dylan promised he wouldn't let this person down, until he hung up and rubbed his chin with a deflated sigh. I assumed he'd been talking to his brother. He looked worried and I wondered how much was riding on him getting us to sell. For a second, it made me falter. But I knew I didn't owe him anything. He was a stranger who had picked our farm and showed up out of nowhere to try to take it from us. Even if his brother was giving him a hard time about getting us to accept their offer, it wasn't my problem.

This was my home.

Our family business.

My future.

Pushing back my shoulders, I carried on walking to the car and opened up the passenger side. 'Ready?' I asked as I slid in.

He jumped a little bit but nodded, closing the car window and setting off down our driveway. 'Where are we headed?' he asked, nodding at the screen in front of us. I gave him the postcode of the jeweller's and he typed it into the satnav, and then we left the farm. 'Jewellery?' Dylan asked, glancing across at me quickly before returning his eyes to the road.

I decided it was best to be honest about what I was doing. 'I'm going to sell a necklace my mum passed down to me. I need money to make this pumpkin patch happen, and I've resisted for a long time using what she left me, but this is a last-ditch effort. And Dad agreed she would want me to do this.' I looked out of the window but the sight of the leaves on the birch trees fading into yellow didn't raise the smile they usually did. 'It doesn't make it any easier, though.'

Dylan was quiet for a moment. 'I wouldn't let my brother and my dad clear my mother's things for a long time. It made me so angry to think of them even touching any of her possessions, let alone getting rid of them. So, I understand more than most.'

I looked over and saw his knuckles were stretched white on the steering wheel. 'Did you eventually clear them?' I asked curiously.

'Yeah. My grandmother persuaded me to. She said they were just things; they weren't memories. I'd always have memories of my mother. She advised me to keep just a couple of things that meant the most then let the rest go. And I did feel a little bit better once I'd done that. But what made me feel the best was...' He pushed back the sleeve of his jacket and tilted his wrist so I could see a tattoo there. It was a black outline of a robin. 'My mum's name, and her favourite bird.' He quickly covered it again and I saw him swallow hard.

I pulled my own jacket sleeve up and held my wrist out to show my black outline tattoo of a tree with the bark and bare branches. 'My mum's name was Hazel. She called me Willow. My dog is Maple. A tree just seemed fitting,' I explained as Dylan glanced at it, his eyes widening in surprise. I shook my head. It was another strange coincidence. We had lost our mothers and both had tattoos. 'The exact same place as yours,' I added softly as I pulled my wrist back and covered it again.

'Crazy,' he muttered. He cleared his throat. 'So, the money you make from the necklace, have you thought how you will use it?'

'I've been looking at farms in the surrounding areas that might sell me pumpkins in bulk, but I need to know exactly how much I will have first. I will also need hay. I might need to hire a marquee and I need to buy props so people can take photos. I've been trying to think about how I can do it all as cheaply as possible but good enough that people enjoy it, spread the word, come back again...' I trailed off. It was a lot to work out. There was no point in spending a fortune if I couldn't make a profit out of it all, but it also needed to be a place people wanted to visit.

'Are you going to charge an entry fee?'

'We don't for pick-your-own season; we just charge a small fee that people can use towards the fruit and veg, then they usually spend more anyway.'

'This is more of an event though, isn't it? It's not just about people buying a pumpkin, so you could charge an entry fee.'

'If I can make it worth people spending the money,' I said. I leaned back against the leather car seat. There was a lot to think about. 'I learned about business plans at uni but I suppose I've left all the business and money side to my dad over the years. And it took him a long time to tell me just how tough things had become.'

'We can make a spreadsheet. Once you know how much you can spend, you can talk to suppliers and put the costs in,' Dylan stated matter-of-factly. 'And see what profit you could turn with or without an entry fee but personally, I think you need to charge something. It sounds like you have grand plans for it all. People will want to come along, I'm sure.'

I looked over at him. 'You'd help me do that?' I asked, thinking this was more than I had expected him to do.

'I said I'd help,' Dylan replied with a shrug. 'And once the spreadsheet is done and you realise you can't turn a profit, then you know you have another option.'

I let out a puff of air and folded my arms across my chest. 'Right.' I was determined to make that bloody spreadsheet show a profit. We managed to make our summer season profitable, although that wasn't enough now with the cost of everything to keep us afloat, so if I could do the same for the autumn season, we might be okay. And then I could throw Dylan's offer back in his face. I thought back to what I'd overheard earlier. 'How much of an impact would buying my farm have on your brother's business?'

'Well, as I said, it would give us a foothold in this area, which we've never have before, and Birchbrook is really sought after. You have good land that we can build on, and we've been given an unofficial nod that we'd get planning permission. So, it would be great for the company, and my brother really wants to expand and...' Dylan stopped for a moment and glanced at me as if unsure whether to keep going.

But I had a feeling what he was going to say. 'Your brother would be grateful to you for securing our land.'

Dylan looked away and gave one nod. 'I want to make him proud,' he said quietly.

I sensed his family put a lot of pressure on him and as he felt he'd let them down leaving university like he did, this was a chance to show them they could be proud of him. God, we had a lot of weight on our shoulders. I was desperate to do the same for my dad too. 'You could find somewhere else that would work just as well,' I said quietly, looking out of the window again. 'Don't forget that. This is business for you. But it's personal for me. You could find other ways to make your family proud. This is my last shot.'

Dylan didn't answer me and we spent the rest of the car journey in silence.

I gripped the box I'd put my mother's necklace in tightly on my lap and wished things hadn't come to this.

14

When I left the jeweller's, I saw Dylan was outside of his car, leaning against it. The sun was bright against a clear, blue sky, and the town was busy as kids came out of school.

He held two takeaway coffee cups and squinted against the sun to watch me walk over. 'Somehow, I thought you'd want the seasonal drink,' he said, holding out one of the cups. 'It's a pumpkin spiced latte,' he added, wrinkling his nose like the thought of it was unpleasant. He clearly didn't have good taste.

'It's my go-to drink in autumn, thank you.' I took it and had a sip, leaning next to him against the car and tilting my face up towards the sun, breathing in the fresh air.

'How did it go?' Dylan asked me then.

'It depends on your perspective. They bought the necklace and they gave me even more than they quoted when I first reached out as the price of gold is so good. It's worth a lot. They were really excited to have it. We have enough to get this patch going for sure, but I feel sad.'

'Of course you do,' Dylan said. 'What do you want to do next?'

I let the sadness wash over me for a minute. That was all I wanted to allow. I had no time to wallow. I had to shake it off. The clock was ticking. I needed to get this patch open for the start of October and show my dad I could make it successful enough to keep hold of the farm in six weeks' time. 'Go back to the farm and finish clearing the field then tonight, work on that spreadsheet. Get the ball rolling.'

'Then that's what we do.' Dylan opened the door and climbed into the car so I walked round to the passenger side and got in beside him. We set off back towards Birchbrook and I did feel fired up. I had more money in the bank than I'd had since I could remember and I was ready to invest it into the farm. It felt weird though to be planning how I was going to do that sat next to the man who wanted me to do the opposite. This had felt like an almost fun challenge. A way to push Dylan's buttons after he pushed mine. But now I was faced with six weeks with a man who had opened up to me about why this was important to him. And I understood him. More than I wanted to. I couldn't let myself get sidetracked by his agenda.

I cleared my throat and decided to voice my concerns before either of us got in too deep with our hasty pact. 'Are you sure about staying on the farm? I could do with your help, there's no question about it, but we are on different sides. You want me to sell; I want to stay. Maybe you should come back in six weeks instead.'

'Why the sudden change of mind?' Dylan asked me. 'I thought you wanted to use me for my business acumen and prove to me you can make a go of your idea? You're backing down now?'

'I never back down,' I replied stubbornly.

'That's what I thought. Neither do I. So, we finish what we started, right?'

'Fine with me,' I retorted. 'I can't wait for you to admit that you lost the pact.' I pulled out my phone. 'I'm going to start looking up suppliers,' I said, googling *pumpkins for sale nearby*. Something, I have to admit, I never thought I'd be doing.

'We'll see,' Dylan said evenly. His lack of rising to my anger annoyed me further. It reminded me of how I told him he clearly wasn't a passionate guy and for some reason, that made me feel even grumpier.

I didn't speak for the rest of the car journey home but when we pulled up outside the farmhouse and Maple ran out to us, I watched as Dylan got out of his car and bent down to greet her almost as enthusiastically and my annoyance faded. I turned away to hide my smile but I made eye contact with my dad, who had followed Maple back. He gave me a curious look so I quickly adjusted my face and walked over to him, whistling for Maple to join me, which she did.

'They gave me a great price, Dad,' I said. 'But it was really hard.'

'I know it was,' he said softly. 'What's he up to?'

We both turned to watch as Dylan walked away from us. 'I'm going to carry on mowing while it's still light,' Dylan called back.

I reached down to pat Maple. She had taken to Dylan more than I thought she would, and for a city boy, he seemed happy to be around her. 'I hope I'm doing the right thing,' I said, watching Dylan taking off his jacket and starting up the mower.

'I hope so too, love,' Dad replied.

* * *

'I ache in places I didn't even know I had,' Dylan declared when he opened the door to me. He'd insisted I come to the cottage to work on the spreadsheet as he had a much better laptop than the old computer we had in the farmhouse. Dad had made dinner for the three of us. Dylan protested that he didn't need to be included in our meals but Dad said he'd been doing free labour all day so the least we could do was feed him, and he was glad of the male company. I rolled my eyes but I could see Dad enjoyed cooking for us and having Dylan to chat to while we ate. Dylan was better company than I would have thought when he wasn't talking business, which Dad kept steering him away from, and me if I mentioned the pumpkin patch. He seemed to want the dinner table to be neutral so we both gave in and ended up having a nice time talking about all sorts of things from sport to films to the travelling Dylan had done when he was younger.

But now as we walked into the cottage, it was back to business. We'd left Dad watching a film in his armchair with Maple on his feet keeping an eye on things as she always did. I carried a bottle of wine and two glasses into the cottage as it felt like it would be needed if I was going to spend an evening with figures. Not my strong point, I had to admit. I would much rather be outside fixing a fence. Dylan, of course, was in his element and brought his laptop, phone and a notebook to the round, pine table in the open-plan kitchen/living area. I spotted an old candle on the side and lit it, the delicious smell of pumpkin spice taking over the room quickly. This was surprisingly cosy.

'I'm impressed you almost cleared all the grass,' I told him as he sat down, wincing as he did so. 'Maybe you should have a bath to help the aches,' I added, then my cheeks flushed involuntarily. I sat down too and quickly poured us both some wine to avoid catching his eye. 'I think we can get it all cleared by tomorrow; you really have saved me so much work.'

'I kind of enjoyed it – being outside, just thinking about the task in hand. It meant I wasn't worrying about anything else,' he said, opening up his laptop.

I nodded. 'That's how I feel. I've always loved that about doing this job. It's bloody hard work but it's so rewarding.'

'I can see that now. Beats my office job, I reckon. Okay, here's a spreadsheet we can use.'

We spent the next hour going over figures and drinking wine. I had to admit that Dylan's input was invaluable and if I started daydreaming up things for the patch, he pulled me back on track. We couldn't input costs yet, but with estimates it was tight and was dependent on either charging an entry fee or charging a lot for pumpkins. I needed to think about that, and if I was going to turn a profit, try to get what I needed as cheaply as possible.

'My brain hurts,' I declared, leaning back in my chair as the night ticked on. I also felt a little bit tipsy after sharing the bottle of wine with Dylan. 'I haven't studied like this since university. You're a hard taskmaster, Mr Henderson.'

Dylan was taking a sip from his wine as I said that and he spluttered, just managing not to spit it all out. 'Willow,' he said, shaking his head.

'What?' I questioned, wondering why he looked so shocked. I replayed in my mind what I had said. Then I blushed all over again. 'Oh.' I guessed it had come out as a little bit suggestive. I stood up quickly. 'I better go to bed,' I said. 'Alone!' I added quickly, half-knocking the chair over as I scrambled to jump away from the table and him.

Dylan started laughing then. 'Tonight made a change from you bossing me around,' he said with that twinkle back in his eye. That twinkle could be dangerous, I decided.

I backed away further. 'I'll send those supplier emails

tomorrow and we can finish clearing the field, okay?' I said, turning away from his eyes.

'Sleep well,' he called after me as I hurried out of the cottage, torn between embarrassment and attraction which was bad with a capital B. I couldn't start feeling attracted to the man who was trying to take my farm away from me.

The cold air hit me once I was outside and wandered back to the farmhouse, taking deep breaths. I sobered up quickly and thankfully, the idea of being attracted to Dylan soon evaporated. I was just lonely and I needed to pull myself together.

The problem was, as I went inside and up to my bed, flashes of Dylan's eyes as he laughed kept coming back to me.

15

My phone rang early the following morning as I was feeding the chickens and taking a walk around the farm with Maple. Today, the sun had faded into a grey day, an autumnal breeze whipping around me. My dad was in one of the polytunnels checking on crops. We'd had an early breakfast together before the sun came up and then separated to do our chores. I glanced over at the cottage a few times but there was no sign of life. Dylan seemed to still be in bed. I envied him. Our late night and wine had made it tricky for me to get up.

'Hi, Sabrina,' I greeted when I answered my phone, walking out of the chicken pen and closing the gate, following Maple as she ran towards the crop fields. 'What's up?'

I liked to walk the fields as much as possible as we headed towards winter to look at what had grown and sold well in summer, so then I could decide what to try to grow more or less of, what seeds I needed to order, when I needed to plant things. And I had to keep an eye on when frosts came in, so I could protect some of the crops that weren't sheltered in the polytunnels. Winter was slower on the farm but still an important time to lay the groundwork for the following summer season. If I could make an event in autumn, I would need to factor that in and so that was on my mind as I strolled around: whether I could fit in the extra work if I was running things on my own.

'What's up with me? What's up with you?' Sabrina cried down the phone, very excitable for such an early time, shaking me out of my thoughts.

'What do you mean?'

'I just dropped in to the café; the baby had a bad night so I thought a walk would help us both, plus I needed a very strong coffee, and I thought a fresh loaf of bread would be nice for some toast for breakfast,' Sabrina gabbled. I smiled at how she got to her points so long-windedly. 'I was half-asleep in there but I realised everyone was talking about you. Paul was telling everyone what you said at the pub the night before last about the pumpkin patch, which of course I already knew about, but what was news to me – because my best friend clearly doesn't think it's important to tell me things – was that you were on a date with the man who you gave wrong directions to! Which I can't believe, because he wants to buy your farm! What were you thinking, Willow?'

'First of all, breathe,' I instructed, my eyes wide at my friend's fast talking. I heard her do just that. She was clearly walking back from the High Street to the cottage she shared with her husband, probably pushing the pram. The contrast between our lives was stark. 'Second of all, yes, we were in the pub together but it wasn't a date. Dylan is staying at the farm for a few weeks.'

'Come again?'

'I know this is going to sound a little bit mad but...' I told Sabrina about our pumpkin-patch pact.

There was a long silence. 'But he's the enemy. Why would

you want him living there? Won't he just sabotage the patch so you have to sell? Why has your dad let a strange man live with you both?'

I paused and looked over at the cottages. Dylan was emerging from his and with purpose in his step, he headed straight for the field we were clearing. It was weird; Sabrina was right. 'I maybe jumped in like I often do, and it was kind of too late for my dad to stop me; you know what I'm like when I'm faced with a challenge...'

'You are determined to succeed. It's what I love about you. Along with your big dreams. But you can't trust this man, surely? And why has he agreed to it? I'm confused and worried.'

I watched Dylan get down to work then I continued following Maple across the crop fields. 'I know, I almost called the whole thing off but he got under my skin, Sabrina. Everyone seems to think I can't do this but I know I can, and I have to prove it. In six weeks' time, I will watch Dylan leave the farm with his tail between his legs.'

'I want you to succeed, I really do, Willow. I don't want you and your dad to have to leave the farm and Birchbrook. But I think you need to be careful. This man isn't like us, is he? A city boy who wears suits and drives a fancy car, who looks down on people like us and probably has a glamorous girlfriend waiting for him back home.'

That jolted me. I hadn't thought about Dylan having someone waiting for him back home. Surely, he wouldn't be away from her for six weeks? Why was I even thinking about that?

'You and him are different people,' Sabrina concluded.

I looked back at Dylan finishing off mowing our grass. His sleeves were rolled up again and he was working hard. He glanced over then and lifted his hand to wave to me. I couldn't see if he was smiling but I found myself smiling anyway. I waved back and turned to head in that direction, whistling to Maple to come with me.

'Don't worry,' I assured Sabrina. 'I know how different we are. You know I'd never want a man like he was when we met him in Birchbrook Café,' I said, although I had already seen a different side to him. I wanted to keep that to myself for some reason. Maybe because Sabrina might not believe it. 'This is just about making sure he doesn't convince my dad to sell behind my back. Keep your enemies close and all that.'

'Has he made you guys a good offer?' she asked gently as if worried that question would anger me.

I thought back to last night in the cottage. Dylan had shown me the Henderson Homes offer formally in writing, which he'd sent to my dad. It stated the money they were giving us plus the plans for their development and a written agreement that our birch trees wouldn't be cut down. He was working on a virtual mock-up of what the development would look like and a pitch for planning permission. It would be Henderson Homes' biggest ever project, and the one they could make the most money on. I knew that it would be Dylan's biggest acquisition for his brother and he was hungry for it. But not as hungry as I was to stay.

'Yes,' I admitted to Sabrina. 'It's more than enough for both me and my dad to move away, clear our debts then buy a property, or even a small one each.'

'God, the thought of you not living here...' She trailed off with a sigh.

'It won't come to that,' I promised boldly although I bit my lip, hoping I wasn't lying to us both. I thought for a moment about walking away from this place and starting over somewhere new. I just couldn't picture it. I knew people who had fled Birchbrook as soon as they'd turned eighteen, desperate for a faster-paced life, to see the world, or just try something different, but I had never felt that itch.

I had reached the field. 'I better go; there is so much to do if I'm going to get this up and running for the start of next month.'

'If I can help at all, you know I'm here, right? I know I haven't got your imagination but I am behind you, Willow. If this helps you stay here, I am all for it.'

It was more supportive than she had been back in the café and I appreciated it. Not everyone understood my dreams, I knew that, and maybe they dismissed me as being unable to live up to them but I wanted, this time, to make sure I did. 'Thanks, Sabrina. I'll keep you posted and we'll catch up soon.'

'Definitely. I want to meet this Dylan Henderson.'

He looked up then although he couldn't have heard her and our eyes caught.

'I'm sure you will soon,' I said then we hung up.

'I slept through my alarm,' Dylan said with a sheepish look. 'I was up too late working on something my brother needed for today. I'm getting stuck in now, though.'

'Don't worry, I had to get my usual chores done,' I said as Maple ran past me to greet him, her tail wagging as he reached down with a smile to pat her. I tried but failed not to find the way they were excited to see each other endearing. 'You're making great progress.'

Dylan's phone beeped and he glanced down and looked at it, reading a message. He sighed and shoved it back into his pocket.

'Everything okay?' I asked, curious, suddenly wondering if Sabrina had been right about him having a girlfriend back in the city asking what he was doing out here with me. Well, not with me but...

'My brother just being curt as usual, I don't think he's heard of the words "thank you". I was up to all hours but apparently, I still missed a document he needed,' Dylan replied with a sigh.

I wondered about their relationship. I had always thought having a sibling would have been a massive help out here on the farm but maybe I was better off on my own. 'Do you need to go back to the cottage?'

'No. We said we'd finish clearing today,' he replied, getting back on with mowing.

'I'll get on with the bush. I sent a few emails when I got up this morning to suppliers so we can check on that at lunch,' I said, walking past him to start work.

The word 'we' didn't sound as odd as it should have done.

16

'I've had some interesting responses,' I said to Dylan across the kitchen table as I scrolled on my phone to look at some of the emails I'd had from suppliers. I had emailed telling them my plans and asking what they could offer, potential costs and basically seeing if there was any way we could make my idea work without them charging me a small fortune. I'd been thinking about everything I wanted to offer in the way of autumnal activities and pumpkins and made a list of places I could get them from. 'There are a couple of farms that are close to each other; I wonder if I should go and check them out at the weekend.'

'That seems like it wouldn't be a great use of time; can't you just do online research into it all?' Dylan asked as he sipped his cup of tea. 'That's what I do with our properties.'

None of the suppliers were close by, unfortunately, but I was definitely more of a visual person. Long emails bored me. I would rather talk to the owners and hash out a deal that way.

'You came to look around here,' I pointed out.

'Yeah, once I'd chosen it as our best opportunity to target

next,' he countered. 'You don't have enough time to go around the country looking at all sorts of things, do you?'

I hated him viewing our farm as just an 'opportunity'. Once again, my back was up. 'But I need to see the pumpkins in person,' I told him stubbornly. We glared at one another. I knew from experience how much crops could differ. I could order one hundred pumpkins which could turn out to be mouldy or something. I couldn't risk wasting money. That was worse than losing time.

Dad, at the end of the table, munching on one of the ham and cheese sandwiches he'd made us for lunch, shook his head. 'In my day, there was no internet. I had to travel a lot to find suppliers, to go to markets, to meet other farmers; that was all part of the job. Sometimes, there are things you just have to do in person. You make the best relationships that way and seeing things for yourself helps you know if you're getting the best deal.'

'Exactly. What if I get some dodgy pumpkins?' I said. 'If I plan to go to the places close to each other, it will be worth a trip; I'd only have to stay one night. I can tick off a few suppliers all at once and make sure I've found the best. Like you said, Dylan, if I'm going to charge entry, it needs to be worth it for visitors.'

'I don't want you getting ripped off, love,' Dad said. 'Dylan, why don't you go with her this weekend then you can both be sure you're getting the best deals? I'm still nervous about this working, Willow; I want to make sure you're not getting lost in the dream like you can do.'

'Hey, I don't need a man to—' I started, annoyed Dad thought I needed Dylan with me.

'I didn't say that,' Dad interrupted me calmly, as he often did. I definitely took after my mother and not him. 'Two heads are better than one and we both can't leave the farm so you two should go, and I'll hold the fort.'

'Are you sure?' I asked, knowing he would find it difficult on his own for two days.

'I wouldn't say so if I wasn't sure,' he replied firmly.

'Well, I don't want you getting ripped off,' Dylan said. 'I'll come along, and maybe you're right; seeing things in person might help. I never thought I'd be going to look at pumpkins, I must say.'

'I don't think anyone can be unhappy going to look at pumpkins,' I declared, thinking about how cute they were. 'I want to get as many different varieties as we can. Look...' I held up my phone and showed them some pictures I'd found of popular pumpkin patches around the world. 'I mean, the possibilities are endless.'

'Who knew there were so many different types and colours,' Dylan said. 'I thought pumpkins were just large, orange lumps.'

'This is the man you think is going to help me?' I demanded of my father, who chuckled. 'Mr Online Research,' I found myself teasing him, 'sounds like you need to do some before our weekend trip, okay? I know how much you love being on your laptop.'

'What's wrong with online research? It's my job and...' Dylan started hotly then he sighed. 'You're winding me up, aren't you?'

'It's just so easy,' I said with a grin.

'You wait, you'll be grateful I'm coming with you with my laptop,' he said, unable to stop himself from smiling.

'You two remind me of me and my wife,' Dad suddenly said with a wistful look.

'What?' This time it was me who coughed on my drink – spluttering tea down myself with surprise at what Dad had just said. I looked at Dylan, who was watching me with amusement.

I wondered if he too was remembering what happened in the cottage last night.

'We were so different,' Dad carried on, explaining to Dylan. 'I'm practical and logical. But my wife, she was a dreamer like Willow: emotional and sensitive, full of passion and imagination and life.' He pushed his chair back abruptly. 'Excuse me.' The word 'life' had clearly upset him and he left the room quickly.

I watched him go. 'They were so happy together. I could see it even when I was younger. He lit up whenever she came into the room, and she always leaned on him,' I said quietly. 'I always wondered if I'd find something like that.' I forced out a smile. 'Anyway, he's probably just feeling sentimental because autumn is approaching, and my mum loved it so much. What he said doesn't mean anything.' I knew I was avoiding his eyes and he probably did too.

'Your mum sounds like she was really special,' Dylan said softly.

'She was,' I said. Suddenly, I wanted to change the subject. Talk about things that meant less. It felt like Dylan was finding out too much about me.

'Don't feel like you have to come with me this weekend; I can do it by myself,' I told him then. Part of me hoped he would pull out because there was a bigger part of me that wanted him to come.

'I'm coming, Willow,' he said and the way he looked at me suggested he could tell what I was doing. 'I can use the trip to do some work for myself too so it'll be good for both of us. So, what do we need to do before we leave the farm on Saturday?'

It was clear the decision had been made.

'Well, it would be good to get some things on the farm sorted out so I can focus on the patch when we get back and have hopefully started getting the things we need for it. Things that need fixing or cleaning up. For example, when visitors come to the farm, they'll need to park just off the driveway like they do in the summer season close to the birch trees, and I've had no time to do anything to it since the pick-your-own season ended. The whole area needs a spruce-up.'

'Make a list of everything then we can make sure we tick it all off before we leave this weekend,' Dylan said, getting up and starting to clear away the lunch things.

'I should check on my dad,' I said, watching him bustle around as if he hadn't just arrived here in Birchbrook. 'I'll see you out on the field.'

I left him, feeling all kinds of confused, heading towards my dad's room, but then I saw that he had gone out with Maple. I sensed he'd rather be on his own so I went out to carry on with my work instead.

My phone beeped with a message. It was from Sabrina, asking if I wanted to meet her, her husband and the baby tomorrow afternoon at the café. She added that I should bring Dylan along so they could talk to him. Reading between the lines, I assumed that meant they wanted to grill him. Laughing, I told her I'd see how we were getting on with work but I was sort of intrigued to know what they would think of Dylan, plus I could speak to the two Pats about my food and drink idea, thinking they might be nicer about it than their son had been in the pub.

I picked up the wheelbarrow and threw in the rest of the bramble branches I had been clearing. All the grass had been cut now so we had a flat expanse of soil to work with. I stood and looked around. I'd been thinking of hiring a marquee so the patch would work even if the rain came, and it was autumn so that was pretty damn likely, but it would be a big cost for the month of October.

'You look deep in thought.' Dylan came to stand next to me, also surveying the field.

'Yeah, I had a sudden thought that instead of hiring a costly marquee, I could use a few polytunnels to keep things covered. Like what we use for our crops,' I added so Dylan would know what I meant. 'We keep a couple spare in case of damage, but I could ask some of our farmer friends if they have any they might let me use for a month or so without charging me.'

'They would do that?'

I shrugged. 'We try to help each other out where we can. It's a tough industry to be in; we like to look out for our own. I'll make some calls later. I think they could work well, with hay on the floor plus we could also have a few wooden planters with pumpkins in different colours and sizes. I could build those with some cheap wood and I could get hold of a few crates to give a rustic vibe; they should be cheap as well,' I mused, picturing it all in my mind. I felt Dylan's eyes on me. 'Sorry, did you say something?'

'No, I'm just, well, impressed,' he said, almost stumbling on the words. I raised an eyebrow. He clearly found giving me a compliment difficult. I would be the same about him, though. 'You could really build tables yourself?'

I put my hands on my hips. 'Just wait and see.'

Dylan turned away so his words were lost on the breeze but I was sure I heard him say, 'Can't wait'.

17

We worked from dawn on Friday. Having Dylan around was a big help as Dad focused on our farm chores as much as he was able to, with me pitching in when he struggled, so that the two of us could work on the field and the front of the farm – the areas visitors would see. The field was now clear and I put up the two polytunnels we had spare. I needed probably three more to be able to cover the pumpkins and autumn trail and then we set about tidying up the front of the farm, again clearing things that were overgrown or dying, raking fallen leaves and making sure the gravel looked as good as possible. I also organised the places we would visit over the weekend and Dylan booked us a place to stay despite my protests, saying he could put the cost on the company as he was also going to visit a couple of companies Henderson Homes worked with while we were gone, so I reluctantly let him do that.

Afternoon arrived and it started to absolutely pour with rain. I looked out of the farmhouse window with a sigh. Although I was used to working in all weathers on the farm, there really wasn't much we could do when faced with the thick sheets that were coming down, drowning the ground and making it impossible to see even a couple of feet in front of us. Thankfully, the two tunnels would cover some of the field but I knew the rest would get really muddy and we didn't want to tread that all around the areas we had tidied so it felt like it was best to stop work until Monday. I glanced behind me. Dylan was at the kitchen table, working on his laptop and my dad was chopping vegetables for dinner. I was fed up with computer work and really didn't want to do any more.

Maple was sat next to me looking mournfully at the weather. She'd gone out earlier but I knew she was feeling cabin feverish like I was. I decided both of us should get away from the farm for a bit.

'Sabrina and her husband have asked me to join them at the café in town,' I said to Dylan. 'I might take Maple out with me too. There's not much more we can do here now; we need supplies to do anything more. I don't suppose you fancy a coffee too?'

Dylan stretched out at the table, rolling his shoulders, flexing his arms. I tried not to watch. 'You know what? A coffee sounds good. And I liked the one I had in there before I came here.'

'Hang on, that might be a compliment about Birchbrook,' I joked.

Dylan shook his head. 'Well, that day was a disaster thanks to someone giving me the wrong directions so I've had to focus on the one good part.'

'Hey, surely meeting us was the best part of that day,' I teased him right back.

We were smiling at one another now. Impressive, when I

thought back to that day and how badly I wanted to stop him finding our farm.

'It's okay if I come along then?' Dylan asked me.

'Well, my friends might grill you,' I warned, knowing that once Sabrina saw him, there was no way he'd be able to leave the café without her talking to him.

Dylan looked at me. 'I don't mind, if you don't?'

I shrugged, and said, 'Up to you,' but I was kind of glad meeting my friends hadn't put him off. I wanted their opinion on him. 'Come on, Maple, let's get my coat.' I walked up to Dad first. 'You're okay if we nip out to meet Sabrina and Bradley, right?'

'I'm fine,' he said, carrying on chopping. But he had been more subdued than usual since the conversation we'd had about my mother. 'I'll put all this in the slow cooker then we can eat together later. I might do a puzzle: a perfect rainy afternoon activity.'

I knew he could do with the rest after all we'd done this week. I gave him a quick kiss on the cheek. 'Yeah, you relax; we won't be long.' I looked over my shoulder. 'Ready when you are, Dylan.'

I tried to ignore the smile on Dad's face when Dylan jumped up and followed me and Maple out. I knew that I shouldn't get used to Dylan being around but it felt more comfortable than it should as we left the farm together. I insisted on driving, knowing the roads wouldn't be easy in this weather and my four-by-four was far more capable than his fancy car so the three of us piled in and we headed for Birchbrook.

'I used to walk down here every day with my mum on the way home from school,' I said as I drove along the High Street and looked for a parking space as close to the café as I could.

The weather was giving autumn, that was for sure. The shop lights were all that we could see through the windscreen. 'The café was my favourite – so many treats that I'd beg her for. She loved getting a hot drink and a cake in autumn, and we'd collect conkers on the walk too.'

'When I lost my mother, I felt like I needed to get away from our family home and the town I grew up in,' Dylan said. 'It had changed so much from when I was growing up that it made me miss her more almost, if that makes sense.'

'Birchbrook hasn't changed much,' I said as I pulled in behind a car outside of the café, parking up and switching off the engine. 'That's why a lot of people I went to school with left in a hurry, desperate for somewhere new – bigger and better things, I guess. But it brings me comfort. There's so much change on the farm each season, and I love to see nature doing its thing, but this town has always been there to counteract that. I have the best of both worlds so never felt the urge to leave.' I took off my seat belt. 'Right then, we're here. Shall we make a run for it, guys?'

I jumped out of my side and let Maple out of the back of the car, rushing towards the café with Dylan hurrying after us.

The café was the perfect sanctuary. We walked in, closed the door and shut out the rain. The dark-grey skies felt far away with the bright lights inside. And the warmth soon dried us off. Coupled with the smell of sweet treats, I quickly felt a whole lot better. Scanning the room, I found Sabrina with her husband Bradley and their little girl Dottie at a large table by the window. 'There they are,' I said, pointing them out to Dylan with a smile.

'Hi, Willow, who's this?' female Pat asked, coming to the other side of the counter to greet us. She looked Dylan up and down. I wondered if maybe she didn't recognise him as Mr Suit

Man from the other day. He did look a lot different, I realised. Not only was his hair messed up from the weather but his new boots had arrived and he was in casual clothes, prepared for the farm work he was now doing. His Barbour jacket was starting to lose its brand-newness too. He almost didn't look out of place here. And clearly, Pat was unsure who he was.

'This is Dylan Henderson.'

Pat's eyes widened as she recognised him as the man I had sent in the wrong direction. She glanced at her husband and son, who were now blatantly listening in. 'You enjoyed Birchbrook so much, you couldn't leave?' she asked.

'Well, I'm helping out on the farm for a bit,' Dylan said, throwing me a slightly panicked look. I supposed we hadn't really discussed how we'd explain him staying with me. I knew after the pub that the whole town was probably talking about my outlandish, pumpkin-patch idea; I didn't need everyone knowing about our pact as well.

'I thought you wanted to buy the farm,' Paul called out in his usual blunt way.

I fidgeted on the spot, wishing Paul wasn't working today.

'I'm still deciding,' Dylan said with a glance at me. 'Anyway, Willow, what would you like? My treat.'

I was relieved he'd moved the subject on so we didn't have to explain any more. 'A pumpkin spiced latte, please.'

'I think I'm in a pumpkin mood too,' Dylan said, making me smile. 'Two, please, and how about two slices of your pumpkin pie as well? We might as well go all-out pumpkin.'

'You'll be sick of pumpkins soon,' I said as Pat got our order ready.

'We both might be but this is research, right?'

'Pat, did Paul happen to mention what I'm working on at the farm?' I asked once we were alone with her, Paul disappearing into the kitchen and her husband serving another customer. I quickly told her about the pumpkin patch although by the lack of surprise on her face, I was right that the news was already all around the town. 'Things like this would be perfect to offer visitors,' I said as she passed over a tray with our drinks and pie on. 'I know you bring out your van for the Halloween parade and Christmas-tree-lighting night,' I said, remembering their cream and green food van that they sold drinks and cakes out of at town events. 'It would go down a storm at my pumpkin patch if you wanted to try it out.'

'Well, we could have a think about that, of course, Willow.'

'Maybe for this first year, you could pitch up for free,' I suggested. I saw Dylan frown over at me. 'Think about it and we'll talk,' I said as Dylan paid and picked up the tray.

'I will, thanks, Willow,' she replied. 'And I hope you enjoy your stay in Birchbrook, Dylan,' she added with a curious look in his direction.

We hurried away. 'I thought that maybe since people we are close to are confused about why I'm staying, we shouldn't bother trying to explain it to people we aren't,' Dylan said in a low voice.

'Sabrina knows, I'm warning you now,' I hissed back. 'But yes, no one seems on board with my pumpkin-patch idea so let's give them the least we can to gossip about,' I added.

Dylan nodded and we made our way to join Sabrina at her table. 'Why would you let them sell food and drink for free at the pumpkin patch?' he asked.

'The café is super popular; it will be a real draw for people to know they can get food and drink from them as well as pumpkins,' I explained. 'And Paul was so dismissive about it, I knew they weren't going to pay me a fee to be there until they know it's successful. This way, they get a free slot and it's another attraction I can offer visitors, which is especially useful if I charge for entry. Maybe then after the first year, I can charge them for their pitch. Plus, if the café could publicise the pumpkin patch, it will be invaluable,' I said, wondering if they might let me put up a poster or put leaflets on the tables and talk about it with their customers. The café was a draw for both locals and visitors so I needed them on my side. This felt like the best way to gain it. If I had any food and drink to rival the café at the patch, I would lose their support for sure.

'It does look like a popular place,' Dylan conceded as he weaved around the full tables and we joined Sabrina, Bradley and Dottie. I made the introductions and sat next to Dylan, taking a sip of my latte and a bite of pumpkin pie as Sabrina studied Dylan with interest.

'How are you finding Birchbrook?' she asked him.

'It's very different to anywhere I've lived.' Dylan gestured around the café. 'It reminds me of where my grandmother lives, though; there's a real community feel, which I like. And this place serves good food and drink,' he said as he sampled what he had bought with an appreciative noise.

'I hear you're working on the farm,' Bradley said. 'Must be a shock after working in an office; we always say we could never do what Willow does.' He smiled at his wife. While Sabrina was a teacher, Bradley worked for a communications company.

'I couldn't do what you do,' I returned with a grin.

'It's hard work but it's so rewarding, which I'm not used to unless you count your monthly pay cheque,' Dylan said. 'It feels like you're really building something worthwhile. I like it. And this beats wearing a suit,' he added, gesturing to his outfit.

'We'll make a farmer out of you yet,' I joked.

'Let's not get carried away now,' Dylan replied with a chuckle.

'How's it all going?' Sabrina asked me, so I updated her on the week's work.

'We'll have to come out and look at this patch taking shape,' Sabrina said. 'It sounds like it could really work.'

'You're surprised,' I said, not needing to pose it as a question. She had been sceptical like everyone else about the idea. 'But it's okay, I get not everyone can see my vision. I think it could be something really fun, though.'

'Willow is so passionate about it; her imagination is really impressive,' Dylan told them.

'Speaking of my imagination,' I said, trying not to smile too widely at his praise. I enjoyed it more than I should have done. 'I've been thinking that I should name the pumpkin patch something so it's memorable for people. I wondered about...' I turned to Sabrina. 'Pumpkin Hollow. What do you think?'

She grinned. 'A nod to the *Gilmore Girls*? I love it! It feels cosy and autumnal and inviting.'

'The *Gilmore Girls*?' Dylan asked me, raising an eyebrow.

'It's one of my favourite TV shows to watch at this time of year. It's so cosy and they have lots of autumn-themed episodes. And they drink even more coffee than we do,' I told him with a chuckle. 'I hope other fans might like I've named it that. Plus, I think I can create cute graphics and leaflets and a sign with it on, right?'

Sabrina smiled. 'I think it's inspired, Willow. What do you have to do next for the patch?'

'I need to meet with suppliers,' I said.

'She is taking me away to find everything the pumpkin patch needs this weekend,' Dylan added.

'Oh, yeah?'

'A couple of days away from the farm as all the suppliers are so far away. That will change soon once I'm selling pumpkins, though.'

Dylan glanced at me and smiled and after I returned it, I glanced across the table to see Sabrina and Bradley staring at us. Then they exchanged a look and I wished I knew what they were thinking.

18

'Sabrina said to call if you need anything,' I said to my dad as I stood in the doorway bright and early on Saturday morning. Yesterday's rain had eased to a drizzle but it was windy out and the sky was grey. I hoped we were going to get all the rainy weather out of the way now so that October would be crisp and dry and encourage people to come to the farm. If I could get my autumnal world out of my head and into reality before then. The clock was ticking and it felt like this weekend was make or break as to whether it would work. I didn't want to leave Dad, though. 'Are you sure you'll be okay?' I hadn't been away from the farm for any significant time since my university days, and the thought of him being alone was making me hesitate.

'Willow, I'm a grown man, perfectly capable of being on my own,' he said, shaking his head at me. He stood in the hall with Maple, who was giving me a sulky look as she had seen my overnight bag and had worked out I was leaving her. I'd given her extra cuddles and treats but she was still sad, which was making me hang in the doorway while Dylan sat waiting for me in my car, our things already loaded into the boot. 'And you have to do this to save the farm, right?'

I nodded. 'I know, but I just want you to be okay. Both of you,' I added, giving Maple a worried look.

Dad reached down to stroke the top of her head. 'She will be fine too. We'll have a nice day together. I'll take things easy, and will call for help if anything goes wrong. Which it won't. You get out there and find what you need for your plans. Send me a picture of all the pumpkins you find,' he added with a grin.

I was relieved he seemed more cheerful this morning. 'Okay, I better get going. I said I'd be at the first place by 10 a.m. And we'll probably need to stop for coffee on the way. Right then, keep in touch, yeah?' I took a deep breath and with more promises from Dad that he would contact me lots, I waved and left the farmhouse with a heavy heart.

How could I ever leave this place permanently if it was this difficult to go away for the weekend?

I glanced back to see Dad in the doorway. He waved once more then closed the door and I climbed into my car, hoping that my big idea was going to help us keep the farm. I smoothed down my leggings and long jumper which I was wearing with my knee-high boots and Barbour jacket, a chunky scarf round my neck, my hair its usual bun, and gloves on to drive in. 'Right, I think I have everything; are you okay to go?' I asked as I put my seat belt on and took a deep breath.

'I'm all set,' Dylan said. He had on blue jeans, a flannel shirt, his Barbour and new boots, and a leather satchel with his beloved laptop in by his feet. I liked the country-casual look on him. 'I would still prefer to drive, though.'

'I told you, we're going to farms and country businesses, and it's been raining, there will be mud everywhere, and the roads might be slightly flooded; your car can't handle the journey,' I replied. 'Haven't you noticed no one around here owns the same car as you?'

I took off, trying not to look at the farm in the rear-view mirror in case it upset me further. I turned up the heating as the morning was chilly and put the radio on softly.

'I love my car,' he said. 'I'll never give it up, even if I do get stuck in the mud.'

'That sounds pretty stubborn,' I remarked as we drove out of the farm and onto the road.

'Ha. Coming from you?' He gave me a grin though so I just shook my head.

I knew I was stubborn but I also knew it meant I didn't easily give up, so I was glad that it was one of my traits.

'So, how did you become friends with Sabrina?' he asked. 'You seem… different.'

'We are,' I agreed. 'We were sat next to each other first day at primary school and she was this doll-like little girl in a cute dress, whereas I wore dungarees and had short hair. I didn't think we'd ever be friends. But at break, some kids were trying to upset me by saying I smelled like a cow,' I said, rolling my eyes at the memory. 'And Sabrina marched up to them, she was the smallest by far, and told them that our farm had a wolf and if they kept picking on me, we would set it on them.' I chuckled. 'God knows why they believed her but they did. I was left alone and we started hanging out.'

'She's feisty,' he said with a smile.

'Yep. A few months later, she came to the farm and we had a family staying and the kids tried to pick on her for wearing dresses out in the field, calling her a princess, so I turned the hose on them. They didn't do it again, and Sabrina declared we were best friends, saying how we'd always look out for each other. And we have ever since.'

'I'm almost jealous. I've never had someone like that in my life,' Dylan said. He turned to look across at me. 'God, what must she think of me then?'

I thought about the message Sabrina had sent me once Dylan and I had left the café yesterday.

> When you're back, I'm coming to the farm to see how you're getting on. I'm sorry I wasn't as supportive as I should have been from the start. I think I panicked about you having to leave. I want to help however I can! And remember even if Dylan does seem nice, he wants you to leave. Be careful, okay?

I had replied promising everything would be fine but her words had stuck with me. I supposed we had become friendlier than I'd expected when Dylan first waltzed onto the farm, but Sabrina's message had been a stark reminder that, at the end of the day, we were on opposite sides. 'Sabrina wants to help all she can, and because you don't want my idea to work, that means I doubt you'll ever be friends, right?'

Dylan stared at me for a moment, then looked away out of the window. 'I'm glad you have a supportive friend like her,' he said. I frowned, wondering why he hadn't agreed with me but then I had to focus on heading in the right direction so I didn't push him on it.

* * *

We reached our destination right on time. We were starting out at a farm that grew pumpkins. Dylan had an appointment later on but for now, he was coming to look around the farm with me. We drove in and parked out the front. The rain had ceased now but as I predicted, the ground was wet and muddy.

One of the farm owners met us and led us to the pumpkin fields out back where there were rows of orange pumpkins as far as the eye could see. A harvesting machine was at work at one end harvesting the fully grown pumpkins ready for October and a few workers were checking some closer to us to see if they were ready or not. There must have been thousands of pumpkins ready to be sold.

'We had a good crop this year,' the farmer told us, bending down to show us one of the pumpkins. It was perfectly round and orange and I could see the field looked healthy. 'You're opening up a patch on your farm, you said? You'll just have piles of pumpkins to sell?' he asked, standing back up and giving me a curious look.

'Yes, but it's going to be more of an autumnal destination so there will be lots of things to do and enjoy as well as just buying a pumpkin.' I gazed out at the field. I wondered if one day, I could have one like this back at the farm. 'I obviously need lots of pumpkins for it, though. I'll need to shop around for a good deal as I haven't grown them myself, so the margins will be small.'

'That's true.' He nodded and we carried on walking across the field. Dylan was watching the machine pulling the pumpkins from the soil with interest. I wondered if he'd ever thought he'd be walking a pumpkin field with two farmers one day. 'We'd sell to you at wholesale price but people don't like to pay a lot for their pumpkins nowadays; you'll have competition from supermarkets and the like. We sell some of our crop out front in October direct to customers but we make more from selling to shops and garden centres.'

'Would you consider us selling the pumpkins for you?' Dylan suddenly asked out of nowhere. I threw him a glare, thinking it had been obvious I was supposed to be doing the talking and negotiating here.

'What do you mean?' the farmer asked.

'Instead of Willow putting in a large order then selling them on to customers at a higher price, you just give us some pumpkins to sell on your behalf and you keep all the money from the sale of the pumpkins. Willow doesn't have to pay out anything for them.'

The farmer raised his eyebrow while I was too stunned to speak. 'What's in it for you, though?'

'As Willow said, it's going to be much more than selling pumpkins; we will be selling tickets for the attraction so we will make money that way,' Dylan said, steadfastly ignoring my glare.

'Well, it's a unique idea. How can I know you'll sell what I give you, though? I might miss the opportunity to sell the pumpkins to another supplier or sell them myself here at the farm.'

'We'd have to guarantee to sell a particular number,' Dylan agreed with a nod. 'That would make it worthwhile for you.'

'Hang on...' I managed to splutter out. 'Dylan, we need to talk. Excuse us.' I grabbed the sleeve of his jacket and yanked him away from the farmer, who was staring as if he'd never seen anyone quite like us before.

'What's wrong?' Dylan asked after we were a few feet from the farmer, looking down at my annoyed expression.

'What the hell are you talking about? Why would you offer him that kind of deal? For starters, this is *my* farm and *my* pumpkin patch, and secondly, how can I guarantee ticket sales? How will this idea of yours make me money? Huh?'

'I just took your idea of asking the café to serve food and drinks on the farm for free. The more you can offer visitors, the higher you can charge for an entry fee.'

'That's all well and good but if no one wants to buy a ticket, then what? I'll have to pay for pumpkins I haven't sold.'

'But surely that's better than paying out for them now? I thought you were sure people would come to the patch. So, then you'll make a profit from ticket sales. You can put all your money into making it a destination people want to come to, rather than paying out for pumpkins that you might struggle to sell.'

'Can I make enough profit just from ticket sales, though?'

'You could sell some pumpkins but it will need to be a large order; I just thought it would be a good way of working with this farm. Then next year, you could grow your own pumpkins and build on the profits that way.'

I stared at him, my anger fading away onto the breeze. Now, I was just stumped. 'Why are you helping me so much?'

19

'Sorry, guys, excuse me!' the farmer called out then, as my question hung in the air between me and Dylan. 'I'm needed back in my office now, so what do you both think?'

I kept my eyes on Dylan. 'You don't want this patch to succeed but you're talking about what I can do next year to make even more profit,' I hissed at him, confused.

Dylan shook his head. 'I just saw the business opportunity... That's what I do. Find opportunities,' he said, frowning. 'I guess I wasn't thinking about me. I was thinking about the farm,' he added, now looking as shocked as I had been. 'I didn't mean to overstep or anything, I wanted to help. I'm sorry, Willow. Maybe I should... yeah.' He abruptly turned and took off back towards my car.

'What the hell?' I said under my breath. I hurried back to the farmer, deciding that Dylan and his confusing behaviour would have to wait. 'Okay, let's go through two options – what it would cost me to buy pumpkins to sell, and the second idea of you giving me them to sell for you, and how that would work. I'll walk with you.'

We headed towards his office and struck out two kinds of deals, ending with me promising to confirm by Monday which option I wanted to go with. I needed time to think about Dylan's idea rather than him just springing it on me.

Then I marched back to the car to find Dylan buried in his laptop. I climbed in to the driver's seat and slammed the door shut, making him jump.

'Willow, I almost dropped my laptop,' he cried as I glared at him.

'Do you think I can't handle negotiating deals or something?' I asked with an icy tone.

Dylan sighed, leaning his head against the seat. 'Of course not. I think you can handle anything. I know you don't understand, but I really did just want to help. That's all I want to do,' he said, looking back at me with those wide, blue eyes that made it really difficult to stay furious with him. 'I promise, Willow.' The way he said my name sucked the wind completely out of my sails. Gruff and almost... desperate.

I inhaled deeply. 'Okay. I just want to make a success of this, you know?'

He nodded. 'Of course I know. We are more alike than you think. I feel how much you want this and honestly, if I wasn't trying to succeed myself, I would be doing everything I could to make this work for you.'

There was a short silence after his frankly passionate words. I had told him he wasn't passionate but there was so much fire in his eyes and tone that I felt like I had done him a big disservice. 'Why?' I asked so quietly, I wasn't sure if he had heard me.

Dylan stared back at me. I wasn't sure if I was imagining the electric current in the small space between us. The car suddenly felt too small and too warm, but I also didn't want to be anywhere else but here. My mind was a muddled swirl. Dylan was the enemy. I hated him.

Didn't I?

'I've never met anyone like you,' he finally answered me, also softly that if we'd been any further apart, I wouldn't have heard his words. But I did hear them. And they made my heart beat faster.

I opened my mouth to tell him I hadn't met anyone like him but suddenly, his phone rang. We both jumped this time. He looked at the phone where it was perched on the dashboard and sighed. 'It's the person I'm meeting next,' he said. 'I should...'

'Take it,' I supplied. I twisted in my seat. 'We need to go anyway, or we'll both be late for our appointments.' I started the engine as Dylan answered his phone and we left the pumpkin farm to head to the neighbouring town.

As we drove out, I saw a bunch of horse chestnut trees, conkers scattered beneath them, and I wasn't sure why but I was suddenly desperate to speak to my mum. Maybe it was the reminder of us collecting conkers walking home from school or having to sell her necklace due to the prospect of losing the place she loved dear, or maybe it was the conflicting emotions I now felt towards Dylan, but the sadness that I couldn't talk to her about all of it was piercing.

'Dylan?' I asked once he'd finished his phone call.

'Yeah?'

'Do you ever just really wish you could ask your mum's advice?' The farm was behind us now and the countryside stretched out in front of my car. The trees here were turning like my birch trees, and watery, September sunshine poured through the gaps in them, creating shadows on the windscreen. Golden and dusty orange colours were slowly taking over green. When the wind blew, leaves scattered across the car like butterflies you couldn't catch. It wouldn't be long until there were no leaves left to look at until spring.

'All the time,' Dylan replied. 'Especially when I feel lost. She was always good at getting me to realise I knew which way I wanted to go even if I didn't think I did.'

'That's a definite talent. Mine used to set me a task to do that allowed me to clear my mind and by the end, I usually found my answer.'

I wondered if he felt as lost as I did, but I couldn't ask him that.

'Ah, this is the place,' I said, spotting the town sign at the side of the road. It was much larger than Birchbrook with a wide, busy High Street and lots of shops and businesses lined up along it, and a car park at one end. I pulled in to drop Dylan off for his meeting. 'So, I'll move on to the next farm and you'll ring me when you're done and we can head on to the hotel?'

'Yeah. Call me if you need me, though,' he said, climbing out of the car.

I watched him go and almost wished I could call him back and ask him to come with me to this supplier too. But I drove on, telling myself sternly that I could handle it fine on my own.

I followed the directions the farm had given me, and my eyes widened when I saw the sign outside of the town. I turned the car to see one of the biggest farms I'd ever seen. These farmers were food and plant suppliers to farm shops, garden centres, supermarkets and, of course, when it came to pumpkins – pumpkin patches. The farm was twice as big as the one we'd just visited and about four times larger than Birch Tree Farm. I parked in front of the office and met with one of the owners, who took me into their farm shop to show me the varieties of pumpkins they could offer me.

'Wow,' I couldn't help but say when I saw them. They had every colour, size and variety you could imagine, of both pumpkins and squashes. Small Munchkin pumpkins, a green, striped one called Harlequin, Goosebumps pumpkins that had warts on their skin, pale-orange Autumn Crown ones, and Casperita, which were white. I instantly pictured them all on wooden planters in my polytunnels. They would look so appealing and were perfect to use as autumn décor. Everything was grown to perfection. This place was a huge operation but the owner told me it was still family-run, which obviously appealed to me. I took pictures of everything, then over a cup of tea, we talked about how we could work together. They couldn't offer a deal like the other farmer, I would have to just order a bulk supply from them so again, I left saying I would be in touch on Monday once I'd worked out my budget and how much I could afford as they were pricier than the first farm due to the unusual varieties. Then I asked about crates and they gave me directions to a wine supplier a couple of miles away who sold them cheaply.

I left the wine supplier loaded up with crates and a couple of bottles of wine which once I'd tasted, I had to have, then – to make use of the spare time – I looked online and found somewhere that sold wood cheaply. I ordered enough to build my tables, letting Dad know when it would be arriving so he could sign for it and get it all put into the barn to stay dry.

By the time I drove back to the town to pick Dylan up, the day had dimmed, the sun fading into evening. I was tired and hungry and keen to get to the place he had booked us into for the night. We set off with Dylan navigating the way and grilling me about my supplier meetings.

'I think the best plan is to order as many pumpkins as I can afford from this farm for the tunnels, then ask the first farmer we met today to give us some to put in crates out front that we will sell on his behalf. Then I won't be forking out a small fortune all at once. And if we can make enough from ticket sales, it should be tight but possible to turn a profit. I asked the second place about pumpkin seeds and how best to grow them on my farm for the future too,' I added, trying to show Dylan that I was already thinking about next year.

'You would definitely make more money growing them yourself,' he said evenly.

'How was your meeting?' I asked.

'The man I met owns a large piece of land outside the town that could be a possible place for one of our developments. I had a good look around and spoke to him about what he's looking for if he does sell. I need to do my research and look at the figures to see if it's a viable option. But it looks like a nice area, doesn't it?'

'It reminded me of Birchbrook but bigger,' I said, hoping that if Dylan thought it was a good option then he might start to think Birch Tree Farm wasn't his only option in this part of the country. 'This must be it.' I saw the sign for the Harvest Moon Inn. It was down a twisty lane and was a large, two-storey building painted black and white with a large, wooden door. We carried our bags inside and I smiled at how cosy the inn felt. The ceiling was low with wooden beams, there was a large, wooden bar and lots of comfortable booths to sit in. At one end was a roaring log fire and around the wall hung paintings of the local area.

Up the twisty, narrow staircase, we were greeted by a woman called April who showed us to our rooms which were next door to each other. I went into mine and dropped my bags onto the floor. It was a quaint room with a sloping roof, a large, four-poster bed and a free-standing bath under the attic-style window. It was decorated in white with lots of floral touches, which, coupled with the beams and wooden floor, made me feel instantly at home.

There was a knock on the door and when I said, 'Come in', Dylan stood in the doorway. 'Is it okay?'

'It's lovely,' I said, smiling at him.

'Can I take you to dinner?'

'Excuse me?' I checked, wondering why he'd phrased it like it was a date. I mean, we were both hungry and in need of dinner and a drink, but I supposed I hadn't really thought about us eating together.

'Let me buy you dinner, Willow,' he said. 'Please?'

I took a breath but nodded. 'Sure, okay.'

I followed him of the room, telling myself that the churning in my stomach was just because I needed to eat and not because I suddenly was both nervous and excited.

20

Back down in the inn, we secured one of the booths close to the log fire as the evening had turned chilly. Dylan got me a glass of wine and a beer for himself then we both ordered the steak pie with mash and vegetables. It felt like the most comforting item on the menu – a perfect autumnal meal after a long day, in my opinion. I looked at my phone and the picture Dad had just sent of him and Maple walking through Birchbrook, and it made me smile that they both seemed to be doing okay without me.

'You and your dad seem so close,' Dylan said after I had shown him the picture. I sent Dad back the one I took of all the pumpkins and squashes in the farm shop I had visited.

'We are. Always have been but when my mum became ill, we really leaned on one another. It was such a tough time. And now it's just us running the farm so we only have each other, you know? It must be the same for you with your brother and dad?'

Dylan took a sip of his beer then shook his head. 'Honestly, not really. I think losing my mum had the opposite effect. Dad threw himself into his work and my brother set up Henderson

Homes. I just kind of drifted, which they didn't like. I feel like maybe we don't really understand each other.'

'But you enjoy working with your brother?' I asked, thinking it was a shame he wasn't close with them like I was with my dad.

'It's taking some getting used to. He's always acted like a second father and he's very bossy, has incredibly big expectations, is a workaholic and really wants this business to succeed. I totally get that but I suppose, if I'm honest, it's hard to be as committed to it as it's his business; I'm just not as...' He trailed off as if struggling with how to describe how he felt.

'Not as passionate about it?' I supplied the word without thinking it through. There it was again. The word 'passion'. I hoped Dylan would blame the log fire for the tint to my cheeks.

'Like you are,' Dylan said with a nod. 'About the farm, I mean,' he corrected quickly, his own cheeks looking decidedly pinker all of a sudden. 'Yeah, I'm not loving the job as much as I hoped I would. Or where I'm living. The flat has such an impersonal feeling. I don't know. It's like you said earlier: sometimes, I wish I could ask my mum's advice about life.'

'That would be nice.' I tasted my wine. It felt good after such a long day. 'But as you said, both our mums would probably remind us that we know how we feel deep down. Sometimes, you just want someone to agree with you. If you don't like working for your brother then maybe you shouldn't be doing it.' I shrugged.

'You like working on the farm? Or was it something that was expected of you?'

'Hmm.' I tilted my head to consider that. 'My parents inherited the farm and I think they were unsure about it at first but they quickly fell in love with it and when I was born, the farm was thriving. It was an idyllic childhood. I was outside all the time, with fresh food to eat, and there were always people around. It was fun, although I learned quickly as I grew up, it was hard work too. But my parents' love for the place was infectious. I wanted to help as soon as they let me. I wanted to take on more responsibility as I got older. I never really considered doing anything else. I didn't especially enjoy university as it took me away from the farm, and studying isn't what I'm drawn to. I'm drawn to nature. I thrive outside and doing hard work; it's so rewarding growing something from seed and then seeing people take it home to make recipes with, or eating it yourself for dinner.' I sighed. 'I just wish I was better at the business side of it all.'

'You're doing pretty well with this pumpkin patch,' Dylan said. 'It sounded like such a crazy concept to me but you're going to turn it into a reality, I can see that now.'

I felt a prickle of pride in myself at his praise. He wasn't the only one to think it was a crazy concept. Even I had my moments wondering if this was a bigger dream than I could make come true. Hearing him say I was going to be able to do it meant a lot. 'But if I do make it happen then you'll have to walk away,' I reminded him. Our food arrived then. I took a bite of pie and mash and moaned. 'Ooh this is so tasty.'

'It is,' Dylan agreed. He looked at me across the table. 'It's going to be hard to walk away.'

'You'll have to admit to your brother you couldn't get me to sell,' I agreed with a small smile.

'But maybe I'll convince you to sell in the end. I mean, you can open up your pumpkin patch but it might not do well enough to make a profit, enough to see you guys through a hard winter, and maybe you'll decide that you want to move on, start somewhere new.'

I shook my head. 'One minute, you say you want to do all

you can to help me; the next, you're saying I might fail. It's confusing.'

'That's the pact we made, right?' He raised an eyebrow and I couldn't argue with that but that pact had been impulsive, born out of anger and desperation. Now I knew Dylan better and we'd spent this week together, it didn't seem like such a good idea as it had in that moment.

I changed the subject back to safer ground and as we finished our hearty meal and drinks, I asked him about his grandmother, the one family member he seemed to be genuinely fond of.

'I think I said me and my brother would stay at her house every summer when we were growing up. She lives on the coast in this lovely house that steps right out onto the beach. It's a bit like you said about growing up on the farm – it was an idyllic way to spend the summer. And she is like my mother – calm and kind, and she loves to bake. After my mum died, I stayed with her. She provided a sanctuary, I guess, during that difficult time. I always felt safe there.'

'That's how I feel about the farm,' I said softly. When he spoke about things he liked, his blue eyes lit up and I could see there was a spark in him that seemed to diminish when he put his suit back on and got behind his laptop. I wondered if he realised that was the case.

We both ordered the apple pie for dessert. Two bowls arrived with big slices of shortcrust-pastry-topped apple pie with a generous dollop of whipped cream on the side.

'This looks just like what my gran used to make and we'd eat it on her balcony and look out at the sea. It was pretty perfect,' he said with a wistful smile.

I glanced behind Dylan then and saw lights outside. 'Come

on.' I stood up and picked up my bowl and spoon, grabbing my coat and draping it around my shoulders.

'What?'

'Follow me,' I said, walking behind where Dylan sat and opening up the door that led to the inn's garden. They had LED lanterns strung across the sheltered area. The tables looked out to the river which glowed under the moonlight. It was chilly but they had heaters under the tables so when we sat down, it was actually quite cosy. 'Thought this might be the second-best thing,' I told Dylan as he joined me, gazing out at the water. I was pleased to see a smile on his face.

As I put my bowl on the table, I put my finger into the whipped cream. 'Oops,' I said as I sat down. I put my finger in my mouth to lick off the cream. 'Vanilla flavour,' I said when I tasted the sweetness.

Dylan cleared his throat. 'Good?' he asked in a gruff tone. I realised he'd stopped looking out at the river and was now watching me.

'Delicious,' I replied. 'What?' I added when he didn't stop looking at me.

'You missed a bit.' Dylan leaned over the table and reached out with his fingertip, wiping cream off of the corner of my lip. His eyes tracked the movement of his fingertips. I found myself holding my breath as his finger touched me and when he put it in his mouth and licked off the cream, I found myself staring at him in turn.

'You're right – it's good,' he said with a smile.

21

I was so stunned at what Dylan had done, I froze. He started to eat his dessert and I wondered if what happened had affected him at all or not. I realised I was feeling something else other than surprise – I was ever so slightly turned on. God. This was bad. With a capital B.

'Try it, Willow,' he encouraged me then.

I snapped out of my trance. 'Oh, right, yeah,' I said, looking quickly down at my bowl. The apple pie and cream were delicious but I was now thoroughly distracted.

'Fancy a little walk down there?' Dylan asked once we'd finished the dessert. He pointed to a jetty, which had a gazebo draped with the same lanterns stretching out onto the dark, still river. I agreed and we strolled to the spot.

The moon was right above us, like a guiding light in the dark sky. There wasn't a sound around. The inn with its warmth and merriment felt very far away. 'It's beautiful here,' I said, looking at the river moving slowly on the calm night.

'It feels like it's just the two of us in the world,' Dylan

murmured as he paused beside me. 'Do you ever get lonely on the farm?'

I glanced at him in surprise. 'Yeah, sometimes,' I admitted. 'Do you feel lonely where you live?'

'I do,' he replied.

We were quiet for a moment. I had the strange feeling that neither of us felt lonely tonight.

'Look.' Dylan pointed behind me and I could see the silhouette of a willow tree leaning over the dark water. 'I think maybe every time I see one, I'll be reminded of you now,' he said with a smile.

'Fuck,' I blurted out before I could stop myself.

Dylan looked amused. 'You okay?'

'Nope,' I said, realising how close we were standing to each other. I looked up at him, his eyes catching the moonlight. I shook my head. 'You say these things and I forget for a moment that we're enemies.'

'All I can think about is you asking me if I feel passionate about anything,' Dylan said, taking a step towards me so we were almost touching.

A shiver ran down my spine.

'You told me passion is overrated,' I reminded him as our eyes locked.

'Because I had never really felt it, but that day, when you challenged me to make that pact with you, I felt it then.'

I chuckled. 'Yeah, we really wound each other up that day. And quite a few times since. You push my buttons, Dylan Henderson.'

'I can't stop thinking about you,' he murmured.

'You can't... huh?' I spluttered, confused. 'We're enemies,' I said, freaked out by the way he was looking at me – all soft and tender. 'You hate me. Um... don't you?'

'All I know is I really want to kiss you.'

'Me? A farmer,' I said, shaking my head. 'I'm nothing like the women you usually go for, I know that.'

'I told you – I've never met anyone like you before.'

'You're nothing like the men I go for,' I told him a little bit harshly. 'You turned up all preened and clean and tidy, and tailored in that fancy suit in your fancy car with your perfect hair and those bloody blue eyes that I could get lost in...' I said angrily, my chest heaving, the words escaping my mouth like they had been desperate to get out since we met. 'It's so... annoying!' I jabbed a finger towards him but he grabbed it and pulled me closer, his hand wrapping around mine. My breath hitched as our faces drew even closer.

'Why can't you stop thinking about me too then?' Dylan challenged, sounding just as breathless as me.

'I don't know,' I said helplessly.

His eyes lit up like I'd told him a precious secret.

And maybe I had.

Dylan drew me even closer and let go of my hand, his hands reaching down to cup my face gently. 'I might not be like the men you usually go for, Willow. But I can be just as passionate as them. Maybe even more so,' he said, his voice husky and urgent as his eyes looked deeply into mine. He leaned down and touched my lips ever so softly like he was waiting to see my reaction. I gave him a small smile and his eyes flicked from my eyes to my lips back to my eyes and then he leaned down again and this time, he kissed me properly.

And he made good on his promise. His lips met mine with fire and soon, his hands moved from cupping my face to the back of my head as his mouth moved urgently on mine. I murmured, wrapping my arms around his shoulders, pulling him closer to me as he caressed my tongue with his. He pulled back to search my face with his eyes. 'Are you okay with this?' he murmured.

I dropped my hands from his shoulders and grabbed the sides of his coat, drawing him back down towards me. 'Kiss me again,' I demanded and we both smiled before our lips came back together, desperate for another taste, the kiss sweeter and much more satisfying than the apple pie and whipped cream we'd just eaten.

* * *

'Did you enjoy it?'

'Huh?' I stared at our waitress in surprise when she came over to clear our table. After we had both started shivering, we'd reluctantly let go of one another by the river and come back inside the inn. When the waitress asked me that question, my eyes had flitted straight to Dylan's lips involuntarily. 'I did,' I said, earning a smile from Dylan. He had nice lips. He was a good kisser. Quite possibly the best I'd ever had, which was extremely confusing when I thought about what an unlikely couple we made. We didn't make a scrap of sense on paper but that kiss had had boatloads of passion in it. I had definitely been wrong about Dylan not being passionate. He claimed I brought it out in him, and that made me feel good even though it really shouldn't have done.

'Can I get you anything else?' she asked, clearly missing the fact we were just staring at one another across the booth, not paying her any attention.

'I think we're okay. It's been a long day; we'll go up to our rooms soon, I imagine,' Dylan told her.

She bounced away with our empty dessert bowls and glasses, leaving us alone, the table empty.

'We have to be up early,' he reminded me.

I nodded. Dylan had one more meeting to do for his brother and I had arranged to go to a farm owned by an old family friend of ours. Brian had known my parents for years and his farm was nearby to where we were so I was hoping I could pick his brains as he was so experienced. Plus, Dad said he always had an abundance of hay, which would be really helpful as a floor inside the polytunnels.

Then I needed to hit the shops nearby as they had several large home stores that might have some props for the autumn trail I wanted to create through the polytunnels. I then had arranged to meet one of our summer workers to ask for his help.

So, Dylan was right; it would be a busy day. It was just that I was finding it hard to stop thinking about his lips. 'We do. Let's go to bed.' I coughed. 'Separately, of course. Get some sleep.'

'Some sleep,' he agreed with a nod. We got up and headed upstairs. 'So, you said you've been thinking about what you want to put in the tunnels along with the pumpkins?' he said as we walked towards our bedrooms. The inn was quiet now, lit dimly upstairs, and I wondered if we were the only ones who would be sleeping here tonight.

'I want lots of photo opportunities as people love that, plus it helps publicise the patch if we can get people to tag it on Instagram or something. I was also thinking of fun things for kids to do as they walk around,' I mused, my eyes lighting up as I thought about it. 'I'm hoping I can find some props tomorrow. Maybe like an autumn section with scarecrows, autumn leaves, hay bales and corn, then a Halloween area with skeletons and witches and cobwebs, more of a spooky vibe...' I babbled. We reached the doors to our rooms. 'What do you think?' I asked, turning to face Dylan.

'I never thought I'd become so invested in autumn and pumpkins and Halloween,' he said, smiling at me.

'I'll make an autumn lover out of you yet,' I joked but then my smile faded at the hungry, hooded look in his eyes. 'What are you thinking?' I asked him, my heart pounding inside my chest.

'I'm thinking I really want to kiss you again.'

'You said we needed an early night,' I reminded him.

'You're right.' He turned to go into his room but I grabbed his arm and he paused, looking back at me.

'I'm suddenly not very tired, though,' I said, arching an eyebrow.

'Thank God.' He pulled me to him, pressing his lips against mine.

22

I opened the door behind me and we stumbled into my bedroom, our lips still locked together like we'd been stuck by glue. I wouldn't have minded that either. Dylan's kisses were becoming addictive.

Dylan kicked my door shut behind him and I shrugged his coat off his shoulders, letting it fall to the floor. He did the same to mine and then as we moved backwards, my legs hit the four-poster bed. Dylan broke from my lips to smooth back my hair, giving me a sexy smile, then he kissed my cheek, moving down to my jaw then behind my ear and down my neck, leaving goosebumps behind his kisses.

'Willow,' he said, lifting his gaze to look into my eyes. His were darkened with lust. 'Are you okay with this? I know we haven't known each other long...'

'You have driven me crazy since we first met in the café,' I said breathlessly.

'You have too,' he agreed, and I reached for his shirt buttons and began unbuttoning them. I'd been so angry and exasperated by him but all I could think was that no man had ever made me feel like that before. Dylan made me feel alive. And I craved more of it.

He pulled me back in closer by my waist as I finished unbuttoning him, then let go of me to pull his shirt off. I smiled at the sight of his bare, muscly chest. He might not work outside like me but his body was lean and strong, no doubt from a fancy gym membership, but I wasn't going to complain about how he got it. I ran my fingertips over his skin.

'Willow, can I please take your clothes off?'

I chuckled at how politely he had phrased the question. I wasn't used to that in the bedroom. Previous partners had mostly been fellow farmers and rolling around in haystacks wasn't a cliché for nothing. 'I think we should get naked and see how comfortable this bed is,' I told him. I lifted my arms. 'Take my jumper off.'

'God, I love how bossy you are,' he said gruffly, reaching up and yanking my jumper off. 'Sit on the bed and let me take your boots off.'

I flopped down immediately and Dylan crouched on the carpet and began unzipping my knee-high boots. Somehow, this was just as hot as his kisses – watching Dylan, shirtless, unzipping my boots, keeping his eyes on me and then pulling them off slowly. 'Hurry up,' I urged him, not caring if I was being bossy. I wanted us both to be naked.

Dylan grinned and quickly took off my other boot then he sat up on his knees to reach for my waistband, pulling my leggings down my thighs along with my knickers all at once, yanking them both down my legs and then tossing them aside.

I sucked in a breath. 'That was a time-saver,' I murmured approvingly.

'Take your bra off,' he said huskily, back on his knees in between my legs.

'Say please,' I instructed, my voice just as husky. My pulse was racing with desire now.

'Please, Willow.'

Reaching behind me, I unhooked my bra and let it fall off me so I was in front of him completely naked. 'Your turn,' I said.

Dylan stood up and pulled off his trousers and I saw how he was straining to get out of his boxers. 'Anything else?' he asked.

'All of it,' I commanded, loving being in control right now. I watched as he pulled down his black boxers then stood in front of me just as naked as I was. 'I liked you on your knees,' I told him.

'Fuck, Willow, you're so hot,' he said, getting back on his knees in front of me. He reached up and wrapped his arm around my neck, pulling me in for a kiss. Then he leaned towards my ear. 'Take your hair down, please.' He leaned back to watch me undo my bun, my dark hair falling over my shoulders. His breath hitched. He reached out to thread his fingers through it and then leaned back for another kiss. His hand trailed down my hair to my chest and then he ran his fingertips over my bare breast. I let out a contented murmur. He leaned down and put his mouth there too, pulling my nipple into it and then letting out a contended noise of his own.

'We should have brought the whipped cream up here.' I blurted out what was on my mind as he licked my nipple.

'Hmm.' Dylan continued kissing down my body, kissing down my chest and my belly button, making my back arch. 'But you taste just as good as the whipped cream,' he said then, continuing to kiss me, moving down to my thighs as he settled between them. He dropped gentle kisses on each one and I reached down, threading my fingertips through his hair. My legs trembled with desire as he kissed down each one, and even dropped a gentle kiss on my feet and then the tips of my toes, clearly relishing completing the phrase 'from head to toe'.

Dylan pulled one of my legs over his shoulder and kissed the spot he had missed. I gasped as his tongue found me and clutched his hair as pleasure swirled inside. My last night with a man had been a drunken blur. I was right here in this moment with Dylan though and it was so much better.

When Dylan slid a finger inside me, I moaned out loud. He really knew what he was doing. I squirmed on the bed, heat pooling in the pit of my stomach as he tasted and touched me. He soon tipped me over the edge. I cried out as my body shuddered underneath him, gasping with pleasure, flopping back against the soft bed, my leg dropping from his shoulders.

'Dylan,' I said, breathlessly. 'Get on this bed now.'

Dylan chuckled but he did as I asked. I shuffled back and we both laid down on the pillows, rolling onto our sides to face each other. 'You are so sexy,' he said, reaching out to cup my cheek with his hand.

I leaned in to kiss him gently while I reached down to touch him. He was rock hard and when I stroked him, he groaned. 'I didn't think I was your type,' I said when I pulled back to look into those gorgeous eyes of his.

'Fuck, I think you can tell that you are,' he said, looking down to where I was touching him. 'Mmm, just like that,' he said, pulling me to him and giving me a deep kiss, our tongues meeting as we scrambled closer to one another. Desire was quickly building again.

'I want you,' I whispered, pulling away from his lips for a moment when he ran a hand down my thigh, which was draped over his.

'How much?' he whispered back to me.

'So much,' I said. 'Do you want me?'

'A crazy amount.'

'I need you inside me,' I said then and our lips met again. Dylan moved on top of me, pulling my hair to one side and kissing me with such passion, I felt almost light-headed. When I was about to beg him again, Dylan lifted off me and reached over the side of the bed and when he came back, he had a condom. He sat up then to slide it on, his eyes never leaving mine.

'You thought you might need one?' I teased as I watched impatiently for him to finish.

'I didn't dare hope for this, but I have wanted to kiss you for a while. I've thought about it... a lot.' Dylan smiled. 'Have you?'

'Honestly, no. I was trying to pretend I wasn't attracted to you,' I said, reaching up to pull him down on top of me. 'It didn't work all that well,' I added with a laugh.

'I'm glad it didn't,' Dylan said, giving me a kiss as he parted my legs and slid inside me. We both let out a moan at how good it felt. He held me tightly as he moved inside me and I held on to him just as tightly in return. 'You feel so good.'

'So do you,' I said. 'Faster, Dylan,' I gasped as we moved together on the bed. My body and his seemed to move perfectly together even though this was our first time together. Could it get even better than this if we did it again? I pushed that thought away. I needed to stop thinking and just enjoy what was happening here and now.

'Are you okay?' he asked, looking down at me, as he responded to my command, making us both moan again.

'Yes. Better than okay... Don't stop,' I gasped, wrapping my legs tightly around him so he moved even deeper inside me. I moaned again, losing control along with him as we rocked together, our bodies hot and sticky in the best way, clinging to one another. 'Oh my God,' I breathed as pleasure rolled over me again, taking me by surprise.

'Willow, baby,' Dylan gasped as he trembled on top of me, letting out his own moan, kissing me as we both slowed down.

He stroked my arm as he rolled off, lying back on the bed beside me, and then leaned in to give me a soft, sweet kiss that made me shiver all over again. Our ragged breaths were the only sound for a minute until Dylan reached out and took my hand in his, entwining our fingers together. 'I think that might be the best first time with any woman I've ever had,' he said.

I smiled. That felt good to hear. 'Shame it has to be both the first and last time, isn't it?' I replied with a sigh as my body relaxed into the duvet, fully satisfied by what we had just done.

23

Dylan was quiet for a minute then he shifted over on the bed before propping himself up on an elbow to look at me. 'Why does it have to be the last night?'

I raised an eyebrow. 'Because...' I said, gesturing between us. 'We're enemies, remember?'

'Enemies don't kiss like we do; they don't fuck like we just did,' he said, his tone harsh.

I sat up on the bed. 'Are you mad at me? Why? We just had a great time.'

Dylan sat up too. 'That's why I'm confused you don't want to do it again.'

'Have I dented your ego or something?'

Dylan jumped off the bed. 'I swear, you are the most frustrating woman I have ever met! How can you keep saying we are enemies when we just went to bed together? I told you, I can't stop thinking about you. You have been driving me crazy.' He threw his hands up in the air then back down. 'And you're still doing it now!'

'Right back at you,' I said dryly. I got off the bed too and walked over to my overnight bag to pull out my pyjamas. 'Look, we're tired; maybe we should just sleep on it and talk in the morning,' I suggested as I started to pull them on, not wanting to be naked with him any more.

Dylan grabbed his clothes and pulled them on with a sigh. 'I meant what I said about wanting to help you.'

'But you still want me to sell the farm,' I pointed out.

'But what if that's in your best interest? I really like the patch idea, I can see you might be able to create something that will bring people to the farm, but will it be enough? What if you do all this work, spend money, put in loads of effort and time, pin all your hopes on it and then it fails anyway? I'm asking this because I care about you. I'm not sure I can watch you fail, Willow,' he said urgently as we both got dressed, not looking at one another.

'You don't care about me; you hardly know me,' I snapped. 'What you care about is pleasing your brother. You want him to respect you, and you see this deal as the way to do it. You just want me to sell. Maybe this was all about that too...' I gestured to the bed. 'That's why it can't happen again. Why we should just keep things business between us. We both have so much at stake. This will just distract us.'

'This was just a distraction to you?' he asked quietly then.

I turned to face him and I couldn't ignore the hurt look in his eyes. 'We just need to focus on the next few weeks, don't we?' I said in a slightly softer tone because it had been hot being with him. My body did want more. But I needed to think with my head instead. I wanted to save my farm and he wanted me to sell it. It couldn't end well between us. Why set ourselves up to get even more hurt at the end of our pact? One of us had to lose. We should just forget tonight had happened, surely?

Dylan looked away from me. 'I guess so. I'll let you get some sleep. See you for breakfast.' He picked up his coat from where I had slung it on the floor and left my room without a backward glance.

I let out a puff of air. Somehow, he had made me feel bad. But I knew I was right.

I walked into the en suite to get ready for bed and glanced at my reflection. My hair was loose and tousled, my lips were pink and puffy from Dylan's lips and my cheeks were flushed.

When I thought back to the feeling of his touch, a small smile appeared on my face.

Then I bit my lip.

I had made the right decision, hadn't I?

* * *

My phone alarm rang out early the next day, causing me to groan as I grabbed it from the bedside table. I'd had a restless night's sleep after going over my conversation with Dylan for hours, like one of those songs you can't get out of your head. I wished I could crawl under the duvet and hide from everything for a few days. That was impossible, though. I had my farm to save. Alongside the man who wanted me to sell it, but who had given me quite possibly the hottest night of my life. It was fucked up.

I climbed sleepily out of the bed and headed for a shower, hoping it would wake me up. I had important things to do today and this made me think that pushing Dylan away last night had been the right thing to do. He had already distracted me from the task in hand. I couldn't let him do that again. Even if part of me wanted him to.

After my shower, I pulled on jeans with a cardigan along with my boots and put my hair back up into a bun, trying not to think about Dylan telling me to take it down last night. But flashbacks kept returning, even though I tried to bat them away. I grabbed my coat and bag so we could leave straight after breakfast, then I headed downstairs, wondering if I should have knocked on Dylan's door but I decided I needed coffee before facing him.

The problem was, when I walked into the inn, Dylan was already sat at the booth we'd had the night before, a cup of coffee and a plate of food in front of him while he scrolled on his phone.

'Having breakfast too?' the landlord called over to me, causing Dylan to look up and see me before I could hide.

'Um, yes,' I said, walking over, knowing it was silly not to as we had to spend the rest of the day together, even though I was kind of dreading it. 'Can I get a latte, please? And...' I glanced at Dylan's plate as I sat down. 'That looks good,' I added, seeing the eggs, bacon, sausage, tomatoes and pile of toast, thinking that was the fuel I desperately needed.

'Just replying to some emails,' Dylan said, barely looking in my direction. 'My brother is firing work at me; I think he's sceptical about how much I'm getting done while I'm staying with you. But I'm doing this meeting for him this morning, which he's grateful for as it's miles away from where he lives.'

There was a babbling edge to his conversation but it was preferable to an awkward silence.

My latte thankfully arrived and I took a long gulp from it before I spoke. 'We have a busy morning ahead then we'll be back at the farm. I mean, if you are still coming back there?' I asked, wondering if he would cut and run after last night. I honestly wasn't sure whether I wanted him to or not. It would make life a lot less complicated, but I couldn't deny the fact I might miss him if he did.

'We made a pact,' Dylan said simply. He nodded as the waitress brought over my breakfast. 'Eat up and we'll get going.' He went back to his phone and I looked down at my plate.

I hated this new-found tension between us. You would have thought the tension would have evaporated after our hot night together but somehow, it was worse now we'd decided that it was to be one night, and one night only.

24

Thankfully, I dropped Dylan off after breakfast so I was on my own for a couple of hours and didn't have to think about him. I didn't have to deal with him next to me in the car looking attractive but not speaking to me. I had no idea how our pumpkin-patch pact had turned into us ripping each other's clothes off and then feeling completely awkward with each other but I was hoping that as time passed, we'd get over it and could go back to how we'd been before the sex. I'd rather have him as my enemy at this point – at least then, we'd talked and fired each other up. I had almost enjoyed arguing with him, I realised now that we were just exchanging bland thoughts about the weather and the traffic. I missed him pushing my buttons, which made me wonder what was wrong with me.

I drove to the next farm on my schedule. My dad had been friends with Brian for years and he'd been instantly agreeable to me coming to see him. His farm was up on a hill, and when I left my car and headed to the field where I could see him walking with his dog, herding his sheep, the biting wind brushed my cobwebs away.

'Hi there,' I called out, waving to get his attention. Sometimes, I wished we had more animals on the farm but I knew that would be even more work. I leaned on the fence to watch as he waved back. He whistled to his dog, and the sheep moved in a perfect circle towards the open gate in front of them.

'Willow!' Brian called, walking over once he'd closed the gate on the sheep, his dog following on his heels. 'Wow, you look just like your mother,' he said, giving me a smile that crinkled his eyes. He was grey now but walked effortlessly and I felt a pinch thinking of my dad, who was unable to do the same.

I gave him a tight hug. 'Yeah, Dad tells me that.' I didn't mind, though; I liked knowing there was a piece left of her in me.

'Let's have a cuppa,' he said, nodding towards his stone house. I followed him and his dog inside, out of the chilly breeze. It was small and cosy and warm inside and I sank into one of his worn armchairs with relief that I could relax for a little bit. I tried not to think about what Dylan was doing while I was here. Brian brought over two steaming mugs of tea and sat in the armchair opposite me while his dog curled up by his feet.

'I regret not seeing your dad as much nowadays but I know he isn't as mobile. Plus, it's just me up here now – you know my son didn't want the farm – so it's hard for me to come to you as much as I used to.' He sighed. 'A real shame but I didn't want to force my boy. I always said Adam lucked out having you as a daughter.'

I smiled as I sipped the tea. 'Thanks, Brian. But I don't know, it's been more of a struggle for us recently than I would like. I'm trying to come up with ways we can make money outside of the spring/summer seasons. I'll be honest, Dad has been talking of selling if we can't.'

Brian shook his head. 'Sad, very sad. But I get it. I think my son will sell once I'm gone, but I couldn't leave. This place is like my other child. It's part of me.'

'That's how I feel.'

'I remember you running around the farm when you were little. You always looked so happy out there. Your mum said she couldn't picture you anywhere else. I'm glad you didn't end up leaving. She'd be proud you stayed and are trying to make it work, I reckon. And if I can help in any way...'

I was touched by his words. I looked at Brian and his dog, all alone out here, and I was sad. I didn't want that to happen to either my father or me. I wished Dylan hadn't flitted through my mind again but the farm had felt far less lonely, and less difficult, with him staying with us. 'I need hay, any that you can give me, for as cheap as possible. I'm going to create an autumnal experience as an attraction, and sell pumpkins. Mum loved the season and so do I, and I've got to try to bring more people to the farm, not just for strawberries in the summer.'

Brian, to his credit, reacted unlike anyone else had so far. He leaned forward. 'Listen, if you're half as determined as your mother and as dedicated as your father, you'll do it. Let's finish these and go to the barn. You can take the hay for free...' He held up a hand when I opened my mouth to protest. 'We stick together. I'll do you a favour and you'll do one for me if I need it in the future. Right?'

'You know it,' I readily agreed. I hesitated but it was rare to speak to someone that knew my parents as well as Brian did. 'My parents were happy together, weren't they?'

'They were. They made a good team. We lost your mother far too soon. My wife left this place before my son did, they chose to go but your dad, your mum, neither of them would have ever left the farm, each other, or you.' Brian sighed. 'I chose the wrong partner. It's not about liking the same things or even having the same personality but you need the same values, the same dreams for the future... My wife, and then my son, they wanted more than the farm but I didn't. That's where it went wrong. Do you know what you want?'

His words sank into my skin. 'I was worried I was being selfish trying to cling on to the farm. I wondered if I should let Dad sell it so he can retire and not worry so much but I can't imagine living anywhere else or doing anything else. And when I asked him if he did want to stay, he admitted he did. So, I felt less selfish but I'm so worried. What if I can't save it?'

'You shouldn't worry about doing anything other than your best, Willow. Your dad doesn't expect miracles from you. He just wants you to be happy and to live a good life. He's proud of you, I know that; he always has been. And you sound passionate about trying this pumpkin idea so I say go for it, but don't beat yourself up about the outcome. Sometimes, in life, things happen. Shit things. Or good things. Things that are unexpected. We just have to decide what to do next when they happen. So, don't worry yet. If it doesn't work out then you can choose what to do next. But for right now, focus on the task in hand.'

'I need to open the pumpkin patch on the first of October and then you're right, I'll just have to wait and see what happens next. But that, I can make happen.'

'What are we waiting for then?' He grinned at me and I smiled back, both of us jumping up to walk out to his barn and look at the hay bales.

* * *

I left Brian's farm with a renewed spark. I phoned one of our summer workers, Steve, to see if he could meet me early. It made sense to chat to him before I picked up Dylan to go homeware shopping.

In the summer, Steve helped us with the pick-your-own season but this time of year, he was training to be a vet. He said he was free outside of his studies and work placement to help out with the patch, though. And bonus, he had a van.

I drove to meet him at his house.

'If you could go and get the hay from Brian and bring it to the farm next week, that would be great. And then I thought one thing we could offer at the patch could be tractor rides so you could take people around the farm, weather permitting. And just be around to help out with anything else if needed, for as many days as you can spare me. I'll pay what we pay during summer,' I said briskly as we stood by my car; I'd turned down his invite to come inside. I didn't need any more tea. I just wanted to get things done.

'I always need the money. You got it, Willow,' Steve said with a nod. 'My sister is away studying, and when I told her about your idea, she said there's a pumpkin patch near her and she and her friends love it. Apparently, it's very "Instagrammable" and autumn is big on TikTok.' He gave a bemused shrug. 'So, I think you'll get her age group in, no problem.'

'Tell her she and her friends can come for free if they share it on social media,' I said as I climbed back into my car. 'Let me know when you can drop off the hay.'

I called Dylan as I drove away. He'd finished his meeting so I headed into the town to meet him. This trip had been successful so far so I was hopeful I could pick up more things for the patch from the homeware shops here.

I parked in a retail area that had four big homeware shops and spotted Dylan waiting for me outside one, two takeaway cups in his hand. He was in a suit again, although he had undone his tie, and his jacket was slung over his arm as he sipped his coffee and scanned the car park. When he saw me, he broke into a smile, before seeming to check himself and look away. I found myself smiling back almost involuntarily.

I walked over and told myself to quit it. I might still fancy him like mad but I couldn't let anything else happen between us.

'How did it go? My meeting was boring as shit but my brother seemed happy when I told him how it went. Here, I got you a latte,' Dylan said as if we hadn't had a frosty morning together. It was confusing.

'Uh, thanks. Yeah, Brian let me have the hay for free and I have someone bringing it to the farm this week. Thanks for the coffee.' We fell into step as we walked into the first homeware shop, the area by the doors full of autumn and Halloween-themed décor. I let out a gasp of excitement. 'This is exactly what we need.'

Dylan smiled and didn't hide it from me this time. 'I'll get you a trolley; seems like you'll need one. At least.' He hurried off and I watched him go, wishing things weren't so complicated between us.

I needed to remind myself of my conversation with Brian – about choosing someone who wanted the same things in life that you did. Dylan couldn't be more different to me. His life was opposite to mine. He must want different things.

Even if I did fantasise about me and Dylan going back to bed again, that's all it would ever be and I didn't want to get hurt. He would leave the farm in five weeks' time just like Brian's wife and son had left him, so our night together had to be a one and only experience. And I knew he must feel the same way too.

Turning away from Dylan, I focused on finding props for the farm because that was far less complicated.

25

The sight of Birch Tree Farm warmed my heart. 'Oh, it's good to be home again,' I said as I drove through the gate later that day and looked at my beloved birch trees. They were on their way to full autumn bloom – swaying in the gentle breeze, the crisp sunshine shining down on them, making the green leaves turning yellow look more like glistening gold instead. They scattered across the drive as we made our way to the farmhouse. Dylan had left his laptop and phone alone for the journey back, looking out of the window at the countryside and listening to the radio, and he seemed in almost as good a mood as me to be back home again. The car was piled high with things we had picked up and I felt more optimistic than I had all week for what I could do now.

Up at the farmhouse, the door was thrown open when I started to park my car outside. Maple ran out barking followed slowly by my dad, who waved and smiled and looked just as pleased as my dog that we were there.

'That was a long weekend without you,' I cried when I got out and Maple jumped up at me, trying to lick me with her tail wagging, making me laugh. I knelt down and buried my face in her fur as Dylan greeted my dad.

'Adam, it's good to see you. How were things while we were away?' he asked, shaking hands with my dad.

'Boring. I can't wait to hear about what you both got up to.'

I coughed as I stood up, causing both men to turn to look at me.

'Fur ball,' I muttered.

Dylan raised his eyebrow but didn't say anything. 'We have a lot to unload from the car.'

'Let's do it after a hot drink. I have cake too. Come on, you can tell me all about it inside. Oh, Willow, the two Pats phoned and told me to tell you, "Yes". You know what that means?'

I beamed at him. 'I sure do.'

I watched as Dad walked inside and Dylan followed, telling him about the pumpkin farm we visited first. He had taken off his jacket and undone a couple of shirt buttons and changed out of his polished shoes into his farm ones so he was now half Mr Suit Man and half Farm-Dylan. I knew which one I preferred. And he seemed to get more relaxed as the farm grew closer so I wondered if he disliked the suit just as much as I did.

'You coming, love?' Dad called back from the doorway.

'Yep,' I said, hurrying after them, Maple trotting beside me, making sure her fur brushed against my legs.

The kitchen felt even cosier than normal after a couple of days away from it. Dad brought over thick slices of carrot cake with mugs of tea, and then we sat at the kitchen table to talk about the trip. Maple stayed by me like she was worried I'd leave her again. I kept a hand on her and wished she would understand if I promised I never would again.

'The pumpkin farm was impressive,' Dylan said over lunch.

'Although Willow told me off for getting too involved...' He grinned over at me.

'Well, you started to negotiate with the farmer without me when clearly it's up to me what I pay for his pumpkins,' I retorted hotly.

I was annoyed to see his grin only became wider like he was enjoying himself.

'But what deal have you decided on?' Dylan asked, raising an eyebrow. I could feel Dad watching us closely and I felt flustered. He leaned back when I didn't answer. 'That's what I thought.'

Damn it. His idea for us to sell the pumpkins on behalf of the farm had been a solid idea for the first try at a pumpkin patch, and would allow me to spend money on the more unusual pumpkins that would look pretty inside the polytunnels. The large, orange ones could be stacked in the crates I'd come back with from the wine place. 'You still should have discussed it with me first before saying anything to the farmer,' I replied stubbornly.

'It just came to me in the moment,' Dylan said. 'Anyway, I thought that was one of the reasons you wanted me to stay here for six weeks – to use me...'

I spluttered on the tea I was drinking.

'You okay, love?' Dad asked me while I tried to compose myself and Dylan chuckled under his breath.

'What was I saying?' Dylan asked when I quietened down. 'Oh, yeah. I thought you wanted to use my ideas while I'm here to help your business, as well as manual labour... Actually, I feel like you are getting the best out of this pact we made.'

I took a breath now I had calmed down and threw him a glare for throwing me off like that. I thought we mutually had agreed not to mention our night together but now it felt like he was almost flirting with me about it. And in front of my father too!

'I suppose you have been convincing Willow to take your deal over the weekend, though,' Dad said, with a worried look in my direction.

'I just reminded her that if things don't work out, there is a pretty good second option on the table but I didn't expect Willow to find so much over the weekend. You should have seen her in the homeware shops; she was a woman on a mission!'

'In my pumpkin element,' I said, laughing as I remembered Dylan following me around the shop chuckling as I got excited over all the décor pieces. 'So, you admit that things are coming together well?' I teased him, to get my own back. 'That maybe you will have to make an offer on that piece of land you visited yesterday instead of our farm?'

'We still have five weeks to go,' he reminded me.

I didn't reply, not wanting to admit that was the reason I was scared to kiss him again. It felt like a long time with him, but also not long enough.

After our tea break, we unpacked my car and moved everything I had bought into the polytunnels. Then Dylan went to his cottage to unpack and do some work, leaving me and my dad in the field alone.

'Brian was so generous about giving me his hay bales,' I said after I filled him in on my visit to his farm. I didn't mention our chat about Mum as Dad seemed so cheerful to have me back and I didn't want to dampen his spirits. 'It feels like it's slowly coming together,' I said, eyeing the props I'd stacked at the start of one of the tunnels to make sure they stayed dry before I set everything up. I had found pumpkin décor pieces, skeletons, cobwebs, fake flowers, lanterns and even a giant fabric scarecrow couple.

'I'm glad he's doing okay; I've always worried about him alone there. Speaking of old friends... Sabrina came over with a lasagne for my dinner yesterday. She said she felt bad for not being as supportive about your idea as she could have been, and I don't think I have been either, love.' Dad gestured to the pile of things I'd bought at the shops alongside the stack of crates I had picked up over the weekend. 'I was just worried you were getting your hopes up. And also that maybe I should let the farm go. I don't want you to feel tied to something that isn't working, that you might start to resent or even hate one day. Like Brian's son did, you know?'

'I'm not like him, though,' I replied. 'He never felt the same way about his farm as I do about this one. Brian made me realise that all I can do is my best. I can try to make this work and if it doesn't then I'll have to accept it. But I really hope it does because I want to stay. This is my home.'

Dad smiled. 'I hope we get to stay too.'

We left the field and Dad showed me that the wood I'd ordered had been delivered safely and was in the barn ready for me to use. I ended up having to hire the other polytunnels we needed and they were due to arrive tomorrow so I could start setting up the trail.

We started to head back to the farmhouse as twilight crept over the farm, the sky above us turning a pretty indigo blue that reminded me unwittingly of the river behind the pub where Dylan and I had kissed last night.

Dad slung an arm around my shoulders and I leaned into him. 'We are going to all pitch in and help from now on, I promise. This isn't all on you. I'm sorry if I made you feel like it was. Sabrina wants to help too; she said she had an idea and took off in a hurry. She's always been a whirlwind, that one.'

I smiled. 'That's true. Thanks, Dad. I could use all the help I can get.'

'You have Dylan to help too,' Dad said, startling me. It was as if he could read my mind or something.

'I don't know. He wants us to sell. I know he has helped but he doesn't want it to work out really, does he?'

'Well, if anyone can change his mind, it's you, love. And the way Dylan was talking over lunch... He seemed impressed with all you achieved over the weekend; it sounds like it was a good idea to go away. How did you get on with him?' Dad asked me as we walked inside and started to remove our muddy wellies and coats.

'Um...'

'I was a bit worried as you've clashed so much but I also wondered if—'

'Don't say it,' I cut Dad off as he gave me a twinkling look. 'We're not you and Mum,' I snapped. 'Sorry,' I quickly added because I knew that had been too harsh. 'I just mean, Dylan is way too different to me. And he's only here for a few weeks. I can't get distracted. And I definitely don't want to get hurt.'

Dad followed me through into the kitchen. 'So, you got on well then? If you're thinking about the possibility of being hurt when he leaves...' He was smiling now and I rolled my eyes. 'I just see something when he looks at you, that's all. And I know you've been lonely sometimes. Even if you never tell me that or try not to show it. All I'm saying is don't shut yourself off because you're already thinking about the end.'

I watched him go over to switch the kettle on. I wondered if he still would have chosen to marry my mum if he had known that she would leave him so early. But I realised I already knew the answer. And if I had the choice of their love even for a short time, knowing me, I would make exactly the same choice.

But what was between Dylan and me was nothing like my parents, I knew.

26

I was up before it was light for the beginning of a new week, and the last full one before the start of October and the deadline I'd set to open up the pumpkin patch. I had a steamy shower to wake myself up along with a large cup of coffee before I headed out with Maple to give us a both a walk and to get ahead on as many chores as I possibly could. The sky gradually grew lighter with every passing minute. Then the farmhouse lights all switched on and the smell of cooking drew my attention as I fed the chickens but I stopped in surprise at the sound of a car driving through the gate.

'Who's that at this early time?' I said to Maple, who gave a curious bark as we watched the car come up the drive, passing the birch trees which stood still and calm this morning, the promise of a crisp, sunny day ahead. The sky above was turning the same golden colour as their leaves. Then I recognised the car and lifted my hand in a wave. 'This is a nice surprise,' I called out as I walked towards Sabrina, who parked outside the farmhouse.

Sabrina jumped out of her car and smiled. 'I couldn't wait; I decided to come on the way to drop Dottie at my mother's before work,' she said, holding out her arms.

I stepped into her hug. 'Is anything wrong?'

'I have something for you,' she said, excitedly, letting go of me and heading around her car. I peeped inside and gave Dottie a wave and was rewarded with a cute smile. I heard a noise behind me and saw that Maple had rushed off when she spotted Dylan strolling over from his cottage, dressed in warm clothes like me.

'Hey, girl,' Dylan greeted Maple with a big smile and pat before his eyes caught mine. 'Morning, Willow.'

'Sabrina has something for me,' I said as he came over, Maple following adoringly by his side. She really had taken to him. We both watched as Sabrina started to lift something large out of her boot.

'Need a hand?' Dylan asked quickly, stepping past me to help her get whatever it was out.

'Oh, thank you, it's a bit tricky,' Sabrina said gratefully. 'I've worked on it all weekend; I really hope you like it,' she said to me as together, they took it out and propped it up on the ground in front of them. 'I thought it could go next to the sign for the farm so people know the pumpkin patch is here.'

It was a wooden sign with painted lettering and pictures on it. I moved closer and realised what my best friend had done.

'Sabrina! Oh, wow, it's amazing,' I said as I read the words *Pumpkin Hollow* she had painted in orange on the sign. There were pumpkins and birch leaves in a border all around the letters as well. 'You are so talented.' I remembered how good she'd been at art while we were at school and I knew she still did lots of crafting and painting with the kids she taught, but this was next level.

'I didn't want you to have to pay out for a sign to be made when I could do it. If you really like it?'

'I don't like it, I love it!'

'It's brilliant,' Dylan agreed, smiling over at me.

'It's perfect. I'll put it up just inside the gate, I think. Wow, Sabrina, I'm so grateful.'

'I've been feeling so bad about how I first reacted to your idea.' She looked over at the field we were turning into our autumn experience. 'I am desperate for you guys to stay in Birchbrook; I want to do all I can to help.' She eyed Dylan next to her. 'Sorry, Dylan.'

'Don't ever apologise for being there for Willow. I'll put it over here and then we can fix it up later,' he said, carrying the sign by himself over to prop it up against one of the birch trees, which matched the sign perfectly.

I pulled my friend into another hug. 'I really am so grateful for this.'

'How was your weekend away?' she asked softly as she hugged me back.

'It was, um, eventful...'

Sabrina leaned back, her eyes searching mine. 'Willow,' she scolded.

I pulled away from her. 'What?' I asked, trying to look innocent, ducking my head to avoid her suddenly piercing gaze.

'I'll get the toolbox then see you inside for breakfast,' Dylan said, making us both jump as he passed by, heading towards our barn behind the farmhouse. Maple followed him eagerly and I heard him chatting to her as they walked away.

'Did something happen between you two?' she hissed as soon as he was safely out of earshot.

'Aren't you going to be late for work?'

'Willow Connor!'

'Fine,' I grumbled, knowing I had always been useless at keeping anything from Sabrina – not since we were too young to have any secrets anyway. 'Something did happen... We kissed and a little bit more...'

'How much more?' she demanded.

'Jeez, Sabrina. Fine, we slept together.'

She gasped then clapped her hands. 'I knew there was chemistry between you both! The way he was staring at you when he first came into the café and when we all met up before you went away, he hung on your every word.'

'That's an exaggeration,' I said, but inside, I couldn't help but hope she was right. 'It has to just be a one-night thing, though. All I care about is saving the farm, and he wants the opposite to happen.'

Sabrina sighed. 'It is complicated,' she admitted. 'But I mean, how did you feel when you were with him?'

'It was a pretty amazing night,' I had to say. I looked at Dylan and Maple heading into the barn. 'I told him though that it can't happen again. And I was right to say that. I need to focus. There isn't much time until October.'

'Follow your heart; you've always been good at that,' Sabrina said as she walked back around her car towards the driver's seat. 'I need to go but we will have to talk about this more over a drink soon.'

I smiled. 'Okay. Thank you again for the sign, I think it's perfect.'

I stood back as she got into the car and waved as she left the farm. There was no time to think about what she'd said about Dylan. I went inside and after breakfast with Dad and Dylan, we set about our work.

We put Sabrina's sign up by the gate and then we brought the crates out of the polytunnels and put them in rows on either side of what would be the entrance to the pumpkin patch. The polytunnels I'd hired arrived so we now had five to cover the autumn and Halloween trail. They stood ready and waiting to be filled.

Then I went into the barn where Dad had put the wood I'd ordered along with whatever we already had spare around the farm to start to build wooden planter tables. I asked Dylan to contact the farm we'd visited to arrange an order of pumpkins that we'd sell on his behalf then to order the more unusual pumpkins from the large farm I'd gone to by myself. He was much better at laptop work than me, and even though I had been pissed off at the time, his idea to cut a deal with the pumpkin farm had been a good one. I asked if we could ensure all the pumpkins arrived before 1 October and Dylan said he would also organise hiring Portaloos for the same time.

Dad got the tractor and the trailer we could attach to it out of our other barn to service and clean them both so we could offer rides around the farm.

The afternoon sped by and it was intensive work but I ploughed on, knowing how good the planters would look when I was finished. I wanted to build five to place throughout the tunnels. I needed to saw and nail the wood into tables then sand them down and polish them so it would be a couple of days' work. I took off my jumper as I'd got hot and threw it onto my toolbox, carrying on in a strappy vest top. Maple lay down in the doorway to the barn, enjoying the sunshine on her back. I played music from my phone, whistling along, and I only noticed Dylan coming in when he finally cleared his throat to get my attention.

'Oh.' I straightened up from where I had been crouched down. I pushed back a stray hair that was over my face. 'Sorry, I was in the zone.'

'I can see that,' he replied with a smile. 'Your dad thought you could do with a drink; he's made us all a fancy-looking coffee,' he said, looking down at the mugs curiously. 'Can you take a quick break?'

'For that, I can,' I said, taking one of the mugs he held out eagerly. I leaned against the doorway to the barn and Dylan did the same. I looked down at the mug. 'Whipped cream, he's gone fancy.' I dipped my finger in to taste the cream topped with chocolate sprinkles. I caught Dylan watching, then he quickly looked away. I wondered if he was remembering our dessert at the pub on Saturday night. I hid my smile by taking a sip, tasting the vanilla syrup. 'Mmm, sweet coffee, just what I needed.'

'I've never had so many fancy coffees as I have had here,' Dylan said after he also tried it. 'I'll be on a sugar and caffeine high,' he added but he took another sip anyway. 'How's it going?' He nodded towards the pile of wood behind me.

I couldn't hide my smile then. 'You're covered,' I teased, leaning forward and touching the cream that was at the corner of his mouth. I felt his whole body tense at my touch. I wiped the cream away then pulled back, blushing at what I'd done. It had felt instinctive, though. 'Sorry,' I said quickly, trying to avoid his scrutiny.

'The thoughts you give me about whipped cream...' Dylan said gruffly.

'Huh?' I looked at him and we were quiet, watching each other. My mind started to race. What was he was thinking about? I longed to know but I also knew it was a bad idea to ask. I moved away from him. 'Yeah, it's going okay,' I said, looking at the two tables I had made so far to try to change the subject from the very dangerous and suggestive one we had suddenly got ourselves on.

'Okay? They look great,' Dylan said, stepping forward to look. 'How did you learn to do things like this?'

'A lot of it was from my dad, watching him, learning from him, working with him... As he struggled more and more with his arthritis, I've had to step in around the farm. They certainly aren't works of art but they are sturdy and will show off the pumpkins well, I think.'

'Don't sell yourself short,' Dylan said, giving me a serious look. 'They are amazing. I couldn't make anything like this. Most people couldn't either. You just set your mind to something then do it, don't you?'

'My dad always said I'm a dreamer and I am; I can get lost in my head and not want to deal with bad shit. If I think I can't fix or solve it, I'd rather run away then but if I know I can do it, then I get stuck in.'

'You're not running away right now, though.'

'It was a wake-up call getting your letter and Dad saying he was actually considering selling. I had been avoiding how tight things had got,' I admitted. I finished my coffee, set the mug down then picked up the hammer again, eager to do something with my hands while we talked about serious stuff. 'I feel bad that I kept hiding from it for as long as I did. I was just scared, though. I really want to be able to stay and make a success of this place. I lost my way for a couple of years and I feel terrible about it but I can't go back and change it now, can I? I'll just do my best from here on out.'

'That's how I feel,' Dylan said with a nod. 'I fucked up and made mistakes and got lost on the way but I want to do better now.'

'Well, you are. You're working hard for your brother. And around here, even if I forced you into it.' I looked up and gave him a quick, teasing smile.

Dylan shook his head. 'I like helping you guys. This place gets under your skin, doesn't it? It's hard out here but it's beautiful and the work is rewarding. I didn't understand when I walked onto the farm. I didn't get how you could be passionate about this place. But I get it now,' he said quietly.

I looked up in surprise. Our eyes met and understanding floated between us. Suddenly, we didn't feel quite on such opposite sides any more.

Dylan's phone rang and we looked way from each other. 'My brother,' he said. 'I better...' I gave him a nod and watched as he walked out of the barn. 'Hey, Nate, yes, I saw your email... Give me a chance; you only sent it half an hour ago. I was just having a coffee... I told you, I can keep up with the work...'

His voice faded away but he sounded different when he spoke to his brother to how he was when he was talking to me. He seemed frustrated but also smaller somehow. I shook my head and went back to my work. It was none of my business but I definitely got the feeling his brother and him had issues they still needed to work on.

27

Steve arrived with the hay bales from Brian later the next day so along with Dylan, we stacked them all in the field and then the long process of laying the hay down as a floor inside the polytunnels began. Thankfully, the weather was dry so we didn't need to worry about the hay getting wet. Steve left at the end of the day, promising to return when we opened to help out and run the tractor rides around the farm.

Now that was done, the more fun part of arranging the props I had bought and creating areas for kids and photo opportunities could begin. The large, orange pumpkins were due to be delivered at the end of the week and the smaller, fancier pumpkins at the weekend and then Monday was 1 October so things were getting scarily real.

'You need to think about publicity now,' Dylan said as the day faded into twilight. He'd vanished for about an hour and I assumed he'd been doing something for his brother. I hated that I'd missed his presence around me as I worked.

I had placed the scarecrow couple in the autumn tunnel, stacking up hay bales so people could sit on them with a scarecrow on either side. I took a picture to send to Sabrina because I was hoping she could create another painted wooden *Pumpkin Hollow* sign for me to hang in between so we were publicising the patch. I would also add pumpkins to the scene – when they were delivered – which would look cool.

'I really don't know how to do that,' I admitted. I had been so focused on making this patch look great and be fun to visit but Dylan was right; I needed to think about how to get people through the doors. 'The two Pats said they'd put leaflets and a poster up in the café. Sabrina is designing them and I found a local printer who's offering me a reasonable deal to print them.'

Dylan nodded. 'Great. But you need to be online nowadays. We can't rely on local word of mouth. And you said Steve's sister is coming to show the patch off on Instagram and TikTok. You need to encourage everyone to do that.'

'Okay, I'll look into that...' I said, turning away to hide my furrowed brow. If I was honest, social media by and large had passed me by. Everyone I knew and wanted to spend time with lived in the same town, and work days were long and hard on the farm; I rarely used my phone in the evenings as I was so tired. I had social media accounts but rarely posted on them and I definitely had no idea what was trending or how to go viral on there. And I only knew those terms in the first place from hearing Sabrina use them!

'Willow, you have a problem asking people to help, don't you?'

I spun around. 'You don't even know me!'

'No?' he taunted. 'How many people in Birchbrook did you tell that the farm was having problems? How many people have had to offer help instead of you asking for it?'

'I asked Brian for his hay,' I disputed.

'You're getting a bit better because you realise how much this needs to work.' Dylan gestured around us. 'But you still don't like it, right?'

I shrugged. 'So what if I prefer to do things myself?'

'Now is not the time for that though, is it?'

I folded my arms across my chest. 'You really are irritating.'

'Take our pact – you knew you needed my help but you couldn't ask me so you challenged me instead.'

He looked so smug, I wanted to throw some hay at him. I stalked off. 'Don't worry, I won't ask you for any more help...'

Dylan hurried after me and gently took my arm, encouraging me to slow down. I stopped. 'Look at me, please.' Reluctantly, I lifted my face and met his eyes. 'Have I ever once said I don't want you to ask me for help?'

'But you shouldn't be helping; you don't want this to work,' I said, wondering why I suddenly felt on the verge of tears. My mind flashed back to his lips on mine but I stubbornly pushed the image away from my mind. I couldn't ever think about that again. Dylan was here to get me to sell the farm. He wanted me to give up, right?

Dylan shook his head. 'It's a complicated situation, for sure. But I like helping you. I can't seem to stop myself.' His hand was still on my arm and he gave me an almost fond smile. It was so confusing. 'Come and see...' He let go and my body instantly missed his touch although I tried desperately to ignore that. I followed him out of the tunnel and across to the cottage where his laptop was open, as usual, on the kitchen table. 'I started to make this...'

I stared at the screen. He had created a website for *Pumpkin Hollow at Birch Tree Farm*: a dazzling orange and cream themed page with space for pictures of the pumpkin patch and the ability to book online for a slot to visit. He then showed me new social media accounts he'd set up and ideas for hashtags we could ask people to use when sharing their pictures. 'I had a look at the nearest pumpkin patches to here and what they charge and I think this is fitting for your first year. Then this is what the farmer wants us to charge for his pumpkins and then this is the cost for the smaller ones you ordered. You could reduce the price per pumpkin if people buy more so it would look like this...' He showed me the spreadsheet he'd created with the prices, which I looked at in awe. I guessed I could have come up with this with time and research, but he had really made my life a whole lot easier by doing this himself. I struggled for what to say. I felt grateful but was anxious about being obliged to him.

'I get worried when you're quiet,' Dylan said after a moment, frowning as he looked at me. It was as if he was trying to work out what was going on inside my head. Which made two of us.

'Are you doing this so I feel like I need to sell to you?' I blurted out.

'How does helping you make the patch successful do that exactly?' he asked slowly, his voice tight like I'd upset him.

I sighed. 'I don't know, Dylan. This is confusing. Things between us are confusing after...' I abruptly stopped myself. Neither of us had said any more about our night together. I took a breath. 'Sorry, this is just really nice of you; it's making me feel a little bit discombobulated.'

Dylan nodded. 'It's okay. I know we want different things here. But I also like helping you. That's all this was, I swear.' He sounded sincere.

'What would your brother say though about you going above and beyond for me?'

'He doesn't get what I'm doing here, that's for sure.' He ran a hand through his hair. 'But to be honest, I'm not sure he ever really gets me.'

'I'm sorry,' I said softly. 'Sometimes, my dad has made me feel like he wished I was different, that I'd change, that I'm too much of a dreamer.'

'Yeah, Nate thinks I should be more like him, I know that.'

I thought back to him speaking to Nate on the phone and how different he had sounded. 'Maybe you shouldn't help the pumpkin patch so much then,' I suggested. I knew that wasn't good for me but I also hated the hurt look in his eyes when he talked about his brother not believing in him. I knew that feeling well. I was worried I'd let my dad down, and my mother too.

'He doesn't know what I'm doing here,' Dylan said with a shrug. 'You want to post on social media about the patch?'

'Saying what?' I asked, panicked by the idea.

'You took a good picture yesterday of Sabrina's sign once we fixed it up by the gate to show her.'

I pulled my phone out of my pocket and looked at it. It showed the *Pumpkin Hollow* sign with the farm behind it, the birch trees in shot looking beautiful as they were now almost completely golden in colour and you could also just make out Maple by the farmhouse door. It was a pretty picture if I did say so myself. 'It would be a good start,' I agreed. I sank into the chair at the kitchen table and put my phone on the table. I added Dylan's Birch Tree Farm accounts to my phone and I created my first posts using the caption:

Pumpkin Hollow: Birch Tree Farm's Pumpkin Patch is opening 1 October.

With shaky fingers, I shared the post everywhere and then both Dylan and I reposted it from our personal accounts. I asked Sabrina to do so as well and I would ask the café too when I went in next. I sucked in a breath. 'I guess there's no going back now, is there?' I glanced at Dylan and he was giving me a pleased smile. I smiled back and had a crazy thought that I wished we'd met under completely different circumstances so there were no complications between us.

But life wasn't that simple.

28

The final week of September was rushing autumn into town. I walked down the High Street with Maple on Wednesday morning and looked down at my feet, smiling to see pretty coloured leaves crunching under my boots as I walked. Orange maple leaves and golden birch tree leaves with even a scarlet red and rusty brown colour mingled in. Change lingered in the air with the promise of new beginnings not far behind. I hoped this season was going to be good to me and the farm.

Maple let out a bark then when a large, yellow leaf landed on the tip of her nose. She jerked her head and it floated off, making me chuckle. More pumpkins had been added to shop doorways in the High Street, most businesses having decorated now as we edged towards October. I looked carefully at them as I walked past and was sure that the ones I'd be selling were better quality, and I hoped visitors would realise that too.

I also saw shiny conkers having burst open as they hit the ground and I picked up a few and put them in my Barbour jacket pocket, thinking I'd put them in a bowl in the farmhouse to deter spiders like I'd done when I was younger. I had just picked up the leaflets and posters from the printers and was going to ask some of the businesses here to display them for me, starting with the café.

Pushing open the door, the smell of cinnamon and coffee hit me. It was mid-morning so the early rush had cleared and lunch was yet to start so it wasn't busy.

'Morning,' I greeted female Pat as I made my way to the counter, Maple bouncing at my heels, clearly hoping for a treat. To be fair to her, my stomach rumbled on cue too.

'Willow, how is everything going? I was hoping you'd come in. I went through the van with Paul last night and we've come up with some things to sell at the farm. He is willing to be there every day for three hours from 2 to 5 p.m., to make the most of the after-school time until half-term and then we can see how it's going and change the times if it'll be busier earlier in the day that week.' She slid a small menu across the table. 'What do you think?'

I glanced at it. They would be offering visitors pumpkin spiced lattes, autumnal hot chocolates, coffee with pumpkin or vanilla syrup, if wanted, tea, and then a selection of cake and sweet treats – pumpkin pie, pumpkin spiced muffins, apple and cinnamon cake, banana bread and a cupcake of the day. My mouth started watering. 'Wow, this looks amazing; I'll be your best customer, I think.' I pulled out a poster and a stack of leaflets from the satchel slung across my body. 'I was wondering if you could display these, please; maybe we can get your customers to come along. Do you think I'm charging an okay amount? I'm worried no one will want to pay to come but I need to charge an entry fee if I have any hope of, well, keeping the farm,' I said, still nervous being honest about what a predicament we were in, but Dylan had been right when he said I needed help, so people should know the truth.

Pat screwed up her face in sympathy. 'I really hope this works for you, Willow. I think that's a reasonable amount for entry and then people can either spend more on pumpkins or just have a nice day out. We would have come along with Paul when he was younger, I'd say. We loved coming to the farm in summer so I don't see why people wouldn't enjoy this just as much. We are all autumn fans in this town.' She dropped me a wink and I smiled back, glad she thought this could work.

'People seemed to think it was an outlandish idea when I first mentioned it, though.'

'Well, this town likes its traditions. Perhaps we are all a bit stuck in our ways. After you mentioned it, I looked up pumpkin patches and they seem to be popular in larger places. So, once everyone tries it out, why can't it be so here? I had to talk my husband and son into trying this café van idea out. But if it works out, no doubt they will claim credit.' She rolled her eyes, making me chuckle. 'Listen: Birchbrook needs you and your father here. Oh, and Maple, of course.' She glanced over the counter to smile at Maple, who was wagging her tail like crazy. 'So, people will be on your side, I'm sure.'

'Fingers crossed. Thank you, Pat.' I knew if she was on board, she could convince others as she was such a Birchbrook stalwart. 'I'm so nervous for the opening on Monday.'

'That's only natural, dear. A few people have mentioned that young man is still staying with you and helping you with the patch?' She looked at me and I knew that meant we'd been the source of town gossip.

'Yes, in one of our cottages. He's working from the farm, helping out with the business side of things. He'll head off once the pumpkin patch opens,' I said, trying not to think about that. I just hoped he'd leave with the endeavour a success and not with my dad's agreement to sell the farm.

'He's very handsome,' she added with a sly smile.

'I guess so.' I shrugged, trying to come off as nonchalant as I possibly could. 'Right, I'm going to ask the other businesses if they'll display these too so I should get going. But can I have a takeaway drink?'

Pat gave me a look that suggested she knew I was changing the subject but she didn't press me any more, thankfully. I didn't want anyone in town apart from Sabrina to know that Dylan and I had spent a night together. 'What would you like, Willow? And would Maple fancy a Puppuccino?'

* * *

It had been another long day. I was feeling slightly defeated by it as evening came around. Only a few of the businesses I had visited after the café had been happy to display anything relating to the pumpkin patch. A couple had said there was no space for advertising or were against it, and then a few were openly sceptical about a pumpkin patch in town, which had been really disappointing.

Why would anyone want to go somewhere just to buy pumpkins when you can get them at the supermarket?

Sounds like a gimmick and a fad to me. I bet no one will be interested in pumpkin patches in a couple of years' time.

Won't the farm be muddy? What will you do if the weather is really bad? People won't want to traipse around in the rain.

Dad came over to the sink I was washing up dinner dishes in as I let out a heavy sigh. 'Don't worry too much about what they said today,' he told me, guessing the reason for my melancholy. 'Pat is right about people round here not being open to change. Think about it: we do the same things every year – the Halloween lantern festival and the tree-lighting ceremony. And most of us have lived here since birth. What about how outsiders are treated when they first move here? Once they come to the farm and have a great time, they won't remember being sceptical about it.'

'Maybe. But the initial reaction hasn't been what I hoped. Think about how you and Sabrina reacted at first too. What if people around here won't even try it out because they don't think they would enjoy it? And Mary at the florist's had a point about bad weather. I know the actual patch will be covered but people do have to come up to the farm and walk over from the parking area. Plus, the café van will be outside. It *is* likely to get muddy...' I rubbed at the dish in the sink harder than was strictly necessary.

'We're country folk; what's a bit of mud, eh?' He nudged me and I gave him a small smile. 'Where's Dylan this evening? He would have cheered you up over dinner.'

'What do you mean?' I asked, hiding the blush that Dylan's name instantly caused. 'He said he had too much work so is in the cottage,' I added, wishing Dad would stop grinning at me. If I was being honest, I had missed Dylan at dinner. He seemed to add an extra spark to the conversation. I didn't want to get used to him eating with us, though. One day soon, he wouldn't be here.

'I just mean, he's very encouraging of the pumpkin patch and he'd reassure you. I know you're worried and we don't know what will happen but I've never seen you so fired up about something. It's nice to see. And it's looking really good. I should have been more supportive from the start.' Dad picked up the clean dish and began drying it, our familiar routine providing some comfort.

'You were worried, though.' I remembered my conversation

with Dylan about my dad, and his brother. 'I guess sometimes, it does hurt when you say I'm just a dreamer.'

'Oh, I never mean to hurt you, love. You know what a worrier I am. I worry about you. I don't want you to be upset if this doesn't work out. You wear your heart on your sleeve, always have done. Maybe when you told me about this idea, I did think it was just a big dream. But you have worked really hard. You're making it happen. You're a dreamer, yes, but you're a doer too.' Dad smiled at me and I returned it, glad that he was no longer angry with me for sticking my head in the sand. I had faced it now. And yes, I would be heartbroken if it didn't work out but this experience was teaching me that I could do things if I put my mind to them.

'Knock knock.'

We both turned to see Dylan in the doorway. Maple jumped up from her bed where she'd been enjoying a bone to greet him. 'I thought I'd go to the pub for a drink now that I've finished work – anyone fancy joining me?'

'I have a date with my jigsaw puzzle but Willow—' Dad began but I jumped in before he could say that I would go along.

'Sorry, but I'm knackered; I need a bath and an early night,' I said quickly. I turned back to the washing-up.

'Oh,' Dylan said. 'Sure, okay. Well, I'll see you both tomorrow then.'

I heard him leave and I exhaled.

I felt my dad studying me.

'Care to tell me what that was all about?' he asked. 'Dylan looked really disappointed.'

'I just don't think it's a good idea to spend too much time with him outside of the farm work. It'll be too hard when he leaves.'

'Stubborn,' Dad muttered as he walked away.

Alone in the kitchen, I went over to the window and watched Dylan heading towards our gate. Part of me really wanted to rush after him and have a drink together but surely, it would bring back memories of last weekend when we'd stayed at the inn. And I'd thought about it enough. I didn't want the temptation to kiss him again, and being out at night alone together felt like it would bring a whole heap of temptation along with it.

I knew I'd done the sensible thing in not going, but I also knew I'd think about Dylan all evening.

29

I stood in the driveway to watch the Birchbrook Café van come in through the farm gate. Friday had started bright with a cool breeze that was causing our birch trees to sway in harmony, as if they were doing a dance. I could hardly see any green left on them now, their golden hue as bright as the sunshine. I remembered my mum telling me that autumn was a chance for nature, and for people, to let go of anything that was holding them back.

My eyes drifted to Dylan's cottage. After he had gone to the pub last night, I had tried to relax but found myself peeping through my curtains to see when he came home. If I was honest, I was dreading the idea of him coming back with another girl. He returned alone though, at 11 p.m., and I sank into my bed with relief. It was disconcerting.

Now, the cottage door opened as if I had manifested him, and Dylan emerged and made his way towards me on the driveway.

'Looks like it's Paul; he was at the pub last night,' Dylan said as he approached me, nodding over at the van. Dylan was wearing warm clothes too, his hands in his coat pockets, his hair blowing like the leaves around us. 'He was complaining about his mum making him work in the van, saying it would be cold and there might not even be customers to make it worthwhile for them.'

I rolled my eyes. 'Paul loves to complain,' I said, watching him park up and climb out of the van. It was painted cream with *Birchbrook Café* written on it in green letters, a chalkboard by the hatch that would open to list the menu they would be offering. 'Ever since we were teenagers, he's said he wants to leave Birchbrook but he's still here.' I lifted my voice. 'Morning!' I called out as Dylan chuckled under his breath. We exchanged an amused smile. And I wondered if Dylan ever thought about how he'd feel when it was time for him to leave Birchbrook. I wondered what it would be like to let him go, like the birch trees were letting go of their leaves. My traitorous mind whispered that I didn't want to have to do that.

'So, where do you want me to park next week?' Paul said, without bothering to greet us. He looked around and saw the set-up in the field behind me. 'Is that where everything will be?' he asked, nodding his head.

'That's right. We're setting up Portaloos here,' I said, pointing to the side of the farmhouse. 'And Steve is coming to offer tractor rides that will go from here so I was thinking—'

'The van should go here,' Paul interrupted, stomping over to the edge of the field. 'Right in the middle of everything. Where are you having people park – over there?' He gestured to the field the other side of the farmhouse close to the chickens, directing his questions at Dylan.

'Why don't you ask Willow where she would like the van to go?' Dylan suddenly said, frowning at Paul's attitude. I was used to it after knowing him all my life and didn't need anyone to defend me. I threw him a glare but inside, I did secretly enjoy the fact he was trying to stand up for me.

'Actually, I think...' I walked over to the field, forcing the two men to follow me. 'We could put it to the side of the polytunnels so everyone has to walk past the van; you might get more trade that way and Steve will finish the rides nearby as well. You can drive this way and stop here.' I stood in the spot. To me, it was the best place to pick up custom.

Paul narrowed his eyes and thought for a moment. Then, he nodded. 'Okay. We'll see how next week goes as to how often we come for the rest of the month.'

'Half-term is the penultimate week, and that is bound to be busy,' Dylan said, earning himself another glare from me but he merely shrugged like my annoyance didn't bother him.

'Shame there is nowhere for people to sit,' Paul said, ignoring us both.

'Any ideas?' Dylan asked him pointedly.

'Benches? I wonder if the school might let you borrow the ones they use for sports day... I'll find out. See you Monday.' Paul strode off.

'God's sake, Dylan, why are you always sticking your nose in?' I demanded once we were alone again.

'Why won't you accept my help?' Dylan threw back. 'You had ten tickets booked overnight, by the way, so people are starting to notice the publicity in town.'

That dissipated my anger. 'Really?'

'It's a start,' Dylan said with a smile.

'I could do with going over the budget spreadsheet later; I want to see if there's anything else I can add to the patch before we open. I might have hit my limit, though.'

'I'll leave my laptop in the farmhouse so you can look over dinner.'

'You're not having dinner with us again?' I found myself asking, wishing I didn't care. 'Dad said he missed you,' I added quickly when Dylan turned to look at me.

'Did he? I can't tonight; someone asked me for dinner last night.'

'Who?' I blurted out. Then we heard another noise on the drive and I looked over to see a large van coming down the driveway from the pumpkin farm. 'Pumpkins!' I cried, moving away from Dylan in excitement. I waved to the driver and went to greet him.

We spent the next hour helping the two guys unload all the orange pumpkins that we were going to sell on the pumpkin farmer's behalf. We piled pumpkins into the wooden crates by the side of the polytunnels. I also made a free-standing stack of pumpkins outside each of the tunnels as welcoming posts for people walking into the autumn trail inside.

'Maybe I should build another table for them as well,' I said as we looked at the sheer number of pumpkins left over. 'For now, stack them behind the tunnels and we can replenish once they start selling.'

'You got covers for them? In case it rains, they might go mushy or mouldy, love,' the driver said to me.

'I'm not your love,' I replied.

I heard a snort from Dylan behind me.

'But yeah, I've got spare tarpaulin that we use to cover the crops in summer if the weather gets crazy. I'll have to get it from the barn later.'

Once they had driven off, I stood and looked at the pumpkins. I carried a few inside the tunnels too for the photo opportunities. I would get the unusual pumpkins delivered over the weekend which I'd stack on the wooden planters I had built, but the orange ones were perfect for the photo set-ups I had created.

Dylan helped me carry them inside and I noticed he kept grinning across at me.

'What's so amusing?' I snapped finally.

'I liked you telling that guy off, and Paul too, and me...' Dylan said, shaking his head. 'You're feisty. I like it.'

'But you're going on a date with someone else,' I found myself saying. I wished instantly I could take it back as the grin faded instantly from Dylan's face. We stared at one another.

'I didn't say it was a date,' Dylan said. 'It's a potential client. But if it was a date, would you mind?'

I couldn't answer.

'Willow...'

I turned away. 'There is too much to do to talk.' I could feel his eyes boring into my back. I sighed. 'We said last weekend was a one-off, right?' I whispered, unsure what I wanted him to say.

'That's what you said,' he replied before ducking out of the tunnel, leaving me alone.

A sigh escaped my lips. What did that mean?

30

'Look what I found!' Sabrina came over on the way home from picking her daughter up from her grandparents. Work had finished for her for the week. Daylight was diming outside so I'd come into the farmhouse, exhausted from another long day. She pulled out pumpkin mugs from her bag. 'I got two sets of four – four for us, four for you.' They were large, deep-orange, pumpkin-shaped mugs with pretty, white, autumn leaves on them. 'How could I resist them?'

'They are so cute. I'd love to sell autumn merch like this at the patch. Sometimes, I think my ideas are too big, though,' I mused as I picked up one of the mugs and smiled at it. 'Like I wish I could build a straw maze. I have to reign myself in; we open on Monday and everything needs to be perfect.'

'You can save those ideas for next year then,' Sabrina suggested. 'Have two for the farmhouse, and two for the cottage so Dylan can use them. Where is he?'

'Getting ready to have dinner with a potential client. Dad is walking Maple. I'm just checking on the slow-cooker beef he made and then I need a shower. I'm knackered but the patch is really coming together now.'

'I'll be over on Monday as soon as school finishes for the day. Oh, Paul came by to see if you guys could borrow our benches; I think Miss Walker has let him have a few,' she said, referring to the headmistress.

'Great,' I said. I gestured to Dylan's open laptop on the kitchen table. 'Ticket sales aren't really going that well, though. There's only been a few today and I'm not sure what to do over the weekend to get more people to book.'

'Maybe people want to wait for it to open; they might not be in the full autumn spirit yet but once October arrives, they will be.' She saw me bite my lip. 'I'll rally everyone at work, don't worry. I need to get home. You look tired; are you going to rest tonight?'

'I'll try. It's hard to switch my mind off. There's only two days to go...'

'Don't stress, it's going to be great. I'll drop these two mugs in for Dylan on my way out. Has anything more happened between you two?'

I shook my head and she looked disappointed.

'Maybe we can have breakfast tomorrow in town to start the weekend off?' she said. 'The four of us?' she added hopefully.

'There's too much to do,' I replied regretfully.

'Okay, well, we could come by afterwards and help out. I'll message you.' She gave me a big hug and I found myself clinging to her for a second. I was trying to be optimistic and when Dylan told me we had sold ten tickets earlier, I'd been thrilled but that was all we had sold. Ten tickets wouldn't make me any profit. What if I ended up losing money on this idea?

Sabrina left and I saw Dylan drive off for his dinner so I had a shower and got changed then sat down to eat with Dad.

Outside, it was dark and the earlier breeze was stronger now. I could hear the wind blowing down the chimney.

I pulled out my phone, feeling a bit worried.

'It doesn't say there's any bad weather on the way but that wind is really getting up.'

Dad looked out of the window. 'Yeah, and it feels like rain is in the air. I'll secure the chickens after dinner and check on the crops.'

'I'll check on the pumpkin patch too,' I agreed. 'Better to be safe than sorry. I thought we would have sold a few more tickets by now. Do you think it's too expensive? Is that putting people off?'

'It's probably too early to tell. Word needs to spread. What has Dylan said about it all?'

'Dad, I can do this by myself.'

'You said yourself – he's good at business and all that online, social media stuff... I think I hear his car.'

We saw a pair of headlights coming up the drive. I relaxed in my chair. Maybe I had been listening out for his return.

'I need to take him back his laptop,' I said. I had looked at the budget and I was maxed out. I would have to try to be happy with what I had bought for the patch so far. I couldn't justify using any more money when we'd only sold ten tickets. I needed to see how the opening week went and then maybe make tweaks accordingly if people still weren't coming to the farm. My hopes were high for the penultimate week of October, which was half-term, but that would only be successful if people who did come by beforehand enjoyed it and spread the word. I worried there wasn't enough going on. It was hard to know. I couldn't put myself in a visitor's shoes. I had created it all. 'I could see if Dylan does have any ideas to increase ticket sales, I guess. I just don't want to rely on him, Dad.'

'I don't know, he seems happy for you to do that.'

'Why, though? He wants us to sell. I made this crazy pact with him but he's still here, helping us, and his brother definitely seems pissed off about it. I can't say I blame him. Dylan's not focused on their business while he's here. And if I keep asking for help, relying on him, it's going to make things really hard once we reach the end of the six weeks and we have to decide whether to sell to him or not. Either way, one of us gets hurt. And then after it all, we won't see each other again.'

Dad leaned on his elbow. 'I did wonder why he agreed to stay for six weeks. You don't do something like make the pact you two made if you're happy with your life. He's looking for something, Willow. Maybe you both are.'

A tiny bit of hope sprung up inside my chest. I let myself imagine for a second that I could rely on Dylan, that I could ask for his help and not worry about it, that after the end of these six weeks, we wouldn't get hurt or have to go our separate ways forever. It all seemed too unbelievable, though. Even if Dad was right and Dylan didn't like his life, I liked mine.

Didn't I?

Maple barked as a gust of wind whipped around the house.

I sighed and looked out of the window. 'We better check on things, I guess. My phone still says no sign of a storm but I'm not sure.'

'Okay, you go and take Dylan his laptop and I'll check on the farm; you look at the patch before you come back for the night. Stay here, Maple; the wind will upset you, girl.'

I headed for Dylan's cottage first, glancing at the pumpkin patch as I went. It seemed all fine as far as I could make out but I knew I better check everything was secure and properly covered just in case. The farm was pitch-black and the stars were hidden by the clouds that had crept over the sky. The wind was noisy and it blew my hair around my face, which I'd left down, still slightly damp from my shower before dinner. There was no sign of rain, though so I was hopeful the breeze would dissipate before morning. It would be a long weekend ahead of trying to get ready for Monday and I was feeling more stressed than I'd admitted to Sabrina and Dad. Everything was riding on this and the pressure was building.

I knocked on the cottage door and wondered if I could be honest with Dylan.

'I brought your laptop back,' I said lamely, when he opened the door.

'Come in,' he said, with an inviting smile.

I hesitated, knowing that I needed to check on the pumpkin patch but I also wanted his advice so when he stood back, I walked inside.

31

'Something smells good,' I noted when I walked through the cottage into the kitchen, which was warm, light and inviting. I felt a bit better already.

Dylan returned to where he'd been stirring something on the cooker. I put the laptop down on the kitchen table as he smiled over his shoulder at me.

'It's Birchbrook's fault. Come and see,' he said, beckoning me over with a nod. He'd changed after the day and now had on jogging bottoms and a T-shirt, his feet bare, and his hair was damp, clearly from the shower. He looked completely relaxed and at home in the cosy cottage; the log fire in the corner crackling merrily, allowing him to just be in a tee. I waited a second to drink him in while he had his back to me. He really was attractive. I'd initially thought he was too much of a city boy for me to crush on him, but the longer he spent on the farm, the more that side of him seemed to evaporate, making me feel like he had never been that type of man; I had just painted him as such when I saw him in his suit that first day.

'So, what are you making?' I asked, stepping over to stand

beside him and peer over into the saucepan. I caught him glance at my black leggings, long, plaid shirt and trainers, and my loose, damp hair. I told myself I shouldn't care, but I couldn't help it. I wanted him to find me attractive too.

'Ever since I had a hot chocolate in the café, I've fancied another one so I found a recipe online and thought I'd give it a go. I was going to bring one over to you but now you're here...' Dylan reached out and touched the small of my back with the hand that wasn't stirring the hot chocolate, sending warmth through my body, although he quickly let go again, as if he hadn't planned the contact and had surprised himself as well as me. 'Want to stay and try it with me? It's an autumnal hot chocolate, apparently.'

'I should go and check on the patch with all this wind... but how can I say no to an autumnal hot chocolate? Plus, I was hoping to get your advice.'

'Oh, yeah?' He smiled as if that pleased him. 'I think we should use the pumpkin mugs that Sabrina bought.'

'What's got into you?' I teased.

'I told you – Birchbrook has changed me. I'm turning into an autumn lover.' He pulled out the two orange, pumpkin mugs from the cupboard and set them down on the kitchen counter.

'You'll be carving pumpkins next,' I joked as I watched him making our drinks.

'If you wanted me to, I would,' he replied quietly, not looking at me.

His words sank into my skin like moisturiser, softening me on the spot. I fought hard not to melt completely. 'What else would you do if I wanted you to?' I couldn't resist asking him, arching an eyebrow, trying to keep my tone teasing and not let him see the effect he was having on me.

I realised then that this was the first night we'd been all

alone since the inn. The spark between us that night seemed to bubble under the surface as we looked at one another even though I was trying not to feel it again. I just couldn't seem to stop thinking about that hot night together.

Dylan let out a wistful sigh. But maddeningly, he didn't answer. Instead, he took the saucepan off the heat and poured the hot chocolate out, dividing it between our two mugs. Then he picked up a bottle of whipped cream, shook it and squirted it on top, finishing the drinks off with a sprinkle of nutmeg and chocolate chips.

'So, what did you want to ask me?' Dylan asked, clearing his throat like he was trying to focus on anything other than how close we were to each other.

'Um, well, I'm worried about ticket sales and…' I tried to remember what I wanted to talk to him about but it was hard to think straight. I watched as a dollop of whipped cream slid off the side of my mug. I reached out and wiped it with my fingertip then sucked the whipped cream off it.

'Jesus, Willow.' Dylan groaned like he was in pain.

'What?' I met his gaze and saw how dark his eyes were. My pulse started to speed up. I knew he was thinking about our night together at the inn then for sure. 'You know I like whipped cream,' I said with a smile. I picked up the pumpkin mug and took a sip, enjoying the way he watched me do it, his breaths coming out loud and ragged in the silent kitchen.

'Oh, wow,' I said as the delicious drink hit me. It was hot chocolate with pumpkin and spice: the perfect autumn drink. 'This is better than anything at the Birchbrook Café; maybe one day, we could sell these at the patch,' I said excitedly. 'We could —' I stopped suddenly because Dylan had moved forward to stand in front of me as I leaned against the counter. 'Aren't you going to try it?' I whispered as his gaze bore into me. My heart thumped at the hungry look on his face. It both thrilled and terrified me.

Dylan reached out and picked up his mug, keeping his eyes on me. He took a sip. 'Actually, that it really good,' he said, evidently surprised at having made something that tasted so yummy. He put the mug back down and I giggled. 'What?'

'You have cream...' I reached out and wiped the corner of his mouth.

As my fingertips bushed his lips, he parted them and I slid my finger inside and he licked the cream off me. I couldn't stop the hitch of my breath as I watched him do that. What was it with us and whipped cream?

'Willow,' he said, his voice low and desperate. 'I have to kiss you. Please, God. Tell me you want me to kiss you,' he said urgently, his eyes on my lips again.

32

My body sagged in relief that Dylan wanted to kiss me again too.

'Yes, please,' I gasped and his hands came around my waist and I arched towards him, tilting my face up as he leaned down. When our lips met, we both let out a contended murmur.

Dylan pulled me closer and deepened the kiss. It quickly turned hungry. He moved his hands to my hair, running his fingers through the damp strands as his tongue played with mine. I moved my hands to his waist and clung shamelessly to him.

Dylan's lips left mine and he looked into my eyes again. 'I've wanted to do that every day since the night we spent together, but I didn't think you did.'

I nodded. I felt vulnerable as he looked at me. 'I'm scared,' I whispered.

Dylan cupped my face in his hands. 'We don't need to do anything more; I just wanted to kiss you again.'

'I want more, though,' I said, with a smile.

Dylan chuckled. 'Oh yeah? That's a relief because I do too.' His lips met mine again and this time, the spark between us was even more electric. 'Can I...?' His fingertips rested on the buttons of my shirt. I nodded eagerly. 'Last time, you seemed to enjoy telling me what to do...' he said softly, watching me as he slowly undid my shirt.

'Did you enjoy it too?' I asked him, wondering if he could hear how breathless I was from our kisses. My fear was still there but it was being overtaken by how much I wanted him to touch me. I had been ignoring it for so long that my body felt like it had been released from jail. It was desperate for more.

'I loved every minute of that evening,' Dylan said as he finished unbuttoning me and slipped the shirt off of my shoulders, tossing it onto the kitchen table behind him. 'I think about it at the most inappropriate times, if I'm honest.'

'Oh yeah?' I reached behind me and undid my bra, letting it fall to the floor. 'I have thought about it a couple of times too...'

'Only a couple? I better make sure this one is so memorable, you can't stop thinking about it then,' Dylan said, giving me a tug so I stood up from the counter and moved closer to him. He gave me soft kisses down my neck, causing goosebumps to appear on my arms. Then he carried on to my chest, kissing in between my breasts, making me arch my back again, willing his lips to move to them. He did what I wanted and softly kissed me there. 'I have an idea...' he said, stopping before he reached my nipple. I watched as he reached behind me and picked up the can of whipped cream. 'Can I?'

I was losing the ability to speak so I just nodded and watched fascinated as he shook the can and tilted it towards me, squirting some cream around my nipple. I gasped at the cold and then again when Dylan's tongue flicked out to lick the cream before drawing my nipple into his mouth, sucking off the rest of it, causing a shiver to run down my spine.

'You taste so good,' Dylan said then, squirting out cream

onto my other breast. I couldn't hold in a moan this time when he licked it off me slowly, his eyes on me as I watched him do it. I held tightly to him, my legs feeling unsteady. 'Here,' Dylan said, moving me back again so I could lean against the counter. 'What now?' he asked, watching me like he couldn't get enough.

I reached down and pulled off my leggings.

'Keep going,' Dylan urged me so I also pulled off my underwear. I was now naked in front of him.

'Your turn,' I said and watched as he pulled off his T-shirt and jogging bottoms and then his boxers, smiling to see how he strained against them before pulling them down too. 'Had enough cream?' I asked him with a smile.

'I could use a little bit more...' He grabbed the can again and dropped to his knees on the kitchen floor, taking me by surprise. He gently parted my legs a bit and I watched as he squirted some cream on my inner thigh and then licked it off, making me gasp again. He then reached for me, stroking me just where I needed him to. 'You like that, Willow?'

'Yes, don't stop,' I begged.

Dylan stood up, kissing me fiercely as he reached between my legs. I hadn't realised how desperate I had been for his touch.

I gripped the counter as my limbs turned to jelly again, letting out another moan while he stroked me. 'Turn around,' he said suddenly, spinning me around so I had my back to him. He kissed my neck as he reached between my legs again. I leaned against him, gasping as he sent pleasure shooting through my body. 'Are you going to come for me, you gorgeous girl?' He spoke into my ear breathily as he touched me. I could feel how turned on he was as he pressed into my back.

I let out another moan and fell against him as I came. 'Oh my...' I gasped as pleasure rolled over me in waves. 'Dylan, that was...' I couldn't get my words out and he laughed into my ear. '...so hot,' I finished as I turned into his arms and pressed my lips against his. 'I need you inside me,' I begged then.

Wordlessly, Dylan lifted me up onto the kitchen counter. 'Wait here,' he said, disappearing before returning with a condom. He handed it to me and I reached down to stroke him before slipping it on, enjoying the small moan he let out when I touched him.

'How much do you want me?' I asked when the condom was on.

'So badly, it's crazy,' Dylan said, stepping in between my legs. He wrapped them around him as he reached up to touch my cheek. 'You are incredible, you know that, right?'

'You're pretty incredible too,' I said back, loving the way he was looking into my eyes, like he couldn't believe his luck. My breath hitched as he slid slowly inside me. His arms came around my back and I hooked mine around his neck as I hung off the counter around him. He moved inside me, keeping his gaze fixed on mine as we both gasped in pleasure.

'I've never done it in the kitchen before,' Dylan said, leaning in to kiss me.

I giggled against his lips. 'Might not be hygienic,' I replied, gripping his shoulders as he pushed deeper inside me. 'That feels so good.'

'It's never felt this good before,' Dylan said back. I let out a moan and he shook his head. 'You'll be the death of me with that noise.'

'You like it?'

'I love hearing you moan, gorgeous.'

'I'm so close,' I cried out then. Dylan reached in between us and touched me, causing me to bite my lip to disguise my moan.

'I want to hear you,' he grunted at me so I stopped biting my lip.

'Just like that,' I encouraged him as he stroked me while he moved faster and harder inside me.

I tipped suddenly and deliciously over the edge, crying out his name as I shuddered against him.

'That was so hot, Willow,' Dylan said as he pulled me even closer, holding me tightly by the waist as he continued to move inside me. He only lasted another few seconds before he cried out with his own climax, collapsing against me with gasping breaths. 'Fuck, that was even better than the first time.' He gave me a long, lingering kiss as our damp bodies clung to each other.

'It was,' I agreed, feeling our hearts thumping in fast, synchronised beats. 'Why did we wait so long?'

Dylan sighed. 'I have no idea. I need to hold you in my arms.' He disposed of the condom and helped me off the counter before leading me by the hand to the sofa right by the fire, which was dying a little bit now but we were both so warm after what had happened, we didn't care.

Still naked, we curled up on the sofa together, Dylan putting his arms around me and me leaning against his chest as we both slowly got our breath back. His embrace felt strong and safe and it took me by surprise how easily I curved into him, as if we had been snuggling up for years instead of this being the first time. Last time we had sex, we had parted quickly and after a heated argument, but this time, we were together. It was peaceful and sweet.

Dylan leaned down and kissed my forehead and I was taken aback by the gentle touch. The fear came back in a rush. I didn't want him to go. Fuck.

'I can't stay here,' I said then, although my body definitely didn't want to move. My brain was fuzzy after the sex high. I felt like there was something that I was supposed to do, but I couldn't remember what and I didn't really want to remember either.

'Relax,' Dylan whispered as if he could feel that I'd tensed up. He encouraged me to scoot closer to his chest so I laid my head against him and he stroked my hair as I watched the fire. 'I've got you,' he added and his words soothed me.

'It is nice,' I conceded sleepily. I felt myself melt into him despite the warning voice in my head that I shouldn't stay here and get attached to this man.

'It is nice,' Dylan agreed, sounding just as sleepy as I did.

My eyes fluttered then, closing as his chest rose and fell with slow, even breaths, mine matching the rhythm perfectly.

33

When I opened my eyes the following morning, I was disorientated. And achy. I stretched out my tightly curled up legs with a groan, looked around and realised I was on the sofa in Dylan's cottage, still naked but there was a blanket over me. Despite the fact I had fallen asleep in his arms, there was no sign of Dylan. The room was light which indicated that it was later than I would usually wake up despite the fact it was Saturday.

I rolled over a little bit so I could see around the cottage but it seemed empty. Sleeping on the sofa after our vigorous encounter in the kitchen meant my body was stiff but I also felt contented and like I had slept deeply. I struggled to sit up but managed it finally and lifted my arms over my head to stretch them out too. It was then I noticed the howling wind coming down the cottage chimney. It sounded worse than it had last night on the walk over here. With a sigh, I realised I hadn't checked on the pumpkin patch as I had planned to. After getting carried away with Dylan, I must have fallen asleep and now I was bound to be behind on the day's work. Speaking of – where was Dylan? Why had I woken up alone?

Climbing off the sofa, I spotted my discarded clothes from last night in the kitchen and walked over to them, hastily pulling them on. I badly needed coffee but I knew I should get out to the farm first and check on everything. I needed to find Dylan, my dad and Maple too. It all seemed far too quiet for my liking right now.

Once dressed, I headed out the front door, which was slightly ajar, but as I reached for the handle, I paused, hearing a sharp voice from just outside it.

'Nate, I told you not to worry; it's all going well,' Dylan said in a low but angry voice.

I knew I shouldn't listen but I also didn't want to interrupt their conversation. It sounded tense so I stood there hesitating for a moment, wondering what to do.

'She's putty in my hands.'

My blood ran cold as Dylan chuckled down the phone.

'I've practically become part of the family. They definitely are going to sell to us. I just need a couple more weeks to get it all signed, sealed and delivered. Anyway, Nate, she's inside asleep so I better go... Yeah, I'll send that over later... I said I would. Okay, bye.' Dylan must have hung up because he let out a loud sigh.

Anger shot through my veins like I'd had a double espresso. Putty in his hands?! He'd clearly told his brother we'd slept together.

Seething, I yanked open the door and burst outside.

Dylan started as the door crashed into the wall, turning around from where he stood to see me coming out of the door. He had pulled on jeans, trainers and a jumper and was holding his phone and a cup of coffee, his hair tousled from sleeping on the sofa. Behind him, the birch trees swayed merrily in the wind as it whipped around the farm, golden leaves swirling around and falling to the ground.

'Having a nice little chat with your brother, are you?' I fired at Dylan, who took a step back, his cheeks flushing. 'Telling him how you slept with me so I would sign the farm over to you? What the fuck?!' I cried, my hair flying around my face with this crazy weather.

'Willow, no... That wasn't what happened,' he spluttered, starting to walk towards me.

'Don't come any closer,' I warned, putting my hands up.

He froze instantly.

'I just heard you, Dylan! Telling Nate how I was now putty in your hands. Why do you need this place so badly? Just to get your big brother to take you seriously for once in your pathetic little life?' I let out a harsh laugh. 'He'll never respect you. And I will never sell the farm to you. Over my dead body. Pack your stuff and get the hell out of here.'

'You have to listen to me,' Dylan begged. 'It wasn't like how you heard, I promise you. Last night was amazing. Willow, please, I don't really think that – Nate is just...'

Dad shouted my name desperately then. We both turned in shock. I heard Maple bark too.

'Willow! The pumpkin patch!' Dad called, his words drifting over on the wind from where he stood by the field. He was waving his arms and my blood ran cold. I ignored Dylan and tore off towards the field, running until I reached Dad and Maple. My heart sank as I saw what had caused him to shout for me in panic. I screeched to a halt by them, trying to catch my breath as I drank in the sight.

The wind had definitely been even worse during the night. One of the polytunnels, despite how hard I'd fixed it into the ground, had blown half-off and then the rain had clearly got in, soaking the hay and props inside. I could also see the *Pumpkin Hollow* sign Sabrina made had been blown halfway across the driveway. And the tarpaulin covering one of the pumpkin crates had also been taken away by the wind so the pumpkins looked soaked. I hoped they hadn't gone rotten.

Then the final blow: a tree behind the patch had fallen down, half of it on top of one of the other tunnels, and I could see it had ripped a hole in it. I'd gone to bed with the patch practically ready for the opening on Monday morning, but now no one in their right mind would pay to come to this.

'I'm sorry, love,' Dad said. 'I checked on the crops and they're all fine but that side of the farm has always been more sheltered, hasn't it? You thought it all looked okay last night when you checked?'

'I didn't check on the field,' I admitted.

'But I thought you were going to?' Dad asked, surprised, knowing that had been the plan when we parted last night.

'I... forgot,' I said dully. I had got swept up in being with Dylan and hadn't checked on the pumpkin patch like I knew I should have done. He had distracted me when I had been determined not to let him. I felt like an absolute fool after what I'd heard him saying to his brother. I'd ruined the pumpkin patch for a man who had been just using me. I felt numb. I had no idea what to do.

Dad was looking at me but I was at a loss about what to say to him. I didn't want him to know I'd spent the night with Dylan now everything had gone so wrong.

'Oh, shit.' Dylan appeared next to me and looked around, running a hand through his hair. I flinched at his presence. 'This is a nightmare.'

Everything just felt out of control. I couldn't cope with it. I snapped. 'Yeah, a nightmare for us; this is your dream come true!'

'Willow,' Dad said, shocked.

'You can't believe that!' Dylan cried at the same time. 'All I've done is try to help you.'

'But why?' I cried desperately. 'I don't understand. I thought you liked it here, liked me, but then I hear you on the phone to your brother saying what you said...' I couldn't be explicit with my dad right next to us. I didn't want him to know we'd slept together. 'You just wanted me to sell. All you've been doing is to get me to trust you so you could persuade me to give you the farm. I heard you say that to your brother. Just admit it!'

'Dylan?' Dad asked him, looking as lost as I felt. I knew he had grown to like Dylan and to trust him too.

Dylan kept his eyes on me. 'You really believe that after all we've been through? That I would be with you just to get you to sell this place to me?' Dylan looked as shocked as I felt.

'I just heard you telling your brother exactly that! How can I not believe it?' I retorted. I shook my head. He was trying to confuse me. I knew he had told his brother I was putty in his hands. I'd felt so close with him last night. But I was clearly a fool.

'Because you know me! What about last night?' Dylan asked softly.

'It meant nothing,' I snapped before I could stop myself. I saw him wince but I knew I shouldn't care. He had hurt me. Why not hurt him back? 'You should just go, Dylan. Now. Okay? The pact is over. I will never sell to you, and you don't want to be here if this can't be yours. I... we... this place – it all means nothing to you, right? So, leave us to sort all this out ourselves,' I cried, gesturing to the mess.

'Willow, maybe we should all go inside and have a cup of tea and talk about this...' Dad began calmly while Dylan stared at me in silence.

Both of them were pissing me off in different ways. There was so much weight on my shoulders – it felt as if I was being pressed into the ground like the roots of a tree. 'I can't deal with any of this,' I said, throwing my hands up in the air. 'I need to be alone right now. This is all just too much.'

I took off before either of them could stop me. Deep down, I knew it was pointless to try to run from my problems but I had to get away from the mess. The farm. Dylan. Dad. The memory of my mother. The feeling I'd let everyone down. How betrayed I felt by Dylan. I was so hurt and scared. And I had no idea what to do.

Maple started after me instantly and even though I didn't know where to go, I needed to leave the farm. So, I let her walk with me, desperate to escape, trying to hold back tears.

34

I could hear Dad calling me from the field but I didn't respond. I marched out of the gate, passing Sabrina's damaged *Pumpkin Hollow* sign, with Maple at my heels as if she knew I needed her support and comfort right now. I marched towards town without even knowing where I was really heading, but I had to create some distance from the place where it seemed like everything had gone wrong. The familiar landscape around me was lost as my head and heart raged against the past few hours. I'd felt so happy just yesterday evening falling asleep naked in Dylan's arms but this morning, everything had changed.

Leaves the colour of pumpkins and butternut squash swayed gently in the calm after the storm as we walked towards the High Street. Then I saw the birch trees lining the road and I swallowed the lump in my throat. Their mustard leaves reminded me too much of home. I looked down at my feet but the road was scattered with them, like yellow confetti had been tossed around to celebrate autumn in the same way you'd celebrate a wedding. Right now though, there seemed to be nothing to celebrate.

My feet moved of their own accord towards the Birchbrook Café and Maple seemed eager to get inside the warm again so I didn't bother calling her away from the door. Once inside, my chest sagged as the cosy café with its autumn décor and delicious, sweet pumpkin smell just reminded me of my failures.

'Willow, I thought you were too busy to meet for breakfast today,' Sabrina said in surprise as she turned around from where she was ordering at the counter, beaming at the sight of me and Maple walking through the door. Then she saw my face and her smile faded. 'What's wrong?'

I let out a sob before I could stop myself and she charged towards the door, threw her arms around me and pulled me into her chest. 'Are you okay?'

Sniffing into her blonde hair, her floral perfume as familiar as my own vanilla one, I felt Maple leaning against my legs as if she wanted to join in our hug too. 'It's been a shit morning, to be honest,' I said, as a tear rolled out of the corner of my eye. I returned her hug tightly. 'I forgot you were coming in; I'm so glad you're here.'

'Bradley and Dottie are at home, I said we'd get a takeaway brunch as we all feel pretty tired but they won't mind if I stay and chat to you. Go and sit down, I'll get us something and then you can tell me what's going on.'

I shook my head in a weak protest.

'Go on.' She pointed to the tables and I was too weary to argue with her so I went to our favourite one and sank into a chair, grabbing a napkin from the box on the table and dabbing my face. Maple sat down by my feet and I stroked her, glad she was with me. I felt even worse now I was away from the farm. I had walked out on Dad, leaving him with all the mess, and I'd told Dylan to go. My heart was heavy. We'd been so close to the patch opening and now I had no idea what would happen.

'Okay,' Sabrina said a few minutes later. 'I hope this helps. Tell me what's going on. You're worrying me, Willow.' She sat down opposite me and slid the tray onto the table. She'd ordered two pumpkin spiced lattes and two almond croissants for us plus the two Pats had given her a dog treat for Maple, who took it from her eagerly and ate it on the floor.

'Are you sure?' I asked. 'You need to get home, don't you?'

'Willow, you're my family too; surely you know that by now?' she chastised.

I let out another sob, making her eyes widen in alarm.

'Have some of your drink and food, have another tissue here, take a deep breath and then fill me in...'

I followed Sabrina's calm instructions. She had always been good in a crisis. I was vaguely aware that the two Pats, and Paul, were keeping an eye on me from behind the counter, plus a couple of customers who I knew glanced over in concern. I hated that I was having a very public meltdown but everything had gone wrong, I couldn't help it. After I'd had a sip of the drink and a bite of the croissant, I dabbed my eyes and exhaled. 'Last night, it felt like maybe there was a storm brewing so I said to my dad I'd check on the pumpkin patch but I had to take Dylan his laptop back and I wanted his advice as well – we've only sold ten tickets so far. But then we kissed. There was a whole thing with whipped cream...'

'Whipped cream?!' Sabrina cried in shock. She saw my face. 'Not important. Sorry. Go on.'

'We spent the night together. And I fell asleep. And I forgot about checking on the pumpkin patch. There was a storm and it's such a mess, Sabrina. All that hard work and it's going to put us behind to fix it all. And then Dylan...' I swallowed the big lump in my throat down. I told her briefly what I'd overheard of his phone call with his brother. 'I told him to go. And I just couldn't deal with him or the patch. I took off and ran away from it all. And came here,' I finished lamely with a big sniff. I stared at my friend in despair. 'What am I going to do?!'

Sabrina sucked in a breath and took a gulp of her coffee. 'I'm so sorry, Willow. Firstly, if Dylan did sleep with you so he could persuade you to sell the farm then he is an absolute dick and you shouldn't waste another breath on him. I don't know, though; I saw the way he looked at you, and you two seemed to make such a good team. Maybe there is more to the story. I got the feeling from what you've said, and when we had breakfast in here with him, that he's not all that close to his brother so maybe he was just trying to get him off his back?' She took in the glare I gave her. 'Let's leave that to one side then; the more important problem is the pumpkin patch.'

'What pumpkin patch?' I asked miserably. 'How can I fix it all before Monday? And even if I can, only ten people have booked to come. I keep checking but no one else has bought tickets.'

'I have!'

'So, three of the ticket sales are you guys.' I shook my head. This was worse than I had even thought. 'What if no one in Birchbrook gives a shit about pumpkins?' I wailed, probably too loudly as all heads swivelled in our direction.

Female Pat came over with a concerned look on her face. 'I don't mean to eavesdrop but I've known you both your whole lives. Has something happened? Can I help?'

'I think I might have to give up on the pumpkin patch and sell the farm,' I said dully. I shook my head. 'I can't believe all that work was for nothing. Well, I'm not selling to Dylan and his brother. I'll find someone else, then I'll have to leave Birchbrook and—'

'Willow!' Sabrina interrupted in such a sharp tone, I shut up instantly. 'You need to stop catastrophising for a second, okay? You're jumping to the worst possible outcome. Why don't I come to the farm with you and assess the damage? Surely, with a few of us helping out, we can fix it so you can still open on Monday. And we can brainstorm about how we get people to come along. This is Birchbrook! We always help each other out. Everyone will help you if you need it, I'm sure of it.'

Pat nodded along with what Sabrina said. 'I'll come too; we will sort it all out, I have no doubt about it.' She saw me open my mouth. 'If you are about to argue with us, Willow Connor, then you really are out of sorts because when has that ever worked?'

'Good point,' I mumbled. Sabrina had been a force of nature since we were kids and Pat was a Birchbrook institution. The two women were kind of scary right now but my heart swelled with gratitude that they cared enough to give me this tough love, and to offer immediately to help us at the farm. 'I don't know if we can make it work, though,' I added nervously.

'We won't know until we get there.' Sabrina drained her coffee dry and turned to Pat. 'Can we get the food to go, please?'

'Definitely.' She grabbed our plates and called over her shoulder, 'Pat, man the café, darling. Paul, you need to drive us to the farm and you can help out too.' She spoke in such a tone, they didn't dare argue. I knew exactly how they felt.

Sabrina reached over the table to give my hand a squeeze while Pat rushed off to get ready. 'What will you do if Dylan is there when we get back?' she asked quietly so any still prying ears couldn't hear.

'I told him to go,' I said, knowing that had been for the best but my heart still ached to think about him not being there. 'So, he won't be.'

She looked sceptical but I knew things were over between us.

For good.

35

Paul drove us back to the farm in the Birchbrook Café van and kept quiet, thankfully. Sabrina threw me worried looks but I stared out of the window, not up to chatting to her or Pat. It felt like I had been running on adrenaline ever since Dad showed me the letter from Henderson Homes, desperate to save the farm, and I'd thrown myself into it, but now all the energy and enthusiasm had been sucked out of me. It felt like there was no point in trying any more. It seemed like I'd already lost the farm. As well as Dylan. Although I knew I hadn't really had him to begin with. He'd been playing me all along. I just hoped Dad and I could find someone, anyone else really, to sell to. I didn't want Dylan to have Birch Tree Farm. And I sure as hell didn't want his brother to get his grubby hands on it.

We passed through the gate then and I saw Dad was in the pumpkin-patch field. Dad was pushing the wheelbarrow and I felt guilty for having left him here with all the mess. He shouldn't be trying to clear it up by himself. He stopped to look at the van, smiling when he saw me climb out even though I knew I didn't deserve it.

'There you are,' Dad said as Maple galloped over to see him and he waved at Pat, Sabrina and Paul who followed me over to the field. He peered at my face and saw that I'd been crying. 'Oh, love.' He slung an arm around my shoulders and gave me a squeeze.

'Don't, Dad, I don't deserve it,' I said, shaking my head at his affection.

'This wasn't your fault.'

'I should have checked on everything. I could have secured the coverings. I might have seen the tree was close to falling down too. I should have kept on checking… but I fell asleep.'

'With Dylan,' Dad said softly before the others joined us. It wasn't a question. He knew we'd been together. I nodded miserably. 'He took off in his car. I've never seen a man look quite so broken.'

'That tree is a nightmare in itself,' Paul said without preamble as the three of them stood beside us and surveyed the damage. 'Gonna be a big clear-up job.'

'But doable,' Pat said, giving her son a stern look.

He just shrugged.

'And we can patch up the tunnel, right?'

'With all of us working, we can clear that tree by the end of the day, I bet,' Sabrina said, her hands on her hips as she stared at it.

'What about the pumpkins? They are likely ruined,' I said with a sigh.

'Let's move them into the barn to dry out. You could contact the farmer you got them from, see if he can come up with any ideas to save them,' Dad said. 'There are two broken crates, but we don't need them. And your sign, Sabrina…'

'I can easily make a new one,' she said eagerly.

A noise behind us then caught our attention. A large lorry started coming down the drive.

'The rest of the pumpkins,' I wailed. 'But the tunnel is damaged and I haven't checked on my planter tables, and it looks like more rain is on the way,' I added, glancing up at the greying sky.

'We'll get them to put them into the barn for now,' Dad said quickly.

'Let's get started; who else can we call to help?' Pat asked, rubbing her hands together, ready for action.

'Wait,' I said as they all started to head off to work.

They paused.

'I can't ask you to do this. We'll have to work all weekend to try to fix this all if there is any hope of opening on Monday. And even if we can get it looking perfect – is there any point? We've only sold ten tickets so far!'

'One step at a time – let's try and clear the damage first then we can work on getting people here,' Dad told me calmly. He could tell I was still freaking out. 'Right now, there is no pumpkin patch for anyone to enjoy.'

'We want to help,' Sabrina said, nodding along to what Dad had said. 'I grew up on this farm too; we have to fight to keep it. You're my family.'

My eyes started to well up. 'If you're sure...'

Pat gave a firm nod. 'My husband is fine in the café on his own. Paul and I are happy to pitch in. Aren't we?'

'Let's stop talking and get it done,' he replied, walking off before anyone could stop him again.

'I really am so grateful,' I said to them. 'But I messed up; I can't ask you to fix it.'

'We're going to fix it together, like we do everything,' Dad replied. 'Now, love, stop trying to talk us out of it; we're losing time.'

'Come on, Willow, this isn't like you – you were so excited about this idea; you can't give up now you've hit a hurdle,' Sabrina added as we all followed Paul to the lorry to help carry the pumpkins over to the barn.

I couldn't help but glance over to the cottage that Dylan had been staying in, and where I'd slept last night. That felt like a dream now. But Sabrina and my dad, and Pat and Paul, were right to give me a kick up the arse. It was a bad day but I'd had plenty of bad days on the farm. I couldn't give up on it all now. Dylan wasn't here and what happened between us hurt a lot but I had made the pact with him in the first place to save our farm, and that's what I needed to do.

'Okay, guys, thank you for helping. Let's get started!'

And we did.

We spent the rest of the day working to sort things as much as we possibly could. We moved the pumpkins into the barn for shelter to try to dry out the ones that had got caught in the storm, and then we cleared away the fallen tree and resulting debris.

Sabrina worked on making a new *Pumpkin Hollow* sign for the front gate and then another one at the start of the patch. No farmers I reached out to had a spare polytunnel I could get before Monday and the hire company didn't either so, armed with the limited sewing knowledge my mother had given me, I tried to repair the tear in it to stop any further wind or rain from getting inside. Pat sorted out all the autumn and Halloween décor inside the tunnels and swept up the hay that had been blown around and got rid of anything that had been damaged. Then Bradley and Paul collected the benches the school were happy to lend us for the month and they found a couple of crates from a builder friend, which we could use for pumpkins.

I spoke to the pumpkin farmer and he seemed to think most of the pumpkins would be okay once they'd dried out but the dozen or so that looked destroyed, he wouldn't charge me for as he could tell how upset I was.

As we were so close to 1 October, the day finished earlier than we would have liked. Twilight fell over the farm and then it was tricky to see what we were doing.

Sabrina came to find me in the polytunnel as I looked at the patch-up job I'd done. I'd decided to drape one of the fabric cobwebs I'd bought across it so it wasn't visible; people would just see the web, especially when I stuck a plastic spider up there too.

'You wouldn't know anything had happened to it,' Sabrina said, smiling.

'I just hope the weather won't get in again,' I replied, unsure if I'd done enough to protect against another storm.

'The signs are done and Paul is fixing them tightly into the ground as we speak,' she added. 'Your dad is making dinner for anyone who wants it. I think Pat and Paul are going back to the café though, and I need to see Dottie and Bradley. But we will all be back early tomorrow morning. No arguments from you about that.'

I shook my head. 'I don't know what I would have done without you all today. I was ready to give up. I panicked.'

'It's understandable, but it kind of looked worse than it turned out to be, right? Once we cleared that tree away, it hasn't been too bad.'

We both looked around the tunnel. It did look like a fun and festive autumnal trail for people to walk through and get photos in and pick up a pumpkin. Pat had also had the idea to bring out two large barrels we had in the barn so we could let kids go apple bobbing in them.

'Things are always hardest before you start,' I agreed with her as we walked out slowly together. I looked over at the farmhouse lit up, smoke coming out of the chimney, and I was filled with gratitude that I was about to go inside into the warmth and have dinner and think about how people had rallied around me today. 'Today is a prime example of why I love living here,' I said. 'I was lost but everyone stepped in to help without me having to ask.'

'It's always been like that,' Sabrina agreed as we walked over to her parked car so she could head home for the night.

'I want to stay,' I said quietly, my voice mingled in with the gentle breeze.

'We'll find a way,' she promised. She climbed into her car and we said goodbye then I walked into the farmhouse. My phone beeped with an email as I headed for the kitchen.

> Hi Willow, I was given your number by Dylan Henderson. I would love to come and do a piece about your pumpkin patch for the local paper and our website. Would Monday at 2 p.m. be okay for me to come by with our photographer and speak to you?

It was quickly followed by another email – this time from a woman whose name I vaguely recognised.

> Hi Willow, I have been speaking to Dylan Henderson who I went to school with. I am always looking for places I can visit to vlog for my YouTube channel and other social media and I am a huge fan of pumpkin patches. He thought that I could

come by to see yours if you're happy for me to take some content while I'm there?

I stared at my phone, pausing before I went into the kitchen. Dylan had been contacting people about the patch. Before he walked away today, or afterwards? Either way, it was surprising that he cared enough to try to get publicity. Once again, I was confused by how much he seemed to want to help the patch be successful when it wasn't in his interest to do so. And went against his boast to his brother about me being definitely ready to sell the farm to them. I had no idea what the truth really was.

How did Dylan feel about the farm and me? Maybe now I'd never know.

Scrolling to the pumpkin patch website Dylan had made, I checked ticket sales and they had gone up to fifty. My heart leapt. Then a text message came through from female Pat explaining the increase.

> Pat has spread the word while we were at the farm today, letting everyone know that coming to the patch will save the farm and keep you and your dad in Birchbrook. See you tomorrow! Keep the faith!

'Willow, you okay? You look... stunned,' Dad said, standing in the kitchen doorway, frowning to find me stood there staring down at my phone.

'I am a little bit,' I told him but I smiled. 'Maybe it will be all right. People really do want to help us, don't they?'

'I think we should have told people we were in trouble sooner,' Dad said. 'We're both a bit stubborn, aren't we, love? Come on, let's have some food, and a glass of wine feels in order.'

'Good idea.' I remembered my mum telling me that my stubbornness came from my father. I followed him, wondering if she was looking down at us and having a little giggle at my dad saying that.

36

I woke up at dawn after a restless night.

My brain wouldn't stop thinking about everything that had happened over the past couple of days. It was like I was on an emotional roller coaster. One minute, I had been so excited about the pumpkin patch and curled up in Dylan's arms like we had been starting something special then both had been ripped from under my feet, leaving me unsteady and unsure.

And then everyone had stepped in and it looked like maybe we could pull off the patch but it was still touch and go, especially when it came to getting enough people onto the farm to turn a profit and pay off some of our debts. Dylan was nowhere to be seen or heard although he had clearly been doing some things to try to help from wherever he was now. I had no idea what the day was going to bring and part of me wanted to stay in bed, pull the covers over me and pretend Sunday hadn't arrived.

Then I heard my dad get up and go downstairs, greeting Maple as he walked into the kitchen, turning on the lights and then switching on the kettle – something I'd heard every day for so many years. That made me sit up and throw the covers back because this might be the last month that I would hear those sounds if I didn't get out of bed too.

After a quick shower, I pulled on my leggings, a long jumper, a thick scarf and put my hair into a bun then I went downstairs ready to drink a very large mug of coffee.

'How are you feeling today, love?' Dad asked me gently as I leaned against the kitchen counter to take a big gulp of coffee. He was feeding Maple and had made us scrambled eggs but I couldn't face eating anything. I was too keyed up.

'Ready to get started. We *have* to open tomorrow; this needs to work,' I said determinedly. 'I had a panic yesterday. I thought there was no hope but you gave me six weeks to try and I don't want to give up until the end of October.'

Dad looked worried. 'Maybe I put too much pressure on you; maybe it's impossible, we're in too much trouble and—'

'Dad,' I cut him off sternly. 'You gave me six weeks, right?'

Reluctantly, he nodded.

'So, it isn't over until the fat lady sings as old Jim down the pub likes to tell us every New Year's Eve.'

Dad chuckled. 'Yeah, old Jim loves that saying. Okay then, we have until the end of October – let's get started.'

We smiled at one another and I finally had a sense deep down in my bones that somehow, we'd be okay, whatever happened. I glanced out of the window at the golden birch trees that were scattering their leaves, ready for new beginnings, and I wanted to be just like them.

* * *

At the sound of a car coming up the driveway, I squinted against the Sunday-afternoon sun, lifting my hand to shield my eyes to see who it was. I was alone outside of the barn, piling pumpkins into a wheelbarrow to take over to the field. We had spent the day so far finishing the clear-up job we'd started yesterday and there had been extra help today with people from the town, the word spreading that Birch Tree Farm needed saving. I'd never felt prouder to be part of Birchbrook. I still didn't relish asking for help but I knew we couldn't do it without our friends, and somehow, I'd return their favours, even if it took the rest of my life.

Now the polytunnel had been repaired and we'd made sure things were secured better and we could cover everything each night just in case the weather turned bad again, we set about making everything inside the best possible for people to experience. So, I was starting to bring the pumpkins over to do just that.

I recognised the car coming towards me and my pulse immediately picked up pace. The sleek, black car pulled around the farmhouse to park outside of the cottages and I watched as Dylan climbed out of it. He wore the clothes he had left in yesterday and he looked around. When he saw me by the barn, he headed my way with a purposeful stride.

I was inclined to walk off and find Dad and Sabrina so I wouldn't have to face him alone but I knew that would be as childish as sending him in the wrong direction had been. I was learning that putting off bad things, sticking my head in the sand, didn't stop the bad things from happening – it just delayed them and sometimes, that made them even worse in the end. Perhaps if I had listened to my dad's worries, we could have done something to save the farm before things had got as bad as they did. I didn't want to have to deal with any more 'what if's' in my life. So, I carried on loading up pumpkins in the wheelbarrow as Dylan walked over.

'Hi, Willow,' he said, pausing a few feet away from me like he was nervous to come any closer.

I stopped loading up the wheelbarrow and glanced at him. He looked the same, if a little tired and dishevelled, and not freshly shaven like he usually was. His clothes were a little bit crumpled. I wondered where he had slept last night. 'Have you come to pick up your things?'

Dad had said, after I fled the farm, Dylan had taken off not long after in his car so I knew he hadn't had time to pack. The cottage was still his. For now.

'I wanted to speak to you. Can you take a break? We could have a cup of tea in the cottage?'

'Let's stay here; there is so much to do to get ready for tomorrow,' I replied, not wanting to go back inside the cottage when the last time I had been there, we'd ended up sleeping together. It hurt to think about that passionate evening together.

He nodded. 'Okay. That's what I wanted to talk to you about. I left yesterday after you asked me to but all I did was think about the farm. I want to help get ready for the opening tomorrow. I made a pact to stay for six weeks and I want to do that.'

I put my hands on my hips and frowned at him. 'But why? I can tell you now if this is a failure, I won't be selling to Henderson Homes. Not after what you said to your brother, how you made me think that you liked me too—'

'I did like you,' Dylan interjected. 'I do like you, Willow. I told you, what you heard wasn't what I really think or feel, I promise. But that's not important right now.'

I raised an eyebrow. 'It isn't?' This man was so confusing. I had no idea how he felt about me or how I should feel about him.

'No, what's important is opening the pumpkin patch and

doing all we can so you won't have to sell the farm to my brother, or to anyone. I know you doubt my intentions, you aren't sure whether to trust me or believe what I say, but I can help. I can work on selling tickets and getting publicity, bringing people to the farm. You have so much sorted, Willow, you have created what will be such a fun, autumnal day out for people and you are great at fixing things, coming up with ideas, bringing it all together – just look…' He gestured over to the field. 'Let me help with the things that you can't do by yourself, the things that I know how to do, that I'm good at. Even if you don't understand why I'm doing it, can you really afford to say no? Why not just let me help and we can talk about us later? Once the pumpkin patch is open tomorrow. What do you think?'

He looked at me so sincerely, I was stumped at what to say. He was serious. He wanted to help and God knew, I needed it. Yes, ticket sales had crept up slightly yesterday but we were way off what we needed to help keep the farm going until the summer season came around again.

But what would happen to my heart if I said yes?

'Willow, I've come to help bring the pumpkins over.'

Dylan and I both jumped as Paul suddenly appeared with another wheelbarrow. He didn't wait for a response but starting to pick them up to put in the wheelbarrow, acting like we weren't even there.

Dylan smiled at me and I couldn't help but smile back.

I had felt my heart break a little bit yesterday morning so the damage was already done. Dylan wasn't mine, and he never would be. But the farm was what was important now. And a tiny part of me was happy to have him back. That yesterday hadn't been our final goodbye. So, even though I was worried about how I'd feel when he did leave for good, I wasn't sensible enough to turn him away again. I needed his help. For the sake of saving my home.

'Okay, Dylan,' I said finally. 'Let's keep our pact going.' I picked up another pumpkin. 'How can we get people to the pumpkin patch?'

'I have lots of ideas,' he said, starting to walk off.

'Where are you going?' I called after him.

'To get my laptop, of course.'

I rolled my eyes. 'Of course.'

37

I wiped my brow, sweaty and tired, as I stood outside Pumpkin Hollow with my dad, Sabrina and Dylan. Sunday was fading away and we were starting to lose the light. We were the only ones left on the farm now. Somehow, all the work had been done and the pumpkin patch had been repaired and protected. New signs were up to guide people to the patch. The Portaloos had arrived and were in place. The school benches were lined up ready for the Birchbrook Café van to park by them later on tomorrow. Steve had moved into the cottage next door to Dylan, ready to offer tractor rides and help out with anything else we needed. I had installed a table at the edge of the field where Dad and I would check tickets or sell them, as well as any pumpkins, similar to what we did in the summer pick-your-own season. At least we had all that set up in place already.

'Now we just need to do a walk-through,' I said, as the four of us looked at one another. I wanted us to act like we were the visitors tomorrow and see if the patch was good enough to:

1. Give visitors a fun day out.

2. Get them to recommend coming along to people they knew.
3. Make us money!

'I'm nervous,' I added. I almost didn't want to look in case I saw another hundred things that we needed to change or improve. We were all shattered from the weekend's work and I knew we all just wanted to relax now.

'I don't think you need to be,' Sabrina said.

'But tomorrow, the local press is coming, as well as Steve's sister and her social media friends – all first thing, and then we'll have the first paying customers in the afternoon and Paul will arrive with the café van – all of them need to have the best first impression or we will be finished before we even start,' I told her, needing to suck in a deep breath after talking so quickly thanks to my nerves.

'Let's just go inside, love,' Dad said.

I glanced at Dylan. He gave me a reassuring nod. I hadn't seen him much today. He had been on his laptop or phone most of the time, working on publicity and selling tickets while I'd been outside, but knowing he had come back and was there helping us had given me an extra boost, even though I didn't want to admit it. Dad and Sabrina hadn't been all that welcoming to him but he had pretended not to notice and when everyone had left, he joined us at the field and seemed determined to stay. 'Okay then,' I agreed finally. 'Let's go into Pumpkin Hollow!'

We began to mark out the journey the customers would take: as they entered the field, they'd see the table we would be manning and then in front were the polytunnels as well as the crates of large, orange pumpkins. Sabrina had made another *Pumpkin Hollow* sign for the outside of the patch and we'd placed hay bales in front of it with a pile of pumpkins at either end so people could take a photo there as well as it signposting the way into the autumn trail.

Then there were the five tunnels that people could walk through that we'd connected to make one long trail that you'd walk up and down in. Once out the other side, visitors would see the food van and benches, and I had placed another couple of crates of pumpkins there as well. Dad had found an old bathtub in the barn so we had also filled that with pumpkins for a fun end to the trail.

The four of us walked inside the first tunnel. The floor was covered in hay and the first tunnel had two photo opportunities and one of the planter tables for the unusual pumpkins – this one had the white pumpkins on it. The next tunnel had the scarecrow couple and autumn décor in it as well as the green pumpkins, then we moved into the Halloween tunnel with the warty pumpkins and Munchkin pumpkins, and Halloween photo opportunities. We had skeletons and cobwebs and witches. We'd also set up an old table for a creepy dinner that you could sit down and have a picture at. This was the one where I'd repaired the hole with a cobweb and we all agreed that people wouldn't think anything had gone wrong in there.

Next, we'd set up activities – we had two barrels for apple bobbing filled with red, juicy apples, a table with pumpkins that kids could sit and carve at. Another one had face paints that people could use to create Halloween-themed characters, and finally, we had an area where kids could colour in pages we'd printed out online with autumn and Halloween themes on.

The final tunnel was filled with pumpkins. They were on the floor and on one of the wooden planter tables I'd made; we'd stacked more hay bales up with pumpkins on so people could again sit and have a picture, and we'd also created an arch using wires draped in autumn leaves we'd foraged from the farm and in town, in which I'd stuck small pumpkins. I'd also laced fairy lights around so the whole place twinkled happily. This was the last thing visitors would walk past, or have a picture with, and it was a stunning end to the tunnels. I looked up at it and smiled. I was sure people would love it.

The four of us then stepped outside to what would be the food area. The sun was dipping in the sky now, painting it a golden hue that matched the birch trees, and I held my breath as I turned to Sabrina, Dylan and Dad with a raised eyebrow, heart thumping as I waited to hear what they thought about it all.

'You did it.' Dad was the first to speak. He was beaming. 'I know I had my doubts and wasn't fully on board when you came up with the idea but it's great, love. I think anyone who even enjoys autumn a tiny bit would have fun in there. Kids will love it. The pumpkins look so appealing. And even I want a photo at the Halloween table.' He wrapped an arm around my shoulders and gave me a squeeze. 'I'm proud of you.'

Sabrina clapped her hands together. 'Yes, it's amazing, Willow! I should have told you to go for it as soon as you suggested it. It's so much better than the pumpkin patch we went to a few years ago.'

'Really?' I asked, smiling, but then my eyes seemed to automatically go to Dylan as much as I wished they hadn't.

'I think it's going to draw lots of people here this month,' he said in his sensible way. 'I don't know exactly what kind of profit you will make, it's all dependent on how much people will spend on pumpkins and if we can sell enough tickets, but I have no doubt you'll get great publicity and people will recommend it, so I don't see why it's not possible to do well. And we've sold two hundred tickets now.'

'Is that good?' Sabrina asked.

'It's a promising start,' Dylan said. 'But looking online, some of the most popular pumpkin farms and patches can have over three thousand visitors a day.'

My eyes widened. 'A day! That's even more than we've ever had in the summer season.'

'It's a more popular and profitable business than, I'll be honest, I thought it could be,' Dylan said. 'But they are so popular on social media, it's really grown into a big deal. The more I look into it, the more I think if you can spread the word, you can make good money from this.'

'How many people do we need here this month to make a profit?' Dad asked as I still leaned against my father, relief flooding through me that they all liked it. I had seen the pumpkin patch all in my mind but no one else had been really able to picture what I was thinking, but there it was in front of us now. I had created it. I felt a prick of pride. I knew my big dreams had often just been that – dreams – but this time, I'd made the dream come true.

'We need to at least have a thousand people here each week in October and obviously, we want them buying pumpkins too. If you can get more than that, you'll pay back everything Willow has spent and start turning a profit.'

I thought back to the spreadsheet we had made. 'But even if we sell all the pumpkins, we'd need double that amount of visitors by the end of October to clear all our debts so that we can keep the farm profitable long-term.' I thought about how popular our annual Halloween walk was in the town. 'I did wonder if there might be a way we could tie the lantern festival into the patch somehow and then every time they publicise the festival or it's talked about, so will Pumpkin Hollow.'

'I'll speak to the mayor,' Dad said. 'I went to school with

Taylor, she was good friends with your mother, so maybe she'd be willing to help. Maybe part of the walk could happen through the farm or it could finish at the pumpkin patch.'

'That would be perfect,' Sabrina agreed. 'You could light up the patch; it would look so cool and spooky.'

I yawned despite my best efforts to stifle it.

'We should all get some rest,' Dad said when he spotted it. 'It's been an eventful weekend.'

'I need to go home,' Sabrina said. 'I'll come over once school finishes for the day with Bradley and Dottie and my mum – we've booked for the last slot. I can't wait.'

'I'll follow in a bit,' I said, wanting to just have a minute alone here. They all seemed to understand. Sabrina and Dad headed off towards her car and the farmhouse. When Dad opened up the door, I heard Maple bark excitedly – she was likely ready for her dinner. She'd been running around with people all day so had collapsed in her bed an hour ago for a long nap. I was thinking that sounded good to me too right now.

Dylan hovered for a second when they left. 'I know there is still lots to do in encouraging visitors to come here and to look after it all and keep it going for the month, but take a minute to see what you've already achieved. This place is great, Willow. I think you should be really proud of it. I'll see you tomorrow. Goodnight.' He strode off, his words leaving a warm, fuzzy feeling inside me.

I watched him go for a second, confused at how supportive he was. He seemed to want us to succeed and not lose the farm. But what would his brother say about that? I tried not to hope that Dylan had decided the farm was more important. Because that meant *I* was more important. And that just felt impossible. We had only just met and any burgeoning romance seemed over now. My heart ached a little bit for him still, though.

Looking back at the pumpkin patch, I wandered over to one of the benches the school had lent us and I sat down on it. Above my head, the sky was now dark and the stars had come out. When I was younger, I used to sit outside at night to look at the stars. There was no pollution or tall buildings to dim their light. One of the many reasons I loved living here on the farm. I used to make wishes on them. When I was young enough to think that wishes on stars could become reality. I never wanted to lose my dreams but I had lost them, bogged down from grief after losing my mother and then the troubles with the farm and hiding instead of facing them and trying to do something about it all. Finally, I had remembered to dream again but I'd also worked hard to make it come true; I hadn't relied on wishing and hoping.

I gazed at Pumpkin Hollow and I felt proud of myself. I was grateful to everyone who had helped me make it happen too.

I knew it was silly but I looked up at the stars again. There wasn't any harm in making a little wish tonight that all our hard work would pay off. It was 1 October tomorrow. It had always been a month I loved. The month I was born. And my mum had loved it too. I hoped she was looking down and giving her support to it all.

I made a wish on the stars that the pumpkin patch would be a success. I knew though we had done as much as we possibly could so if it wasn't then I wouldn't have any regrets. But I really hoped it would.

After getting up off the bench, I made my way towards the farmhouse. I knew I needed to try to get a good night's sleep. I looked over at the cottages before I walked inside. It was hard to resist. Dylan was in there. My body and heart wanted to return to the night we'd spent together. I longed to know if his did too.

Maple met me at the door. 'Hey, girl, ready to sell pumpkins tomorrow?' I asked as she bounded around my feet. I closed the door behind me and went into the kitchen, hoping that the stars had heard my wish and would grant it. Butterflies danced in my stomach at the thought of it being opening day tomorrow. It felt like the first day of school all over again. I had no idea what to expect. I didn't have a clue really about what I was doing.

But I was excited too. I wished I could take a peek into the future to see what was going to happen but life didn't let you do that. And maybe that was a good thing because it meant we had possibility. Tomorrow could change everything.

I just needed it to be a good change for us.

38

I woke up before my alarm on Monday morning. It was 1 October. I had slept surprisingly well, exhausted from the weekend, so I leapt out of bed, keen to get on with the day. I grabbed my phone to check the website and see the number of tickets sold. It had edged up to three hundred overnight. A great improvement from the ten we had started with, but we still had a long way to go.

After I got ready for the day, I fed Maple and had a coffee with two slices of toast smothered in peanut butter then I took her out with me for a walk so I could do what was needed on the farm away from the pumpkin patch. I was relieved to see it looked like it was going to be a dry day. We'd clearly get more visitors if the weather stayed crisp and sunny, even if most of the patch was protected from the weather. They would likely spend more time on the farm too. And, let's be honest about it, spend more money.

Once my chores were completed, I headed over to where Dad was getting the card machine set up ready to take payments. Dylan was there too, on his laptop sending emails.

'I just have to do a couple of things for my brother before I can work on generating some more publicity for Pumpkin Hollow,' Dylan said. 'The local newspaper will be here in twenty minutes.'

'My sister just messaged me,' Steve said, strolling over from the cottages to join us. Like me and Dylan, he wore jeans, a thick jumper and wellies. 'She'll be here in an hour with four of her friends. They are really excited.'

'Great.' I bit my lip, wondering if their expectations would turn out to be too high or not. 'I really hope they all like it.'

'It looks right up their street,' Steve reassured me.

'The tractor all ready to go?' Dad asked him.

'Yeah, I'll get it and the trailer from the barn now and set up it over there by the sign Sabrina made. I think if I offer one every two hours, that allows most people to have one if they want to, and I can still help you guys manage everything else.'

'Okay then,' I said when Steve had walked off. 'Now we wait for everyone to get here. Maybe I should check everything again...' I started to walk off, feeling too restless to stand still. I had nervous energy running through my body.

'My old friend, Amy, who emailed you about coming to the farm, just messaged me,' Dylan said, falling into stride with me. 'She's on her way. Hopefully, she'll share on her channels. She's pretty big on TikTok and Instagram, it's her full-time job now, so I think she can get us on the social media radar.'

'An old friend?' I couldn't stop myself from asking as I looked over to the gate and was relieved to see the *Pumpkin Hollow* sign was exactly where it should be, and the farm gate was open and ready to welcome people to it.

'We went to school together,' Dylan replied. He looked across at me. 'There was nothing romantic; she dated my brother for a bit when we were younger, but that's it.'

I shrugged. 'It's none of my business,' I mumbled as relief washed over me. I knew I shouldn't care, but I did.

'Of course it is.' Dylan touched my arm but I shook his hand off. 'You've got to stop this,' he said then.

'What do you mean?'

'I know you're pushing me away, trying to act like we are nothing to each other, but you know that isn't the case.'

'How can you say that after what I overheard you saying to your brother?' I asked, incredulous that he seemed frustrated with me. I was the one that should have been pissed off, not him!

'I told you, I didn't mean what I said. The pressure Nate has me under...'

I shook my head. 'I can't talk about this now, Dylan. It's opening day. Give me a break.' I stomped off but even though I heard him call my name, I ignored it. I couldn't believe he wanted to talk about that phone call when I was this nervous. I watched as a car drove through the gate and I took a deep breath.

It was time.

* * *

The morning rushed by. I greeted the local press and Steve's sister and her friends, and Dylan took his old friend Amy around the pumpkin patch. The journalist and photographer seemed impressed but it was Steve's sister and her friends who put a big smile on my face when I heard them squealing with excitement and saw how many videos and photos they were taking with the pumpkins.

After Dylan had shot a video of Amy buying a pumpkin, she came over to me. 'Thank you for letting me come here. I've got some really cute photos and videos. I think it's great. I went to a couple of pumpkin patches last autumn and yours is just as good, if not better because of all the areas you have for photos. And that guy driving the tractor: he can take me on a ride any time.' She winked, making me laugh.

Steve offered to take them all out on the tractor then, so she hurried off to join him for that, along with the rest of the press.

'It feels like it's going well,' Dad said as I walked over to where he was having a rest with Maple before we opened to the public.

'Amy was really impressed,' Dylan agreed as he closed his laptop. 'All my work is finished so I can help you guys this afternoon and I'll keep an eye on everything online through the day too. It's almost time for the first people to arrive. Are you ready?'

'As ready as I'll ever be.'

Dad got up to take Maple inside as we thought maybe she should stay in the farmhouse just for the first afternoon so we could focus on visitors.

When we were alone, Dylan turned to me. 'I'm sorry about earlier. I know this is your focus right now. As it should be. I didn't mean to bring up our stuff. I'm just happy to help you today.'

He looked so worried, I smiled. 'It's fine. Let's just get through the day, okay?'

'I'll be by your side,' he promised me. And although I looked away from him, my heart melted at those words despite all my good intentions.

Once the local press, Steve's sister and her friends, and Amy had all left, the first paying customers started to arrive. We had organised the tickets in one-hour slots to allow everyone plenty of time and space in the pumpkin patch. It was lovely to see families turning up and the excitement on the kids' faces when they saw what was in the field. Sabrina and her family arrived after school with the largest number of people we had booked for the first day. I left Dad manning the ticket and pumpkin sales table to walk through the trail and check on how it was looking, and if people seemed to be enjoying it all.

'Look at this.' Sabrina showed me a picture they had taken in the autumn section and it did look like a great shot. 'I've shared it on all my social media and tagged the farm like Dylan told me to. Where is he anyway?'

'He went to buy us coffees from Paul,' I said. The van was going down a storm with visitors, and the smell of coffee and cinnamon was strong enough on the breeze to reach the pumpkin patch, adding to the cosy, autumnal vibe. I watched two kids carrying a huge pumpkin over to their parents, and a group of teenagers cheering each other on as they bobbed for apples. It seemed to be going well. We just needed everyone here to spread the word.

'I can see a family I know from school,' Sabrina said. 'I'll go and say hello.'

I waved her away and walked through to the Halloween section where I reminded a family taking photos of the dinner table to share them online and tag us – then I'd repost them on the Pumpkin Hollow accounts. Dylan came to find me as I restacked a pile of pumpkins that had gone a bit lopsided, probably from someone knocking against them accidentally. I decided it would be good to walk through every couple of hours to adjust anything that needed it and also spot if any pumpkins needed replenishing from the barn.

'Paul said we had to try these. I asked for pumpkin spiced lattes but he refused,' Dylan explained as he handed me a takeaway Birchbrook Café cup and looked down at the one he still held. 'He kind of scares me,' he admitted with a grimace.

I giggled. 'He is a character, for sure. I'm happy to taste test café treats, though. Let's head outside and check if Dad needs a break,' I suggested. We walked out of the tunnel and I took a sip of the drink Paul had forced upon Dylan. 'Oh, shit, he was right to make you order this,' I said, letting out a moan at the taste. 'Apple and cinnamon latte?'

Dylan nodded. 'Yep.' He took a sip. 'Oh, man, why have I suddenly developed a taste for sweet coffee?'

'Autumn just makes you crave sweet treats,' I replied with a smile. He caught my eye and grinned back. I instantly thought about him making me that hot chocolate topped with whipped cream, and I could tell his thoughts had strayed there as well. We walked out onto the field then, passing families snapping photos by the *Pumpkin Hollow* sign, and wandered over to the table where Dad was currently selling a big pile of pumpkins to a woman who I recognised worked in our nearest supermarket. 'I'm glad we're selling some pumpkins,' I said quietly to Dylan, trying to move my thoughts away from our hot night together. I couldn't let myself wish for any more of that.

'We're being tagged in a few photos on social media already and ticket sales are steady through the website, plus we had two families show up and pay for entry today. I think it's good to allow that while we're still new. Hopefully, the social media influencers will post their content soon and the local press should have their article up online in the next couple of days and in the newspaper by the end of the week, which will all help to spread the word, right?' Dylan raised an eyebrow at the look I gave him. 'What? Do I have coffee on my face or something?'

I shook my head. 'No. It's just the way you were talking – you keep using the word "we",' I said. 'Why do you keep saying "we"?'

We kept looking at one another and I didn't think that I was imagining the way his eyes softened when he met my gaze and then his eyes flicked from my eyes to my lips.

My breath hitched. Was he thinking about kissing me again?

'Why, Dylan? Why do you keep saying "we"?' I repeated my question, desperate to know why he was so invested in the pumpkin patch when he should have been making sure it didn't work.

'That's a very good question.'

We both started at the sudden, deep voice behind us, breaking our eye contact. I turned around to see a tall, dark man who looked a little bit familiar. He wore a tailored, dark suit that looked completely out of place at a pumpkin patch. I saw Dylan stiffen beside me and I glanced at his face. He was shocked and a little bit annoyed. But his face was nothing compared to the expression on the man behind us. He glared at Dylan with open hospitality.

'So, little brother, why don't you tell me what the hell is going on?'

39

'Nate, what are you doing here?' Dylan asked as I stared in surprise at the two Henderson brothers standing by me.

Nate acted much like Dylan had when he first came to the farm in his suit, standing upright and glancing around with barely disguised distaste. He gave Dylan a look up and down and sneered a little bit at his brother's farm clothes. 'I could ask you the same question. You've been fobbing me off since you first came here so I thought I better turn up and see what's really going on.' He seemed to really notice me for the first time then. Again, his gaze travelled from my head to my toes, and again, he seemed to find something wanting in my appearance. 'I assume you're the reason my brother suddenly has a keen interest in farming?'

Nate's accent was posher and sharper than his brother's and his handsome face was completely at odds with his bad attitude.

My back was thoroughly up as I stared at him defiantly while Dylan looked on, evidently still stunned that his brother had shown up like this.

'I'm Willow Connor, this is my farm, and you are?' I asked icily, even though of course I had worked it out.

'Nate Henderson,' he replied shortly. He turned back to his brother. 'We need to talk.'

'I told you on the phone, I'm not coming home yet,' Dylan replied, not making any moves to leave me.

I raised an eyebrow. The last I'd heard was Dylan had practically promised his brother the keys to my farm.

'And I told you, this is getting ridiculous now. You work for me, not *her*,' Nate said, jerking his head in my direction. The way he said 'her' made it clear exactly how he felt about that.

I glanced around. Nate was speaking loudly and we were in earshot of a few families. I didn't want this to spoil opening day. 'Follow me. Now!' I told them both firmly. I marched off and heard them both trail after me.

I led them into the farmhouse and spun round to face them. It was annoying that they both were so much taller than me. I put my hands on my hips and refused to be intimidated, though. This was my home.

'Look, I don't know what's going on with you two but this is the first day my pumpkin patch is open and I don't want either of you to ruin things for me. So, work out whatever your problem is in here alone and leave my farm out of it.'

'Your farm is the problem!' Nate snapped back at me.

'I thought you were desperate to get your hands on it,' I pointed out.

'Dylan made a good pitch for this land,' Nate said. 'But when he said he needed to stay here to persuade you and your father to sell to us, I was uneasy. Usually, people bite our hands off to make the kind of money you could make with this deal. But for some reason, my brother screwed it up and said he had to move in to persuade you. Of course, I quickly realised he was more interested in you than securing this land for us.'

'I heard him telling you it was practically a done deal,' I said, glancing at Dylan, unsure what was real any more.

'I was trying to get him to leave me alone,' Dylan said, looking embarrassed. 'I felt terrible you heard me saying those things. They weren't true. I just wanted to get him off my back and let me stay here longer.'

Nate let out a loud sigh. 'I knew it was a mistake to give you a job,' he muttered.

'So, if it was a lie...' I kept my eyes on Dylan; his brother was just pissing me off now.

'I wanted to stay; I wanted to help this place... I want the pumpkin patch to be successful. As soon as we kissed, I didn't want you to have to sell to us. I've been telling Nate the deal is almost done while I tried to work on getting us land nearby instead,' Dylan confessed.

'Bloody hell,' Nate said, shaking his head. 'Why do you always fuck up?'

My mouth dropped open in shock as Dylan turned to face his brother.

'That's it. I've had enough of all your snide comments,' Dylan told him. 'I'm tired, Nate. Of trying to prove myself to you. Of trying to get you to respect me, see me as your equal, and basically, treat me like your brother. You think you're better than me. But why? Because you've done exactly what Dad has told you to do all your life?'

'I'm successful,' Nate replied coldly. 'And don't forget I gave you this job because you needed one. You couldn't cut it as a lawyer, or at anything else, could you? So, I had to step in.'

'Actually, I only agreed to work with you because you and Dad wouldn't stop going on at me about it, and I thought maybe if we did work together, there might be a chance that we could grow closer, actually be brothers again. But you've treated me like I'm beneath you since I started. I had a vain hope that me finding a good deal in this area, which you've always wanted, might change things. Looks like that won't ever happen.'

'You haven't found me the deal though, have you? For some reason, you've given up on the idea. I suppose you've chosen her over your family.' Nate shrugged. 'I knew you wouldn't be good enough. That's the story of your life, little brother. Just not up to the job.'

'You know what?' Dylan said, keeping remarkably cool in the face of his brother being so rude. I was shocked by what was coming out of his mouth. I couldn't even imagine talking to my dad like this. 'You should go, Nate. We have a lot of work to do. And you don't belong here.'

'And you do?' Nate scoffed. 'Whatever. You'll soon get bored; you always do.' He turned to me again. 'You'll find out. My brother can't stick at anything in life – jobs, relationships, even places to live. He always runs when things get tough or he realises he can't handle something or it becomes too serious for him. He'll get bored of this farm, and bored of you too. And then he'll come running back to me and my father to bail him out like he's done for the whole of his life.'

'I need to get back to work,' I said, not knowing whether his brother was saying things that were true or just being a dick. I didn't like him but I also knew that when our pact was over, Dylan wouldn't stick around. What reason would he have to? I shrugged to show I didn't care despite the fact I had started to like having him back on the farm again. He'd left once before, though. I needed to remind myself it was only a matter of time until he left again. And he wouldn't come back that time. 'We made a deal that he'd stay for six weeks then I'd decide whether to sell or not. That's all this was,' I said as coolly and calmly as I could manage.

'Willow—' Dylan began but I really didn't want to hear any promises that he couldn't, or wouldn't, keep.

'I have to get back outside,' I cut him off. 'This is important to me. I think you should leave, Nate. It's up to Dylan if he leaves with you or not. But I'm breaking our pact.' I made for the door so that neither of them would keep me in here any longer. 'I wouldn't sell to either of you two. If the pumpkin patch doesn't work out then I'll find someone else who wants this land, even if we don't make quite as much money as we would with you. This farm has been my home and work my whole life. I won't give it to you.'

With that parting statement, I walked out of the door and towards the pumpkin patch.

And I didn't look back.

40

The final slot for the patch was at 4 p.m. and we closed up at 5 p.m. as the sun began to set. I shut the gate and smiled at Sabrina's *Pumpkin Hollow* sign. Things seemed to have gone as well as they could for opening day. Everyone who had booked tickets turned up, plus we had a few extras, and we'd had some nice posts on social media. Steve said his sister and her friends had loved it, and Amy had emailed me to say similar and that she would post everything tomorrow. Steve confessed he'd asked for her number, so that was cute.

Paul had driven off with the van saying he'd be back tomorrow so I supposed that was high enough praise from him for now. There was a feeling that half-term would be the best judge of our success so we had until then to drum up publicity and get as many families through the gate as possible.

I walked slowly to find my dad, who was tidying away the payment station with Maple running around now we'd let her out of the farmhouse. I glanced at the cottages. Dylan's car was still here but there was no sign of him or his brother so I had no idea what had happened once I'd left them alone.

I didn't regret what I had said to Nate but nerves swirled in my stomach about what Dad was going to say about it. We had an agreement for six weeks but I'd gone back on that. I had told Nate and Dylan I'd never sell to them, but it was Dad's name on the deeds to the farm. It was ultimately his decision. I knew I needed to tell him but I was scared at how he'd react.

Had I been too impulsive once again?

While I waited for Dad to finish up, I walked into the pumpkin patch and glanced around. We'd sold a few pumpkins that I'd replenished and everything looked tidy so I covered up the pumpkins that were outside and made sure that the polytunnels were safe and secure. It was due to be dry for the next few days, thankfully, but I was paranoid after the damage from the storm and needed to double-check everything.

'How do you feel about it all?' Dad asked, coming to stand beside me with Maple.

'Good, I think. We just need to see what happens with ticket and pumpkin sales over the next few days. The decider is going to be the penultimate week of October though, isn't it? Half-term week. I really hope that will go well.' I took a breath. I couldn't risk Dad speaking to Dylan before I confessed what I had done earlier. 'Dad, I need to tell you something...' I began, hoping he wouldn't be too angry with me. 'Dylan's brother showed up earlier and he really wound me up.' I gave Dad a shortened version of our conversation.

'He sounds awful,' Dad replied. 'I'm sorry he spoke to you like that. If I'd been there...'

'I can handle myself,' I said, although I wasn't sure if I had handled it properly or not.

'I know that but I'm protective of my only daughter. So is this one,' he added, patting Maple, who sat down in between us.

'Don't be mad but I kind of told him he could stick his offer for our farm,' I blurted out nervously. 'I just couldn't stand the idea of someone like him owning this place. Even if we can't save it, we can sell to someone else, can't we? I know I can be impulsive and I'm sorry if you think that I—'

'Willow,' Dad said gently, stopping me from babbling. 'You should have spoken to me about it first.'

'Shit, I know, I let my temper get the best of me,' I said miserably. I'd let him down all over again. I looked down at my feet, wondering if Dad was going to wash his hands of me completely. 'It's your farm. I know that. I'm sorry, Dad. What shall we do?'

'You didn't let me finish. You should have spoken to me about it first. But if you had done, I would have said I agree with you.'

My head snapped up. 'You agree?' I repeated in surprise and relief.

'He shouldn't have spoken to you like that. And I'm not naive to think we'll be able to sell to anyone who will keep this as a farm, this land will be developed if we do have to move on, but I'd want to respect whoever we did end up dealing with. And that is not a man to respect.' Dad glanced over my shoulder. 'His brother though, I did respect him, but I'm not sure if I should or not.'

I followed his gaze to see Dylan walking over from the cottage. He was still here then. I wondered for how long, though.

'I'm not sure either, Dad. I like him but it's not like we have a future, right? His brother is probably right that he'll move on and we won't see him again. And I must admit, thinking about him going back to work for his brother after the way Nate treated us both today – I'm not sure that's a man I could respect.'

'Give him a chance. Look at what he's done for us. He must

care about you too.' Dad gave my shoulder a squeeze. 'We have some leftover lasagne; I'll start heating it in the Aga and make some garlic bread. Come in whenever you can. Let's go, Maple; you can help me.' He whistled for her and set off for the farmhouse, giving Dylan a nod as they passed each other.

I went to sit down on one of the school benches as Dylan made his way over. I could see the moon above the pumpkin patch. It would be full by the time Halloween came around. Perfect for the lantern festival too. I hoped that Dad could persuade the mayor to involve the farm somehow in the event. I had so many ideas running around my head. I wanted to make them all happen. I just needed the chance.

'Hey.' Dylan sat down next to me. 'Okay if I join you? It feels like we need to talk.'

I nodded but I didn't look at him. I felt like it would be too distracting. Looking into Dylan's eyes made me lose all focus for anything other than him. I couldn't risk that right now.

'No good conversations start with that phrase,' I said lightly.

Dylan chuckled softly. 'You have a point. Maybe this can be the first one, though.' He sighed. 'I'm really sorry about earlier. I'm so embarrassed at the things my brother said to you. But also I'm embarrassed by my behaviour over the past few days.' He shook his head. 'I don't want to be someone who lies or plays games. I'm an honest man, I swear it.'

'I really am confused about this weekend,' I admitted. 'I thought we had such a lovely night together, but then everything went wrong.' It had been so strange to have felt so close to him one minute then so hurt by him the next.

'You're right to be confused. I'm sorry, Willow. It really has all been my fault.'

'Just tell me the truth, please, Dylan,' I said. I was tired of playing a guessing game with him and his feelings. We'd started out at loggerheads and then everything seemed to change but maybe you shouldn't go from being enemies to sleeping together.

'I started out determined to get you to sell. The pact we made was crazy. You pushed my buttons that day. I was annoyed that you'd sent me in the wrong direction and that you were trying to stop your dad from dealing with me. I'd as good as promised Nate I would get this land for us, and he seemed so impressed with me, finally. It's embarrassing to admit I wanted my brother's approval, for him to be proud of me for once. It's felt all my life like I can't live up to him. Especially in our dad's eyes.' Dylan sighed. 'I'm ashamed to admit all this, but I want to tell you the truth.'

'I'm glad you're explaining it to me,' I said quietly, knowing this was a big thing for him to get off his chest. I understood the feeling that you weren't good enough. Of wanting your family to be proud of you. I couldn't tell him off for feeling that way. I'd been so determined to save the farm for my family, after all.

'I thought if I agreed to stay on the farm, I could persuade you to give up your crazy pumpkin-patch idea, or I could persuade your dad not to let you try it. I thought you'd soon agree to sell to me. Arrogant, right?'

I turned to face him then. 'Very,' I replied.

'But you intrigued me from that first night. You were so feisty and determined. You had all these big ideas. You didn't let me bulldoze over you. You fought right back. And, God, I admired the hell out of you. And it was more attractive than I was expecting. You drove me crazy. Which is why it got harder to keep trying to persuade you against your ideas. I felt this urge to help you make them all happen instead.' Dylan smiled a little bit. I tried not to smile back but it was hard. His eyes were soft on mine like he really was fond of me. 'When we kissed at that inn, it was better than I'd been imagining it would be. We had such a great night together. I couldn't face hurting you. And I knew by then how much it would hurt if you had to let go of the farm. But it was hard. My brother was breathing down my neck, confused why I was still here but hadn't got your dad to accept our offer yet. And then you said our night together had to just be a one-night thing... That hurt, I have to say.'

'Well, I just felt like I was setting myself up to get my heart broken. I knew you were only here for six weeks, and we wanted different things. We were enemies, basically.'

'No!' Dylan cried. 'We were only enemies for about five minutes. I was hooked as soon as you challenged me to make that pact with you.'

'So, you were happy when we slept together again?' I asked him, really hoping he had been.

'Over the moon. I'm sorry I fucked it all up afterwards.'

'Why did you?'

A yellow leaf floated down then, landing on the bench between us. I picked it up and twirled it between my fingers as I waited for Dylan to answer.

He watched me holding the leaf and sighed. 'Nate phoned me so I left you sleeping. He said Dad was irate that I was still on the farm and wanted me home. Nate said I was letting them down not getting your dad to sign our deal, and I should just give up. He said similar things to what he said today, like I was useless and he regretted offering me a job. Instead of telling him where to stick his job, I found myself telling him that it was all in hand and I'd get you to sign. I wanted for once to shut him up, to prove him wrong. And I suppose for a second, I did wonder why I had let go of my original plan. Why I had let you get under my skin and into my heart. I told him we'd slept together so now I could get you to do what I wanted.'

41

I sucked in a breath at what Dylan had just said. It brought back that cold shock I'd felt when I'd heard him talking to his brother outside of the cottage. I'd been so hurt that he had said those things about me after the great time we'd had together. It had seemed so unlike the man I'd got to know but I had thought that he'd lied about who he was, that I'd got him all wrong. Now, I just wasn't sure.

'And you had no idea I was listening outside, and had heard every word.'

Dylan winced at the memory and looked away from me. 'As soon as the words left my mouth, I bitterly regretted them. I hate lying, but also, I hated saying anything negative about you – about us. It was such a low moment for me. I'm so sorry, Willow. I'll never forget the look on your face.' He shuddered. 'I just wanted Nate to leave me alone so I could be here with you. I should have told him how I really felt, though. I have now.'

'You have?'

'I told him I need a break. Until the end of the month. Until the end of our six-week pact. I made a promise to stay and that's what I want to do. I need to figure out what I want in life. Would you let me stay, though? Despite the fact I was a complete dick and I hurt you?'

I hesitated. Surely this would just make it harder for him to leave?

'I don't know. The pact is done and dusted. I already told Nate, and my dad agreed with me, that there's no way I'd let him get his hands on my farm.'

Dylan nodded. 'I know. And I completely agree with you. You should be here, Willow. This is where you belong. I worked that out pretty quickly, even though I didn't want to admit it to myself or you, and certainly not to Nate. Would you ever be able to forgive me for the things I said to my brother?'

'I'm not sure,' I said.

I thought for a minute. This weekend had been hard. But I'd made it through. Dylan had finally stood up to his brother and he wanted to stay. I knew I could still do it with his help. We still had the rest of October to try to make this work and secure the farm for at least the next year. I didn't want to do it without him.

Finally, I nodded. 'Okay, Dylan. You can stay as we agreed until the end of October. I'm still not sure if I can make this all work out. And I could do with your help still. If it's really what you want.'

Dylan reached for me and I let him take hold of one of my hands. His touch still felt good. He gazed into my eyes. 'I really want to stay with you, Willow.'

My heart skipped. 'You can stay,' I whispered.

The look on his face was so happy, I returned his smile and I knew that whatever had happened, he was sincere about wanting to be here. And I was happy to have him here. I didn't know what was going to come next for us or the farm, but I couldn't wait to find out.

* * *

The rest of the week was a blur.

We threw ourselves into the pumpkin patch. Now that Dylan had told his brother he was staying and working on the farm, he abandoned any pretence of doing work for Henderson Homes and seemed happy to pitch in with me and my dad, and Steve, on what needed to be done. He still hunched himself over his laptop a lot though but that was because I asked him to. He was so much better at dealing with the publicity and social media side of the business while I was happiest working on the patch and my dad liked dealing with greeting visitors and putting through payments. We became a solid team of three somehow, with Steve helping too. It was working better than I could have ever predicted.

Birchbrook got behind Pumpkin Hollow more each day. Word did start to spread, especially after the local newspaper posted a positive review online and then in the physical edition later on. Steve's sister and her friends shared the patch on their social media, and Sabrina encouraged families from her school to come. The two Pats did a great job of publicising it in their café too. And Paul came by in the café van each afternoon to sell food and drink, and every day, the line for them grew longer. By Thursday, I even saw him smile once, although he denied it.

But the best boost to the business came when Dylan's old school friend Amy posted her content on her TikTok and Instagram. She had hundreds of thousands of followers and they all loved the pumpkin patch videos and photos. She tagged us and almost immediately, the ticket sales started to roll in.

'I don't care if she is an ex-girlfriend,' I joked to Dylan when he showed me that we'd sold five hundred tickets the morning after she posted about the patch.

'I told you – there's never been anything between us. I think she still has a crush on Nate. Maybe she thought he'd be grateful for her help.'

'Little does she know he hates this place. She's going on a date with Steve so hopefully, she'll forget all about Nate. I'll call her tonight to say thank you.'

'We should go to the pub to celebrate once we finish work for the day. If this rate of sales keeps going, we're going to smash our target for ticket sales for the first week.'

'You should, love,' Dad said, overhearing as he helped a couple put their pumpkins into a wheelbarrow to carry over to their car. 'You've worked so hard this week, and the weekend will be crazy based on these new ticket sales. Relax tonight; it's Friday, after all!'

'I suppose we could...' I said, hesitating because although letting off some steam after the stressful week sounded really good, I wasn't sure about being alone with Dylan and drinking. 'I'll see if Sabrina and Bradley might be able to get a babysitter and join us.'

Dad walked off to help the couple, leaving Dylan looking at me. He grinned. 'Are you thinking safety in numbers or something?' he asked, a definite flirty edge to his tone, as if he'd worked out my plan.

'Dylan...'

'I'm only teasing,' he said quickly. 'I know I don't deserve a night out with you alone, as much as I want one.' He waved at a family who were looking for help and hurried over to them.

His words left an impression. I liked him wanting to be alone with me. But I was scared to want the same thing after all we'd been through. I wanted to trust his feelings for me. But it was hard.

I pulled out my phone to ask Sabrina if she fancied meeting us at the pub. I wasn't sure if I wanted her to say yes or no.

42

Dylan and I walked into the Birchbrook Arms that night. The evening had turned chilly so the crackling log fire inside was a very welcome sight. The pub was busy as it was Friday night but Sabrina and Bradley had secured a small table in the corner. They had jumped at the chance to have a quick drink with us, and I was relieved to have 'safety in numbers' as Dylan had put it earlier.

'We had so much fun today!' A woman accosted me on the way to the bar so Dylan said he'd get us a drink and I stopped to smile at her. 'I've been telling everyone they need to come along to the pumpkin patch,' she added.

I recognised her then as having come to the farm earlier with her family – she was a newcomer to town and said it was so much more fun than the one she had been to near her old house.

'Thank you so much,' I said. 'That really helps us out.'

'I might bring the kids again in half-term; it's hard to find things to do all week!'

When we said goodbye, I joined Sabrina and Bradley as Dylan carried over a beer for him and wine for me. 'That was some week,' I said as I sank into the chair and took a grateful gulp. I slipped off my coat as the pub was so warm and I felt some of the tension of the past few days slip away.

'You have worked so hard,' Sabrina said, raising her glass in the air. 'We need to toast Pumpkin Hollow.'

'Everyone keeps saying it's the place to go,' Bradley added. 'I told my colleagues all about it and they've all booked tickets.'

'It's like Birchbrook never realised we were missing something to do at this time of year,' Sabrina agreed with a vigorous nod in her husband's direction.

'Apart from the lantern festival,' Bradley said.

'Speaking of, Dad has a meeting booked in with the mayor on Monday to see if she will let us tie in the farm to it this year,' I said, smiling at how enthusiastic they were about it all. 'Maybe people can set off or end at the pumpkin patch and I'll decorate it even more for Halloween and light it up. I think it could be really great.'

'He'll persuade Taylor, I'm sure of it. He said she is an old friend, right? And your dad is so happy with how it's going,' Dylan said. 'Ticket sales have increased so much. I have high hopes for half-term.'

'It's your birthday before that – next week,' Sabrina added excitedly. 'How shall we celebrate?'

'I haven't had a chance to think about it,' I admitted. 'It's so full on at the farm, I don't want to do anything much.'

Sabrina pulled a sad face. 'Okay, well, I'll have a think of something; you have to celebrate it a bit.'

I smiled. 'Okay. We will do something,' I promised, although I was already feeling very tired.

Bradley started telling us a funny story about his work and I leaned back in the chair to listen, glad I didn't need to make much conversation, just relax. I glanced over at Dylan as he laughed at what Bradley was saying. I had a strange feeling that he wouldn't be a newcomer in our group for long. That the four of us would have many drinks together in this pub. Or maybe it was wishful thinking. That I wanted us to do that.

When I went to the loo, Sabrina joined me and, standing in front of the mirrors as we washed our hands, she studied me.

'What?' I asked finally, uncomfortable at her scrutiny.

'You look exhausted. But happy.'

'That sums it up. I'm relieved things are going well.'

'Are you also relieved that Dylan is still with you? I heard that his brother showed up and there seemed to be tension...'

I turned to her and rolled my eyes. 'How does gossip travel so fast in this town?'

Sabrina shrugged. 'Don't deflect. Spill the beans!'

'Yeah, his brother came to the farm,' I said as I reapplied my lip gloss. 'He was angry Dylan hasn't been working as hard for him as he's been helping us, and he wanted to know what was going on. I think he'd guessed Dylan wasn't pushing me to accept their offer for the farm like he'd told Nate he was doing. His brother was pretty vile to both of us. Dylan told him to go and that he's staying until the end of the month and wouldn't be working for him until then. I don't know what he's going to do. But they don't have a good relationship.'

'So, why did he say those things to his brother about you two?'

'To buy more time. Dylan said he knew early on I wouldn't want to sell, and because he liked me, he wanted to help me keep the farm. The opposite of what he was saying he was doing to Nate. So, the conversation I overheard was Dylan lying to his brother. But what he said about me hurt. He says it wasn't true and he's sorry, and he seems determined to stay, but I don't know if I can trust his feelings for me. And I'm not sure if there's any point in any more happening with us. I mean, if he's leaving at the end of October. It's just going to hurt us both, isn't it?'

'But I guess you can't always know what will happen,' Sabrina said. 'I mean, you could find a way to make it work even if Dylan goes back to working for his brother. If you really like each other. I don't know, the way you smile at one another... You have some strong chemistry, Willow. I'm not sure I've ever seen you fit with a man like you seem to fit with him.'

Sabrina's words ran through my mind over and over for the rest of the evening. After we'd had a couple of drinks, Dylan and I said goodbye to everyone else and headed back towards the farm. I was glad of my coat as after the pub, the cold hit us and we walked briskly. Dylan offered me his arm and I took it to stay warm and I did enjoy how strong he felt to lean on. I supposed I hadn't leaned on anyone for a long time. It was nice.

'Do you think you and Nate will make up?' I asked as we approached the farm. It was all quiet as it was late, both Dad and Maple fast asleep inside, I betted.

'I don't know if I can work with him after how he acted the other day. All those things he said.'

'Why do you think things are so difficult between you? If you don't mind me asking...' I found myself walking towards the pumpkin patch and Dylan didn't stop me from steering us in that direction. I wanted to give it a final check before I went to bed, I supposed.

'We were close when we were younger but I think it all changed when my mum died. Nate took on a lot at that time. Our dad expected a lot of him too. And Dad put pressure on me but I didn't handle it well, and maybe I rebelled a bit and Nate was unhappy with me. Or maybe he wished he could do the same, I don't know. We just grew further apart. I wondered if working together was the last shot at being close brothers again. And if it was, it's failed.'

'Is that my fault?' I asked as we walked into the field, the moon casting a silvery glow over the pumpkins and the polytunnels. We paused in the silence to look at it all. In the day, it had been bright and busy but now it was dark and quiet, the pumpkins almost had a spooky vibe to them. I pictured how good we could make it look for the Halloween festival.

Dylan turned to me, my arm dropping from his. 'No. I jumped at the chance to stay here because I wasn't happy. I was so determined to prove myself to my brother, to make a success of us working together, but it wasn't long before I realised I didn't enjoy it. I didn't like working for him. I don't feel motivated to do the work. It isn't what I want to do. And it feels like I'll never make him proud anyway.'

'Maybe he just wants you to have what he has,' I suggested.

'What do you mean?'

'Something you're passionate about. Something you want to stick to and make a success of. Something that makes you happy.' I tilted my head to look at him in the light from the moon. 'Was that too brutal?' I added, knowing that sometimes, I could be too honest.

Dylan gave me a small smile. 'You know I like it how you say what you think. Maybe you're right. Maybe at the heart of it all, he is worried about me. Maybe I have been a bit lost since Mum passed away.'

I nodded. 'I know that feeling.' I looked at the pumpkin patch. 'I think she would be proud of this. Of how hard I've worked. How much I want to save this place. I might have left it a bit late to pull myself together but I am passionate about it now. I don't know if it will work but I know now I won't regret anything about the past few weeks. I've put my heart and soul into the pumpkin patch. I won't have to think "what if", you know?'

'That's how I want to live too.' Dylan stepped closer. 'I've never felt happier than I have being here. With you.'

'Really?' I whispered. I wanted that to be true so badly. Dylan had changed the whole dynamic on the farm for me. I liked having him here. The feeling that we had become a team. And I couldn't deny the spark between us. But I was so unsure about his feelings. Hearing him say he was happy here made me smile.

'I just have this feeling it's only going to get better too,' Dylan said, smiling down at me. He moved closer still, the gap between us just inches now. My breath hitched as he reached out to touch my cheek and then slid it down to cup my chin. 'Can I kiss you again? I won't if you don't want me to but I really want to.'

All I could do was nod. I saw a flicker of a smile on his lips before he leaned down and brushed them against mine. He murmured at the contact, his eyes closing. He wrapped his arms around me then and pulled me into his chest and I kissed him back, relieved to be touching again after wanting to but keeping my distance.

Dylan gave me a long, deep kiss but before it turned hungry, he pulled away from me. 'I'll wait until you're ready for more,' he said. 'Even though it'll be hard. Come on, let me walk you to your door.' He put his arm around me and we walked back to the farmhouse. I was disappointed that he'd just kissed me once but I knew I couldn't jump into bed with him again unless I was 100 per cent sure about him... and about us.

I opened up the door. 'Goodnight then,' I said.

Dylan gave me a gentle kiss on my cheek. 'Goodnight, Willow. I'll be thinking about you.'

I watched him walk off into the darkness towards the cottages.

'I'll think about you too,' I whispered before closing the farmhouse door and sinking against it with a wistful sigh.

43

We now had just one week to go until the penultimate week of October and what would be our biggest test yet: half-term. It was also my birthday week.

Monday morning dawned crisp and sunny, and Amy came back with some of her fellow social media influencers. I wandered over to where they were taking videos and photos of each other walking through the autumn tunnel in their seasonally themed outfits of browns and oranges and creams.

'This is going above and beyond,' I told Amy when she left them to greet me. I'd phoned her to thank her for the publicity she'd already given us after her first visit; I hadn't expected her to return this year. And the fact she'd brought a group that would hopefully also share the farm online really meant a lot.

'I loved it, I told you, and my followers did too. And you have such aesthetic set-ups; it looks so good for outfit photos and fun videos,' she assured me with a warm smile. 'Where's Dylan? We had a chat when I arrived but I'll try to say goodbye to him before we leave.'

'He's helping Dad at the payment table as we're really busy

today.' I glanced around. We were at three-quarter capacity today: our most popular day yet.

'I was really shocked when he contacted me to say he was staying on a farm. I thought he was like me and could only survive in a city.' She laughed. 'It's nice to see him so relaxed, though.'

'You think he is relaxed here?'

'Oh, definitely. Listen, we both come from pretty uptight families and Dylan found it harder than me, I think, to find his way within our world. I assume he told you I went out with his brother for a bit and I always wondered if he was the one who got away but I have to say, now I've met my own farmer, I can see the appeal.' She leaned in. 'Dylan's clearly smitten with you.'

'Oh, we're not a couple,' I said automatically.

Amy looked confused.

'Well, I suppose there is something between us but it's not official or anything,' I added, feeling a bit flustered as I tried to explain what we were to each other when I really didn't have a clue myself.

'I think you go great together, not that my opinion matters, I know. Dylan is a good guy. He really hasn't had it easy what with losing his mother and his family not being particularly caring, shall we say. I think being here has given him the freedom and a fresh perspective that he needed. It's great to see him so happy.' She gave my arm a squeeze. 'I think he'd make you happy too if you want him to.'

She gave me a cheerful wave before re-joining her friends, leaving me thinking over what she'd said. It was nice to hear that someone from Dylan's life thought he was thriving here and that I wasn't just hoping that to be the case.

When I walked outside, the man himself came over with a paper plate. 'I picked up two slices of pecan pie from the Birchwood Café van. Can you take a break with me and have a slice? There's whipped cream too.' He dropped me a wink, which did make me giggle as I thought back to how we'd made use of it in the past.

My mouth watered on cue. 'It's too tempting to turn down,' I replied, also dropping a wink, making him chuckle.

We weaved through the families outside who were choosing their favourite large, orange pumpkin to carve for Halloween and walked over to the cottages where we sat outside on the step to eat side by side.

'Amy's friends should help us get even more visitors for half-term,' Dylan said. 'I'll go into town after we've had this and deliver some more flyers around. Plus, I want to pick up something for tomorrow.' He had a secretive smile on his face.

My stomach somersaulted a little bit, so I hastily tried the pecan pie. 'Mmm. That's good. Pat gets better and better at her sweet treats,' I said. Then I eyed him. 'So, you're picking up something for tomorrow?' It was my birthday and after much pressing from Sabrina and my dad, I had agreed to have a small dinner at the farmhouse with them.

'I am, but it's a surprise.'

'I'm not sure I like surprises.'

'Don't you trust me?' he asked, looking across at me.

I hesitated.

'It's okay, I told you I want to earn your trust. It's a good surprise, I promise.' Dylan's phone lit up on the ground between us and he checked it. 'We're getting more social media tags today,' he said. 'And ticket bookings are flying in for half-term. I think we have a chance of selling out for the week if the next couple of days follow how it's going today.'

I shook my head. 'It's kind of surreal. I can't believe it's happening. I wondered if I was the only one who loved this time of year this much.' I looked over at the bustling field full of smiling faces and pumpkins, coloured fallen leaves scattered everywhere, crunching under people's feet. 'I got that from my mum. She said this was her favourite season. She had this feeling that she'd have a child in autumn. And her love of trees led her to call me Willow.'

Dylan smiled. 'I'm sure you can guess who my mother was a big fan of and called me after. This farm reminds me so much of summers with my grandmother. Which is weird as she lived by the coast and we're on a countryside farm but I think it's the feeling.'

I turned to find him watching me. 'What's the feeling?'

'A feeling of comfort, maybe. Cosy. Wholesome. A feeling of...' He trailed off. 'Anyway, I better head off, unless you need anything?'

Shaking my head, I watched Dylan get up and give me a smile before he walked over to his car. I wondered if he had just been about to say the word 'home'. Did the farm feel like home to him? That thought made me smile. It did already feel like he belonged here. Seeing Dylan climb into that fancy car was jarring now I was used to him wearing jeans, flannel shirts and boots or trainers, his hair tousled from the autumn breeze, a Barbour jacket slung over his arm, working on the farm beside me. That car seemed like it wasn't his any more. I wondered if Dylan felt that way too.

After I finished my pecan pie, I walked back to Pumpkin Hollow when my phone started ringing. 'Hello?'

'Is this Willow Connor?'

'Who's this?' I asked with caution as it could be someone saying we hadn't paid a bill.

'I'm Maddy from *The Star Chronicle* and I've seen lots of talk online about your new pumpkin patch and I'd love to do a feature...'

I stopped walking. This was a national newspaper and website. The reach would be huge compared to the local newspaper we had had come by when we opened.

'Really?' I asked, unable to play it cool, I was so shocked.

I could hear the smile in her voice. 'Really. Do you have ten minutes to chat?'

'Definitely,' I replied.

44

My twenty-sixth birthday started out like most days on the farm, which I didn't mind at all apart from my dad making us pancakes for breakfast after I had completed my farm chores in the darkness of the October morning. I walked Maple to feed the chickens and I thought about my mum, which I often did on my birthday. She had always woken me up early, even more excited than me for the day, and insisted we eat the cake she had baked for breakfast and open my presents in bed. My dad and I had tried to carry on that tradition a few times but it had felt hollow without her so we had tried to create new traditions instead.

I still missed her though as Maple barked excitedly at the chickens. I had thought Mum would have been around for many more milestones than she had been. It was a shame she couldn't see the changes we were making on the farm. But also the change in me. I could feel it. I looked over as Dylan made his way to the farmhouse for breakfast and I knew he had been a part of that change.

'Come on, Maple, the chickens have had their breakfast; it's time for ours,' I said, whistling for her. I had left my hair down today as I'd washed it and was letting it dry naturally and it blew across my face on the morning breeze. I pushed it back as Maple ran eagerly to my side and we walked into the warm house and through to the kitchen where the table was set up for breakfast. It had two cards and presents on it as well as a bunch of pretty orange and yellow roses: my favourites.

Dad was bringing over a large plate of pancakes while Dylan carried coffees and the maple syrup. I fed Maple and then joined them at the table.

'Happy birthday, love,' Dad said. 'We thought we'd have a quick celebration before the day starts and then we can let our hair down tonight with Sabrina and everyone. Not that I have much to let down,' he added, a twinkle in his eyes. It was nice to see. Sometimes, he could be melancholic on my birthday without Mum around so I was glad he was in a good mood. He handed me his card, which had a Border Collie on it, and his present.

I opened it up and smiled at the large, gold-framed photo of me and Maple in the pumpkin patch. He'd taken it the day we opened despite my protests as I wasn't a big fan of having my picture taken. 'That's so sweet, Dad,' I said. We never went crazy on birthdays, preferring thoughtful gifts over expensive ones and in later years, we were glad of that tradition as we certainly couldn't justify pricey presents. 'I'll put it on my bedside table.' We had a big hug and then as he dished up pancakes, Dylan handed me his card and present.

Dylan had chosen an autumn-themed card – it was covered in assorted leaves and said:

Have an unbe-LEAF-able birthday!

I giggled at the terrible pun and opened it up to read his message.

Willow, I hope you have a very happy birthday. Thank you for making me fall in love with October. Dylan.

My breath hitched a little bit. I glanced at him – he was watching my reaction. I smiled across at him and he dropped me a wink. I then opened up his present and unwrapped a small, velvet jewellery box.

'I know what this cost you to part with, and I thought you deserved to have it back,' he said as I lifted the box open and gasped.

'What is it?' Dad asked as he drizzled maple syrup over his pancakes.

Unable to speak, I tilted the box to show Dad the gold and diamond necklace inside. The gold and diamond necklace that my mum had passed down to me and I had sold to make the pumpkin patch and try to rescue the farm.

'Oh my,' Dad said, his eyes widening.

Mine misted as I looked over at Dylan. 'You bought it back...' I was so touched, I could barely get my words out.

Dylan nodded. 'I could see how hard it was for you to sell it, how much you wished you hadn't had to. You've done incredible things these past few weeks. I have been so inspired by your ideas, your determination and your hard work. I knew this should come back to you.'

I jumped up and went over to him. Despite my dad being there, I couldn't stop myself from giving him a kiss on the lips. I reached out to touch his cheek as he looked up at me, startled by my kiss. 'Thank you, Dylan. Will you put it on me?'

He stood up and I lifted up my hair. I felt his breath on the back of my neck as he gently draped the necklace around my neck and then fastened it. He quickly brushed his fingertips on my skin before I put my hair back down.

I looked at my dad, who was beaming. 'What do you think?'

'I always said you should wear it more,' Dad replied, looking a little bit misty-eyed himself. 'Dylan, Willow's mother would be so happy that she has it back. Thank you, son.'

It was Dylan's turn then to be unable to speak.

* * *

My third birthday present was *The Star Chronicle* publishing the article about Pumpkin Hollow on their website. We were flooded with bookings after that. Dylan came to find me just before we closed up for the day.

'Willow, I just checked and we've sold out for half-term!'

I paused in lifting pumpkins out of the wheelbarrow to replace the gaps in the crates in the field. 'What?'

'Half-term is now completely sold out!'

'Oh my God!' I bounded over to him and fell into his arms. Dylan picked me up and twirled me around. 'I can't believe it!'

Dylan put me back on the ground and smiled at me. 'Now we just need to sell out of pumpkins too.'

'I might really save the farm,' I said in wonder. Goosebumps spread down my arms beneath my wool jumper. 'This is definitely the best birthday ever.'

'Well, you deserve it.' Dylan started to let me go but I held on to him. He raised an eyebrow as my gaze flicked to his lips. 'You want another kiss, baby?'

'Yes,' I admitted.

'How much?' he asked, looking into my eyes hungrily.

'A lot,' I gasped out.

Dylan leaned in then but he passed my lips and pressed his close to one of my ears. 'I'll kiss you tonight if you still want me to. Come to my cottage after your party.'

And then he let me go and walked off, leaving me breathless.

I finished unloading pumpkins and helping the last visitors of the day but whenever I had a moment of not being occupied, my mind kept replaying Dylan's words. Him buying me back my mum's necklace had shown that he did know me, that he wanted me to stay here, that he knew what was important to me. I wanted to trust his feelings. I couldn't deny the fact I had feelings for him. He had chosen us over his brother and I knew that had cost him a lot. I liked being with him. We made a good team. I wasn't sure that I could resist the craving I felt to properly kiss him again. This morning, I had longed to deepen that quick kiss and now it was all I could think about.

After I closed the pumpkin patch for the day, I had a shower and got changed for the dinner that my dad and Sabrina had organised. I put on leggings and a long, striped shirt and kept my hair down as it had been all day. Then I added my DM boots and my mum's necklace, and finished it all off with a spritz of my favourite perfume. I glanced out of my bedroom window before I went downstairs and saw the cottage was lit up. Would I go back there tonight? My pulse quickened at the thought of being in Dylan's arms again. The pull to kiss him, to feel his touch, to be naked with him again, was stronger than my fear of being hurt when he left the farm.

Maybe we could make it work somehow.

Maybe this was real.

Maybe I would find out tonight.

45

'He bought your mum's necklace back?' Sabrina hissed at me as we stood together in the kitchen, both holding a glass of wine. She wore a pretty, black dress, her hair curled and red lipstick on her lips. It had been a long time since she'd been at a party so she said she was making the most of it. I had asked for a quiet dinner party but this was Birchbrook and they didn't do quiet.

I looked around at our bustling kitchen. The dining table was covered with food and drink; everyone had brought something along with them. Sabrina and her family were here, Dad, Dylan and Steve, Amy had come along and Steve's sister with her boyfriend, the two Pats and Paul, Brian had turned up, shocking me that he'd left his farm and come all this way to see us, the landlord of the Birchbrook Arms and his wife, even Mayor Taylor had walked in and she was currently talking to my dad in the corner. A few more people had come too who I'd known all my life in town, including even my old headmistress, who was drinking a glass of wine and talking shop with the current headmistress, Sabrina's boss.

I nodded at Sabrina's question. 'He said I should have it

back.' I touched the necklace. 'It was a huge surprise.' My eyes found Dylan chatting with Steve, a beer in his hand, leaning against the kitchen table. 'I feel like maybe I do want to be with him.'

Sabrina clutched my arm. 'Of course you do. There were sparks even that first day in the café when you gave him the wrong directions. God, Willow, that was hilarious!'

'Not my finest moment,' I said with a sheepish smile. 'I thought he was completely not my type that day, although clearly handsome.'

'I think he's been your type all along; it was just hard to see past the suit,' she said. 'He stayed on a farm for you; that should have told you something from the start.'

'It was pretty crazy to move in with strangers.'

'I told you: you were both looking for something. Maybe now you've found it?'

My dad tapped on his glass then and asked for quiet in the room so I didn't have to answer Sabrina. My eyes met Dylan's briefly before my dad came to stand beside me. I hoped Sabrina was right. I felt more settled than I had since we lost Mum. I held on to her necklace as my dad started speaking.

'Well, thank you all for coming,' he said, looking around the room at everyone watching him, drinks in hands. 'I was thinking earlier about when we first arrived at this farm; my wife immediately pictured us having a family here. We didn't have a clue about running a farm but it felt like home instantly anyway. When we had Willow, that family dream came true. And to see her the past few weeks making changes around here, throwing herself into the project just like her mother would have had done, has really meant the world to me. I know Birch Tree Farm is in good hands and I know that my wife...' Dad's voice broke a little bit here so I took his hand and squeezed it. He smiled at me. '...would be so proud if she was here. Hopefully, she can see it wherever she is. So, happy twenty-sixth birthday, love; you have been through a lot for someone so young but whatever life throws at you, you always find a way through it. And I know sometimes, I haven't been as supportive as I could have been, because we come at things so differently, but I really admire that about you. Raise your glasses to my daughter, please!' He lifted his up and everyone followed suit. 'Happy birthday, Willow!'

Everyone said, 'Happy birthday' to me as I hugged my dad tightly and I felt, finally, that he was proud of me and that I hadn't let my parents down like I thought I had. This farm meant so much to us and after selling all the tickets for half-term, I was hoping that we'd done enough to keep it for the next year at least.

My eyes found Dylan across the room again. He was beaming with pride too. And I knew that I wanted to go to him later.

* * *

The party wound down around 11 p.m. as it was a weekday, and Dylan and I walked to the gate to wave goodbye to everyone. Dad said we should clear up everything in the morning and had headed up to bed, which I had no doubt was to give me and Dylan some privacy. We'd spent a lot of the party side by side and I was glad we were now alone.

'Did you have a good time tonight?' Dylan asked as we strolled back down the driveway, the moonlight pooling in the gaps between the leaves on the birch trees as we passed them.

'It was lovely. I thought it would just be us and Sabrina and Bradley so it was a nice surprise to have so many people come along.'

'Let's have a chat out here,' Dylan said, gesturing to the field as we approached it. 'I want to ask you something.'

'Okay,' I replied, curious as to what he wanted to talk about. All I'd been thinking about was going to the cottage for a kiss. And maybe more...

Dylan led us to the benches in front of the pumpkin patch. At night with no one around, the field was quiet and still and the moon shone down on the pumpkins, reminding me that it wasn't long until Halloween.

We sat down beside each other and he took my hand in his. 'I meant what I said the other day about really wanting you to trust me again,' he said softly. 'I really want to kiss you, for you to come back with me to the cottage, but I don't want you to hesitate or not really enjoy it because you aren't sure about my feelings for you, or my intentions,' he added, his skin warm on mine despite the chilly night.

'Intentions?' I couldn't help but give him a teasing smile. 'What century is this, again?'

Dylan rolled his eyes. 'I'm all serious, and you're making fun of me...'

'I'm sorry.' I squeezed his hand. 'What are your feelings, and intentions?' I asked, grinning at the word.

He smiled. 'I don't know why I put up with you, but you're what I want, Willow. I have never felt this kind of connection before. I think I felt it even on that first day when I was furious at you and all I could think about was getting my hands on the farm. Almost immediately, you threw me off kilter and you've been doing it ever since. I want you to know that, and I know it's fast, but I can't help it – I'm already falling for you.'

I couldn't laugh at that. 'Wow.' I let go of his hand and took hold of the edge of his jacket and pulled him towards me. I gave him a lingering kiss and then leaned back slightly to look into his eyes. 'I feel the same but what does this mean? You're leaving soon...'

'I don't know but I spoke to Nate earlier,' Dylan said, his eyes lighting up after I admitted I was also falling for him. It was scary on one hand, but on the other, it felt completely natural. Like we had always been meant to fall for each other. 'I told him that I don't want to work for him any more. I didn't enjoy it. Being on the farm has shown me I don't want to be stuck in a city doing office work and I don't want to be in my car travelling around either, both of which working for him would mean. I like the countryside. Being outside. I like the freedom here. I like being able to follow my own initiative. And build something special. I don't know what the future looks like but if you also wanted me to stay, I don't have to leave at the end of the month. There's no rush in working out what we do. I just was hoping that we could work it out together. What do you think?'

46

I let Dylan's words sink in. He was in no hurry to leave once October ended. He didn't want to work for his brother any more. He had feelings for me.

'You like being here?' I checked, my mind racing. I had been so sure that I wouldn't see him again once the six-week pact we made was over with. But now hope sprang up inside my heart.

'I do. Do you like me being here?'

'Yes,' I whispered. 'I've been thinking that I don't want you to go.'

'Then I won't go,' Dylan said urgently. 'I promise I won't go. I don't know what I'll do here; I'm nowhere up to your farming standards...' He grinned.

'But we could work it out together?'

'That's what I want. Can I kiss you properly, please? I'm going crazy.'

I smiled and just had to time to nod before his lips met mine again.

This time, neither of us were shy or gentle about it. Dylan threaded his fingertips through my hair as he held the back of my head and I wrapped my arms around his neck, moving as close as I could get without climbing onto his lap. But then Dylan moved his hands to my waist and lifted me up on it. My legs fell either side of him while we kissed hungrily, like we'd both been desperate to do it again.

'God, I have wanted to do this every single day,' Dylan murmured when he moved to kiss my neck, making me shiver. 'Are you cold? Want to go into the cottage?'

'Yes,' I breathed, although I hadn't shivered from the cold, but from his touch.

Dylan scooped me with him as he stood up. I squealed and wrapped my legs tightly around his waist as he started walking.

'You can't carry me,' I protested, laughing as he headed for the cottage with purpose.

'I don't want to let you go now you're in my arms again. Is that okay?' he asked, holding me close to his chest.

'Yes,' I said, smiling. 'Very much okay.' I clung to him as he led us to the cottage, kicking the door open. He shut it after we'd walked through. 'Can we go to your room?' I asked, thinking about how last time, we had got carried away in the kitchen then slept on the sofa. I wanted to be in Dylan's bed now.

'Is that a trick question?'

As we made for the stairs though, Dylan stumbled. He struggled to carry me up, making me giggle. Dylan started chuckling too.

'I thought this would be more romantic,' he joked as we made slow progress. We wobbled and I clung to him like a koala.

'Put me down,' I said, laughing and holding the rail as he almost tripped. 'I don't want to fall before we've had sex.'

Dylan paused then, laughing. 'Stop it, I can't breathe!'

We managed to get control of ourselves and he valiantly

carried on and managed to get us to the top of the, thankfully short, staircase and through into his bedroom. He then took his coat off and pulled mine from me before tumbling with me on his bed.

'That was some journey,' I said, flopping back on the duvet as Dylan leaned over me, my legs still wrapped around him.

'You can say that again,' he replied seriously. He gently pushed back my hair and smiled down at me. 'You are gorgeous, Willow. It's been hell in here some nights thinking about you just over in the farmhouse in your bed. I wanted you here so badly.'

'Yeah?' I had to smile at that. 'I looked over here a lot.'

Dylan pressed his lips against mine and the fire between us sparked up again.

'Why are we still dressed?' I complained after a minute.

He chuckled. 'You're so demanding in the bedroom. And I love it. Get off the bed with me,' he said, getting up. I scooted along the bed and jumped up too, my body alive with anticipation.

He reached for the buttons on my shirt and undid them slowly, locking eyes with me as he did so. My heart was beating fast as he unpeeled my shirt from my shoulders and tossed it onto the floor. Then he stepped back and slowly undid his own shirt while I watched, craving his touch.

He seemed to guess my thoughts as he grinned and slowly took off his shoes, socks and trousers until he was just in his underwear. 'Are you going to join me?'

I shook my head at his teasing and pulled off my clothes impatiently. I didn't stop at my underwear, though; I tossed them to the side too so I was completely naked in front of him. 'Is this what you thought about in your bed?'

Dylan drank me in hungrily. 'God, yes.'

'Are you going to come over here then?' I said, sitting down on the edge of the bed and scooting backwards.

He quickly ditched his boxers and joined me on the bed, leaning over me again. 'I want to kiss all your body like I did the first time.' He dropped gentle kisses down the side of my face, brushing his lips on mine, before moving them down to my chest and across one of my breasts, lingering on my nipple. I bit my lip as he carried on trailing kisses along my stomach and then my thigh and then he carried on down my leg and even pulled a toe into his mouth to give it a quick kiss.

I giggled. 'You really did kiss it all.'

'You taste so good. My favourite sweet treat.' He came back and kissed my mouth again, moving his hand back up my body. This time, he parted my legs gently and touched me where I had been desperate for him. 'Have you thought about this too?'

'So many times,' I whispered, arching my back as he stroked me. His lips moved back to my breast, sucking on my nipple, causing me to moan. 'I wanted to be your sweet treat.'

Dylan lifted off me suddenly and he moved in between my legs, moving his mouth there. I gasped as he acted like I was that sweet treat. It felt so good, I couldn't keep quiet. I let out another moan. My body had definitely missed his touch. I clutched the duvet in my hands as I cried out with pleasure suddenly and deliciously.

'You're so good at that,' I said, shaking my head in wonder as my body trembled underneath him.

'Will you sit on me, baby?' Dylan asked as he rolled onto the bed beside me. 'I've wanted that so much.'

'Yes,' I said, watching as he reached for himself and began stroking. 'I want that too.'

Dylan pulled open the bedside table and got out a condom. When he was ready, I sat astride him and looked down at the admiring look on his face. 'You are amazing,' he gasped when he slid inside me.

I leaned down to kiss him as I grinded on top of him. 'We're amazing together.'

* * *

It was the early hours of the morning when we finally stopped kissing and touching and lay side by side in bed.

I looked around the dimly lit bedroom as Dylan stroked my arm and watched me. 'These need refurbishing, don't they?'

'When I was trying to distract myself from thinking about you at night, I thought about what I would do to these cottages. I think they could be a great addition to the farm. If you refurbished the rooms and publicised them, especially with all the attractions you have throughout the year now, you would make good money from people coming to stay here. I think you could—'

'That's it.' I sat up excitedly, ignoring Dylan's protest at me moving away from him. 'You could run this business.'

'Huh?' He leaned on his elbow to look up at me as I knelt on the bed.

'You could take over the Airbnb business for us; you'd be great at it. And we could share the profits. You could stay here and run the business. Um... if you wanted...' I trailed off, suddenly wondering if I was being too pushy. But then I remembered to trust my gut. 'I want you to,' I added firmly.

Dylan sat up slowly, looking at me. 'You would trust me to do that?' he asked quietly.

I remembered what he'd told me about his brother and father. 'I believe in you, like you believed in me.'

His face lit up and he gave me a big kiss. 'Really? I could do it, Willow. I really could.'

'I know,' I told him firmly. 'Do you really want to?'

'I told you – I want to stay. This might be your best idea yet.'

'Well, it was your idea really... Let's talk to Dad about it all.' I glanced at the clock. 'We have so much to do, we should go to sleep, but I am kind of peckish.'

'Want me to get us a snack?'

'No, I will.' I hurried off and when I returned with a tray, Dylan was leaning against the pillows on the bed. 'I brought some snacks but then I couldn't resist this...' I put the tray on the bedside table and picked up the can of whipped cream that he still had in the fridge. I crawled onto the bed and went over to Dylan. I leaned over his bare chest and squirted some cream on it. Dylan's breath hitched as I licked it off.

'I thought you said we should go to sleep,' he gasped as he ran his fingertips through my hair while I cleaned the cream off him.

I looked at him and reached for his boxers. 'You don't want me to take these off and have a sweet treat of my own then?'

'Fuck, yeah, I want that. So much,' he said, watching with dark eyes as I grinned and started to slide them off. 'Forget what I said earlier about falling for you. This is it for me. I've already fallen.'

I paused to smile back at him. 'I've already fallen too,' I said. 'Like the leaves on the trees,' I added; even though it was a cheesy-as-hell line, I was unable to resist.

'Like the leaves on the trees,' he agreed as I slid his boxers off and we ignored all the work ahead of us and concentrated on each other instead.

47

Half-term was suddenly with us, and with a sold-out pumpkin patch to manage, we were busy all day every day for the week. It felt amazing though to see so many families and visitors flock to the farm and leave with an array of pumpkins. It had been an exhausting week but it gave me hope that the patch had done what we wanted it to for the farm.

Then we reached the end of October. Halloween. The 31st. It fell on the Wednesday after half-term and it was the perfect day to close Pumpkin Hollow for our first (but hopefully not last!) year of being open.

It was also the sixth and final week of the pact I'd made with Dad and Dylan. I would soon know if we'd done enough to save the farm.

Anticipation was high then for the night of the Birchbrook lantern festival. Dad had persuaded Mayor Taylor to let the LED lantern trail finish at the farm and in advance, we had made the patch look as spooky as possible, setting up LED lights all over, putting them in lanterns and carved pumpkins, and draping fairy lights over every space possible. Along with Paul's Birchbrook Café van, we'd also invited a couple of other local food businesses to set up vans, and the craft shop in the next town over was going to have a stall for the night.

As the day faded into evening, everyone came over to set up and we closed the pumpkin patch to visitors for the last time.

As I left Dad and Maple outside putting through the final pumpkin sales to last-minute buyers, I found Dylan with his laptop at the kitchen table in the farmhouse. The last visitors had walked through our trail and they left with big smiles on their faces.

I walked over to him nervously as I knew he'd been inputting numbers for the past hour once the last booked slot had been and gone. My limbs ached and I was bone-tired, but tonight was an opportunity to show the town how great the pumpkin patch was and to make it a part of our annual Halloween celebrations. If I was able to keep the farm going for another year, it hopefully would be even more popular next autumn.

'How did we do?' I asked, walking over to sit beside him.

He looked up from his laptop with a serious expression on his face. 'I think we should wait for your father to come in so he can hear this and you both can decide what to do.'

I swallowed hard. 'Okay,' I said shakily.

Dad came in a minute later with Maple barking excitedly. 'Well, that's it until tonight. The last customer has left the farm.' His smile faded when he looked at my face. 'What's wrong, love?'

'Dylan wanted to wait for us both to be here to tell us how well we've done this month,' I said, my nerves now tenfold. Dylan was giving nothing away and I had no idea what I was going to do if I'd been wrong and it hadn't been quite the smash hit it had felt like it was. Dylan had asked if we should sell tickets for the lantern festival but it had always been a free event, unless you bought food or drink or something from one of the shops of course, and I wanted to make sure everyone thought of the patch in a good way so we had made all the money we were going to this year now.

'I've crunched all the numbers, and I've also done a forecast based on how we've done this year for the following five years to look at the long-term profitability of the pumpkin patch, and whether it means you can pay off your debts and turn an annual profit,' Dylan said as my dad sat down next to me. Even Maple wandered over and sat quietly down by my feet, sensing a tense atmosphere in the room.

Dad quickly squeezed my hand. 'Whatever happens, we will be okay, love.'

I nodded but I couldn't speak. I just looked at Dylan.

He broke into a smile. 'It looks great, guys!' He spun the laptop around so we could see his spreadsheet but if I was honest, the sheer amount of numbers made my head hurt. 'You've turned a profit this year that will pay off your current debts and leave some spare that you could invest. If Willow goes ahead and starts growing pumpkins to sell next year then I anticipate with increased ticket sales and making more from pumpkins, plus you could charge for food and drinks vans to have a pitch on the farm, you could easily double the profit from this year. Obviously, we don't know if pumpkin patches will continue in popularity past the next five years but I can't see it dying off any time soon. With the profit you're making in autumn coupled with what you make in spring/summer, the farm is definitely sustainable for the next five years.'

'Really?' I squealed as relief washed over me.

'That's brilliant news,' Dad said, grinning at Dylan. 'You really think we can keep the farm long-term?'

'I do. And as we discussed, if we look into other revenues like the Airbnb business, and think about how we can increase your profits in the pick-your-own season too then I think this farm has a really solid future ahead.' Dylan turned to me. 'You did it, Willow.'

I was finding this hard to take in. 'We can keep the farm?'

'Honestly, I wouldn't be advising you to sell to anyone,' Dylan said, smiling at my stunned expression. 'This is a great business. And I can't wait to help you with it, if that's what you still want.'

'Actually, I have something to say about that...' Dad said before I could respond. He cleared his throat. 'Willow, I am so proud of you, love. This past month has been stressful but you have thrown yourself into saving our farm. And I know you did it because you love living and working here but also because you know I do too, and that this place meant the world to your mother.' He glanced at Mum's necklace, which still hung around my neck, and his eyes grew a little bit misty, but he ploughed on. 'We all know, however, that the farm is getting harder for me to work on. I've loved helping the customers this week and I would want to keep doing that but some of the manual labour is too difficult now. That's why I'm so happy you want to stay here, Dylan, and help my daughter. And hopefully, with the increase in profits, you can bring in more help through the year too as I think I will have to slow things down and reduce my day-to-day involvement in the business.'

'But Dad—' I began.

'Willow,' he stopped me. 'I'm not upset by this. I want you to take the farm over. You're so passionate about it. That's what this place needs. I lost my passion when your mother died. I should have pushed you back then to take on more responsibility. Instead, I let us struggle on and we almost lost this place. I won't make that mistake again. This month, you have more than proved that you're capable of running the farm even better than I ever did. Even better than your mother. So...' He got up stiffly and went over to the sideboard where he opened a drawer and pulled out an envelope. He carried it back to the table and passed it to me.

'Another scary envelope,' I said, looking at it with apprehension as I thought back to last month when Dad had made me read the letter from Henderson Homes. I couldn't have foreseen that turning out as well as it had but I was still nervous to know what my dad was giving me now.

'Not scary. I promise. Open it, please.'

I took a breath, aware of both my dad and Dylan watching me closely.

I pulled out the document from the envelope and my eyes scanned it. I was so shocked, I re-read it. 'I don't understand,' I said slowly. 'Are these...?'

'The deeds to the farm,' my dad confirmed. 'I've signed it over to you, love. The farm now belongs to you. You own Birch Tree Farm.'

I looked up at him, my eyes wide. 'Really, Dad?'

He nodded, smiling. 'Really. It's all yours, Willow.'

'Oh my God.' I jumped up and gave him a big squeeze over his shoulders. 'You didn't have to do this.'

'I know. I wanted to. You deserve it.'

My eyes welled up with tears. I looked over at Dylan, who was beaming happily at us. 'I get to stay here,' I said as a tear rolled down my face.

'You do,' Dylan said. 'You were always meant to stay here, Willow.'

'Thank you, Dad. This means the world to me.'

'I know it does.' Dad sniffed and wiped away a tear of his own. He waved me off and got up. 'I'll go and start dinner.'

I went to Dylan. He jumped up out of his chair and wrapped me in a tight embrace. 'You'll stay too?' I whispered into his ear.

'I'm not going anywhere, Willow,' he whispered back.

48

It was pitch-black and nearing 8 p.m. as I stood with Dad, Dylan and Maple by the edge of Pumpkin Hollow. It was the first year I hadn't walked the lantern festival since I was a child but we needed to make sure everything was okay at the pumpkin patch and be here to greet the town when everyone arrived. Sabrina had sent me a message when they all set off through the High Street.

Usually, the walk took them around the town green past the school then back to the High Street at the end so they walked in a big loop. This year, they would start there and the businesses that usually opened and sold things still would, then they would walk to the farm and finish at the pumpkin patch. It was a prettier walk and I'd promised a big finale so most people were on board, although, as female Pat had said, Birchbrook wasn't great with change so there had also been a few grumbles. I hoped we'd win the grumblers over though so the farm could become an annual part of it all.

I looked at the field in front of me. It was all lit up and looked spooky and cool with the lanterns dotted around the farm with the few pumpkins we had left. We had sold most of them. The farmer we'd sold the orange ones on behalf of was so pleased, he'd already asked about next year but I told him I was hoping to grow my own.

I had also draped fairy lights over the outside of the two polytunnels we'd kept up – the others I'd taken down as we didn't need the autumn set-ups any more. Inside the tunnels, I'd added more lanterns and draped fairy lights across the ceiling and themed them for Halloween with the skeletons and witches and cobwebs, along with more I'd picked up this week. Any remaining pumpkins were also stacked outside and we'd set up a spookily cool photo opportunity under the *Pumpkin Hollow* sign.

'It looks great,' Dylan said, following my gaze. 'Perfect for Halloween.'

'Look.' Dad pointed and we turned to see a line of lights turning into our drive. Against the dark night, they made for a dazzling sight. Coupled with the full moon that was casting a bright beam down on us, the LED lanterns were so pretty and also looked magical. We lapsed into silence as the line of lanterns grew closer, heading up the drive towards the farmhouse. The birch trees currently looked their best, before the breeze would shed their golden leaves completely, ready for winter, and they swayed in the night as if they were welcoming the town to the farm too.

A local band who had offered to play for the exposure started playing 'I Put A Spell On You' as the food vans readied themselves for visitors and we greeted everyone on the trail, directing them to enjoy the pumpkin patch for the final night. We watched as kids ran around, people took photos and others queued for food and drink. A few people even started dancing to the band. Lanterns lit up everywhere and the whole farm glowed merrily.

I left Dad and Dylan with Maple at my heels to walk around and greet as many people as I could. I glanced up at the full moon, remembering the wish I'd made on the stars. Somehow, it had come true.

'This is so much fun,' Sabrina said when I approached her and her family. 'I even heard Paul saying he can't wait for next autumn now.' Her eyes twinkled with amusement.

'The profits the café van made here in half-term surprised him, I think. He muttered about betting I'd charge him next year to have a pitch here. So, I let him take a pumpkin home,' I replied with a laugh. He hadn't gone so far as to say he was sorry for being so disparaging about my idea but I could tell he was pleasantly surprised by how well it had all worked out. He was an acquired taste, for sure, but he had been a huge support in the end. I told Sabrina then that we'd done well enough to not have to sell in the near future and that my dad had signed the farm over to me too.

'Oh, Willow!' She gave me a hug. 'I'm so happy for you!'

'Thank you for all your help. There was a point when I thought it was all over. It's thanks to you I didn't give up that day in the café.' All had felt lost at that moment when I'd seen the storm damage and had an argument with Dylan. My best friend had made sure I didn't walk away from either of them.

'There's no need to thank me. You've done so much for me over the years. That's what being best friends is all about.' She leaned in as she caught sight of Dylan heading our way. 'And is Dylan going to help you run the farm?'

I nodded happily, unable to stop the smile on my face. 'He doesn't want to leave and I want him to stay.'

'Well, I'm pleased for you both. You make each other better.'

Dottie started crying then so Sabrina went to check on her, and Dylan caught me by the waist, wrapping his arms around me.

I looked up into his eyes. 'Hey, you.' I put my arms around his neck and pulled him down to give him a quick kiss. 'Sabrina just said something sweet. She said that we make each other better.'

'You make me better for sure,' he said. 'You were right that day we met when you said I wasn't passionate about anything. I had lost my passion for life. I had no idea what I wanted. I was missing that spark I'd had when I was younger. You've given it back to me.'

'You're definitely passionate now,' I said softly, thinking about last night when we had stayed up late in bed again, unable to get enough of each other. 'You've pushed me to believe in myself and work hard to make my dreams come true. And ask for help. And be a little bit less stubborn. Just a little bit anyway,' I added with a grin.

'I think we didn't know how lonely we were until we found each other,' Dylan said, smiling back. 'I'm so glad I found your farm. I thought I could take it from you but instead, you've given me everything I ever wanted.'

'Dylan, that's the sweetest thing,' I cried, kissing him again. 'You've made me so happy!'

We let each other go and looked around at the people enjoying the Halloween night. In the distance, the farmhouse was lit up and behind it, Dylan's cottage was waiting for us to be alone in it together.

'You know I'm in this for keeps, don't you?' he asked me then. 'I see our future together. Here. Do you?'

I looked out at the farm then. I thought about the year ahead. A cosy winter then Christmas together, followed by a busy spring and summer season when the farm would thrive and then a second year of running the pumpkin patch, hopefully bigger and even better than this first year. Dylan would work on the cottage business alongside the farm too so that might take off. There were so many possibilities.

But each night, whatever the day had brought, we could curl up together in each other's arms and that made me feel ready for whatever the next year was going to deliver.

'I see my future with you,' I agreed. 'We made the most unlikely pair when you turned up, didn't we? But somehow, we belong together. And I can't wait to see what happens next.'

'Me too. I love you, Willow.'

'I love you too,' I replied.

I looked up at the sky again. Next to the glowing full moon were twinkling stars, and one twinkled a little bit brighter than the others, almost as if it were dropping me a wink. It was nice to think that maybe it was a sign from my mum or the universe or whatever there might be out there watching over us that I was on the right path finally. I felt it inside my heart even if that wasn't actually a sign. I was right where I was meant to be and I had the best people around me too.

'I can't quite believe I live in Birchbrook now,' Dylan said with a laugh as a group of teenagers dressed as vampires walked past, all holding lanterns in one hand and drinks from the café van in the other. 'Or that autumn might be my favourite season.'

'Might be?' I teased, shaking my head in mock outrage.

'You're right – I'm sorry. Autumn is definitely my favourite season!' he declared.

He took my hand in his as we walked towards where my dad was talking to the mayor.

Was I imagining a tiny spark between the two of them? I wasn't sure quite how to feel about that but there did seem to be a hint of magic in the air tonight so perhaps it wasn't all that surprising.

'Glad to hear it,' I joked back to Dylan. 'It's the season we met in, after all.'

'Definitely my favourite then.' Dylan winked at me. 'I'll get us two pumpkin spiced lattes. Maple – do you want a Puppuccino?'

Maple was bounding along beside us like always and she let out a bark, proving once again that she seemed to understand whatever we said to her.

I watched them go and smiled. Dylan had said autumn was now his favourite season. Who would have thought that six weeks ago?

I remembered the reasons I'd listed to myself back in September as to why I loved this time of year. How would I revise that list now?

Autumn was still my favourite season for these very important reasons:

1. My mother loved this time of year and named me Willow after her favourite tree from her childhood.
2. I owned Birch Tree Farm where the trees that lined the drive up to the farmhouse changed to stunning colours each year autumn came around.
3. I was born in October.
4. I had created Pumpkin Hollow: a pumpkin patch that opened in autumn and had been a complete success this first season.
5. Autumnal food and drink were the best, especially topped with whipped cream (winky face emoji).
6. I had fallen in love in October.

That last reason had been the biggest surprise of the season.

But autumn was all about new beginnings, and I couldn't wait to start mine with Dylan on Birch Tree Farm, the place I would always belong.

* * *

MORE FROM VICTORIA WALTERS

In case you missed it, *Long Story Short*, Victoria Walters' previous title, is available to order now here:

https://mybook.to/LongStoryShortBackAd

ACKNOWLEDGEMENTS

Thank you so much to my agent Hannah Ferguson for helping to spark the idea that became this book on a phone call. We joked about how much I love autumn and suddenly Pumpkin Hollow was born! Thank you for all your support and encouragement, and hard work always.

Thank you to my editor Emily Yau – you were so enthusiastic about this idea right from the start and I'm so happy you love Birch Tree Farm as much as I do! Thank you once again for all your insights and encouragement.

A huge thank you to the teams at Boldwood Books and Hardman and Swainson – thank you all for your support and hard work on my books. I love working with you all! Special thanks to Niamh Wallace for being such a cheerleader for my books, to my copy editor Emily Reader, my proofreader Anna Paterson, and Alex Allden for such a cosy cover.

And thank you to anyone reading this book! I'm a huge fan of autumn and all things cosy and, of course, pumpkins so I really hope that came across in the book and you too have fallen in love with the season! Thank you for picking up *Love and Lattes at Pumpkin Hollow* and I hope you come back to Birch Tree Farm for future books too.

Sending love to my family and friends and fellow authors who are always there if I need you.

PLAYLIST FOR LOVE AND LATTES AT PUMPKIN HOLLOW

Pumpkin Spice Season – Scotty Orando
Willow – Taylor Swift
Autumn Leaves – Mckenna Grace September – Valerie Rose
Stick Season – Noah Kahan
Falling in Love at a Coffee Shop
Autumn Song – Theo Bleak
Autumn Comes – David Gramberg, Mary Lou
Autumn Town Leaves – Iron & Wine
September Song – JP Cooper
October Eyes – Alt Bloom
Coffee – Beabadoobee
Back to Autumn – Tall Heights
Cozy – Sarah King, EyeLoveBrandon
we fell in love in October – girl in red Things that Fall – Lily Williams
October Sky – Yebba
Rain – mxmtoon
Weathervane – Hunter Metts
I'll Get the Coffee – Kathryn Gallagher
Autumn Leaves – Eva Cassidy
this is what autumn feels like – JVKE

ABOUT THE AUTHOR

Victoria Walters is the author of both cosy crime and romantic novels, including the bestselling Glendale Hall series. She has been chosen for WHSmith Fresh Talent, shortlisted for two RNA novels and was picked as an Amazon Rising Star.

Sign up to Victoria Walters' mailing list for news, competitions and updates on future books.

Visit Victoria's website: www.victoria-writes.com

Follow Victoria on social media:

- instagram.com/vickyjwalters
- facebook.com/VictoriaWaltersAuthor
- x.com/Vicky_Walters
- bookbub.com/authors/victoria-walters
- youtube.com/@vickyjwalters
- threads.net/vickyjwalters

ALSO BY VICTORIA WALTERS

The Love Interest

The Plot Twist

The Paris Chapter

Long Story Short

Birch Tree Farm Series

Love and Lattes at Pumpkin Hollow

Boldwood EVER AFTER

xoxo

JOIN BOLDWOOD'S **ROMANCE COMMUNITY** FOR SWEET AND SPICY BOOK RECS WITH ALL YOUR FAVOURITE TROPES!

SIGN UP TO OUR NEWSLETTER

HTTPS://BIT.LY/BOLDWOODEVERAFTER

Boldwood

Boldwood Books is an award-winning fiction publishing company seeking out the best stories from around the world.

Find out more at www.boldwoodbooks.com

Join our reader community for brilliant books, competitions and offers!

Follow us
@BoldwoodBooks
@TheBoldBookClub

Sign up to our weekly deals newsletter

https://bit.ly/BoldwoodBNewsletter